The Cowboy's

Forbidden Bride

By Cora Seton

Author's Note

The Cowboy's Forbidden Bride is the fifth and final volume in the Turners v. Coopers series. To find out more, look for the rest of the books in the series, including:

The Cowboy's Secret Bride (Volume 1)
The Cowboy's Outlaw Bride (Volume 2)
The Cowboy's Hidden Bride (Volume 3)
The Cowboy's Stolen Bride (Volume 4)

Also, don't miss Cora Seton's Chance Creek series, the Cowboys of Chance Creek, the Heroes of Chance Creek, the Brides of Chance Creek, and the SEALs of Chance Creek:

The Cowboys of Chance Creek Series:

The Cowboy Inherits a Bride (Volume 0)
The Cowboy's E-Mail Order Bride (Volume 1)
The Cowboy Wins a Bride (Volume 2)
The Cowboy Imports a Bride (Volume 3)
The Cowgirl Ropes a Billionaire (Volume 4)
The Sheriff Catches a Bride (Volume 5)
The Cowboy Lassos a Bride (Volume 6)
The Cowboy Rescues a Bride (Volume 7)
The Cowboy Earns a Bride (Volume 8)
The Cowboy's Christmas Bride (Volume 9)

The Heroes of Chance Creek Series:

The Navy SEAL's E-Mail Order Bride (Volume 1)
The Soldier's E-Mail Order Bride (Volume 2)
The Marine's E-Mail Order Bride (Volume 3)
The Navy SEAL's Christmas Bride (Volume 4)
The Airman's E-Mail Order Bride (Volume 5)

The Brides of Chance Creek Series:

Issued to the Bride One Navy SEAL
Issued to the Bride One Airman
Issued to the Bride One Sniper
Issued to the Bride One Marine
Issued to the Bride One Soldier

The SEALs of Chance Creek Series:

A SEAL's Oath
A SEAL's Vow
A SEAL's Pledge
A SEAL's Consent
A SEAL's Purpose
A SEAL's Resolve
A SEAL's Devotion
A SEAL's Desire
A SEAL's Struggle
A SEAL's Triumph

Visit Cora's website at www.coraseton.com
Find Cora on Facebook at facebook.com/CoraSeton
Sign up for my newsletter HERE.
www.coraseton.com/sign-up-for-my-newsletter

Chapter One

STEEL COOPER WAS sick of hiding. Sick of hanging out with criminals. Sick of playing a part that had no bearing on who he really was or what he wanted from life. Sick of watching everyone else live out loud, unfettered by their pasts or their obligations. He'd spent half his life hiding. More than that, really, if you counted all the years he ran cover for his father's petty crimes, the way children do when their parents skirt the law.

As he stood in the shadows of a grove of trees that skirted Thorn Hill, spying on his sister's wedding reception, he vowed that all the secrecy in his life would end soon. He'd finish the job his father, Dale, had started, would catch the killer that had preyed upon Chance Creek, Montana, for far too many years, and would finally—finally—take his place in the sun.

He wasn't sure when he'd hit the wall. Maybe it was witnessing each of his siblings marry this summer, one after the other, finding a kind of happiness that seemed out of his grasp.

Maybe it was knowing that no one but him even believed the rash of overdose deaths in Silver Falls were anything but accidents. He'd been trying to prove them wrong since he'd come back to town with his family several years ago, and so far he'd made little progress.

Or maybe it was realizing Stella Turner was falling for someone else.

Steel looked over the celebration in front of him. Trees had been festooned with fairy lights. A local band played popular dance tunes. Despite the intense heat that had plagued Chance Creek all summer, it was a perfect night—

For everyone but him.

His chest tightened as Stella danced in the arms of another man. Her dark hair had been caught up into a loose bun for the occasion, tendrils coming free and curling in the heat. He wasn't close enough to see her hazel eyes, but he had them memorized, like the sweet shape of her face and her tantalizing figure. If his life hadn't become so damn complicated thirteen years ago, maybe he'd be the one dancing with her. Holding her close. Taking her home.

Getting married—

Steel squashed that thought—hard. He wouldn't be marrying anyone anytime soon. Certainly not Stella, who worked at the Chance Creek county sheriff's department fielding calls. She was smart as a whip, cool under pressure, and damned pretty to boot. Much too good for the likes of him—at least the way he was living his life now.

But a man could dream, and he'd been dreaming about Stella since the day he'd come back to town and caught sight of her walking down main street, the girl next door all grown up.

Completely out of his reach.

Since then he'd done his best to stay out of her way, but that was impossible in a small town, especially since her family's ranch lay across one small creek from his. He saw Stella all the time.

Craved seeing her. Wanted to do a hell of a lot more.

So far he'd managed to keep himself in check, but if he had to watch her in Eric Holden's arms much longer, he was going to lose control.

It had taken him nearly an hour to creep close enough to the festivities tonight to be able to see them clearly without being seen himself, and he'd only managed it because the hot summer days had convinced Tory and Liam to situate the party among a grove of shade trees on his family's property. Once the sun set, he'd slipped from tree to tree from the deeper arm of forest that bounded their pastures.

If he was caught, he'd have the excuse of wanting to congratulate his sister, but it would be for the best for all concerned if he wasn't. Everyone, including his own family, thought he'd returned to Chance Creek to help his siblings on their ranch. Thirteen years ago, when their father's checkered past had caught up to him and Dale had landed in jail, their mother, Enid, had moved the rest of his siblings to Idaho. Steel, already eighteen, had lingered in Chance Creek just long enough to clean up Dale's mess, then had headed even farther west, to Washington. They'd all assumed the ranch had been sold as part of their parents' divorce settlement and hadn't expected to ever get the chance to come home, so when Dale died three years ago, and Steel, Lance, Tory and Olivia found themselves named as owners of Thorn Hill, their surprise was absolute.

Lance and Olivia had jumped at the opportunity to go home. Tory had held off for several years but had joined them recently. Steel wouldn't have come at all if it weren't for the killer.

He wasn't sure if he'd come at all if he'd known how hard it would be to live in the same town as Stella, so close and yet inexorably out of reach of her.

He'd been able to create a new life for himself in Washington, one in which the people who mattered knew who he was and why he did what he did. He'd had a tight group of friends who'd had his back—something he didn't entirely appreciate until he gave it all up to come home.

Still, it would all be worth it if he could just finish this job and put his undercover days behind him—make the kind of life that would give him a chance with a woman like Stella. Until then he needed to keep his distance from his family. He'd made a mistake thinking he could live with them and still penetrate the seamy underside of the area. He found it ironic that all the good people of Chance Creek assumed from the start he was a criminal like his father was, while the criminals who populated Silver Falls viewed him with too much suspicion for him to make any real progress tracking down the killer.

On a night like this one, that irony got under his skin and made him wish he'd never taken the job in the first place.

He'd taken too long, and now he was losing Stella to another man.

Steel chanced another look and bit back a curse when he took in the way Eric had pulled her in tight against him. Steel knew Eric—or knew of him. He was a sheriff's deputy here in Chance Creek county, a powerful, stocky man, fifteen years older than Stella, his dark hair going gray at the temples. He'd been a mainstay at the department for as long as Steel could remember.

Steel kept track of all the law enforcement officers from Billings to Bozeman. Not because he was a criminal, like he'd been trying to make everyone think—but because he was a deputy, too—in Silver Falls, a scruffy hill town a short distance down the highway in the next county over. Silver Falls was a little smaller—and a little wilder—than Chance Creek. He'd expected to fit in there just fine.

He took some small pride in the fact that no one attending this wedding knew what he did for a living. You could say a lot about him—and people did—but he knew how to run an undercover operation. He'd been forced to learn—fast—over a decade ago, but he'd taken to it like a duck to water.

It was a good thing Mitch Bolton, the sheriff in Silver Falls, knew how to keep a tight lid on the workings of the department. To Steel's knowledge, no one had slipped and exposed him.

He wondered how much longer that could last. Wondered how long it would take to finish the job his father had started. Not just because he'd like to be the one out there dancing with Stella, but because he'd like to be a bigger part of everything his family did. His siblings needed his help with the ranch. The wedding he was watching was beautiful, but beneath the festive set dressing he knew Thorn Hill was barely holding together, like many ranches in Chance Creek.

Steel could see the strain in many of the celebrants' faces. Everyone was trying to relax tonight, allowing themselves to enjoy the reception, but there was wear and fatigue behind each smile.

It had been a hard summer for everyone.

Steel ducked behind a tree as a couple wandered close to his hiding place—his sister Olivia and her husband, Noah Turner.

They spoke softly and laughed, and Steel smiled to hear them. He respected Noah, even if he had never been able to show it due to the feud that had until recently defined their families' relationship. Noah was a parole officer who worked for the Chance Creek sheriff's department, so Steel had been surprised when his sister, who'd had her own brushes with the law, had ended up with him.

But she seemed happy, and that was the important thing.

Olivia was working at the library now, putting away money so she could go to school, get her degree and one day take over as head librarian. Noah worked on both their families' ranches, and his parole officer salary helped make ends meet.

Steel wondered how Noah felt about having a supposed criminal as his brother-in-law; since Noah worked for Chance Creek rather than Silver Falls, he wasn't in the loop about Steel's undercover activities, and as a parole officer, he probably wouldn't have known even if they had worked in the same county, but as it was, Steel figured it had to bother the law-abiding man to think his brother-in-law was making bad choices.

But then Noah had managed to overlook Olivia's past. Sometimes people surprised you.

Maybe Stella would overlook his past—if he could ever finish the job he was working on.

Just about everyone Steel knew would get a surprise then. If only it wasn't taking so damn long.

The killer was a patient man. Thirteen years ago a spate of overdose deaths among young women on the fringes of Chance Creek society had alerted William Turner, Stella's father, who had also been a sheriff's deputy, that something more sinister than a series of accidents was taking place in his town. He couldn't convince anyone else to take his theory seriously, so he'd enlisted Dale's help and run a side investigation.

When William and Dale came too close to exposing him, the killer dropped out of sight, and no other deaths that fit the profile occurred—until recently.

When Dale knew his health was failing, he'd called Steel to visit him in prison one last time. "The investigation is yours now," he'd rasped from his position on the other side of the plexiglass. "The killer will be back. I know it."

If Steel hadn't been watching the Chance Creek crime blotter avidly all these years, he doubted anyone would have made the connection when the overdoses started in Silver Falls. At first Steel had burned with the desire to avenge his father, who might not have been caught in his own criminal enterprises if he hadn't been working to uncover the killer. Dale had filled him in on all of it, given him a series of orders to cover up his and William's off-the-books investigation, then had pulled strings through William to help Steel get into the sheriff's department in Washington. Once he'd become a deputy there, he'd continued with undercover work, honing his skills. As the years passed, and there was no sign of trouble in Chance Creek, Steel figured maybe William had been wrong from the start. Maybe there'd never been a killer at all. In truth he'd come to want to shuck off the responsibility Dale had laid on his shoulders before he died. Steel had been busy creating a new life in Washington. He could have stayed there—stepped away from undercover work—

But then the killings started again.

Steel swallowed as he watched Eric bend close to Stella and say something in her ear. What kind of sweet nothings was the man telling her? Steel itched to be holding her himself, telling her all about his life, his past—and the future he wanted to build.

It had taken several deaths in Silver Falls before he'd

spotted the pattern, and it was only because Silver Falls' crime reporting was lumped in with Chance Creek's in the online version of the local paper that he'd seen it at all. It had been easy enough to join his siblings when they came back to take possession of the ranch. It was harder to convince the Silver Falls sheriff to take him on to work the case.

For one thing, the killer's habits had shifted enough to make it difficult to prove it was the same person. Thirteen years ago the victims were young women who were already in trouble: sex workers or petty criminals estranged from their families and known to use drugs.

This time around the killer had changed his way of doing things, and Steel wondered if he'd upped the ante for himself to make his murders more exciting. Now he seemed to be luring women to him. The kind of women—or rather, teenage girls—who should know better.

When Steel had first noticed the surge of overdoses in Silver Falls, he'd wondered if it was the same fentanyl scourge that was hitting everywhere. Several things bothered him right from the start, though. All the overdose victims were young and female, relatively well off, living with their families until they died. Many of them lived in Chance Creek, but their deaths occurred in Silver Falls.

Mitch Bolton, the Silver Falls sheriff, finally took him on and gave him the leeway to work the cases, but he'd always maintained finding the source of the drugs was Steel's true mandate. He didn't believe in a single killer as much as he thought all drugs were far too accessible. Steel was determined to work both sides of the case and hoped to get it done in a year.

He shook his head now at his own folly. He'd underestimated the job, and now he was paying for it. He hadn't been able to let Stella know who he really was. Had managed to dance with her a time or two, and that was it. Now Eric was stealing her—

And it was his own damn fault.

He'd wasted a lot of time building relationships with petty dealers and criminals but couldn't seem to get traction with anyone higher in the distribution chain. In desperation he finally repeated his father's idea: he grew a crop of pot of his own to try to sell—a move he hoped signaled to other dealers he was ready to play ball, a small-time operator who wanted to move into bigger things. He'd planted it on the Ridley property, an abandoned ranch that bordered his family's and the Turners' land.

It had almost worked, too. He'd gotten some interest from an outfit in town to the point where they'd started feeling almost territorial about the crop. They'd started sending their own men out to patrol it, a couple of lackeys who'd first surprised his sister Tory, then her soon-to-be husband, on the Ridley property. Luckily, neither of those occasions had escalated to a serious confrontation. Steel had told them to lay off—and stay away from his crop—and inadvertently unleashed a firestorm.

Literally.

Steel assumed the men had complained around

town about his high-handedness, and the killer, whoever he was, figured it was his chance to deal once and for all with him, a man asking too many questions about the overdoses. He had to hand it to the man. Sending goons to tie him up and burn down his crop had all the hallmarks of an attack those local dealers might have made in retaliation when he'd balked their supervision, and Sheriff Holden had certainly been convinced that's exactly what happened.

Steel knew the sheriff was wrong. He'd seen the two men who'd come after him. They weren't the same men who'd wanted to patrol his crop. In fact, they weren't from around these parts at all. They were hired guns who'd infiltrated his property, disarmed and disposed of him so methodically he knew they'd done this dozens of times before. He had no idea where the killer had found them or how he'd gotten them to do his dirty work.

He was lucky he was alive today. His crop and most of the structures on the Ridley property had burned to the ground.

He'd filled in Mitch Bolton on what had happened. His attackers left town before anyone caught up to them, though, and Steel was none the wiser as to whom they worked for. No one else seemed to know either. He hadn't blown his cover—everyone still thought he was a petty criminal. A not-very-savvy petty criminal, but he'd upped his cred a little.

"Maybe you aren't such a homebody after all," one of the other dealers had remarked a few days after the fire when he'd bumped into him on the outskirts of

Silver Falls.

"Homebody? What the hell are you talking about?" he'd asked in some consternation. Hardly an adjective he wanted associated with him when he was acting undercover.

"Figured you were kind of a family man, living at Thorn Hill and all."

"Fuck, no." But he'd taken the comment to heart. Here he'd thought he'd been doing such a good job establishing his bad reputation, and he hadn't been fooling anyone at all. No wonder he wasn't getting anywhere.

Time to change things up.

If only he'd done so sooner.

Steel had rented a broken-down trailer in Silver Falls some months ago to use as a crash-pad when he didn't want to go home, but now he moved there full time and stopped going back to Thorn Hill. He let his garbage pile up outside. Went out at all hours. Spent his time in dive bars. Let it be known he was available for whatever needed to be done.

Now he was at a loss about what to do next. He hated knowing someone out there held all the cards. The killer, whoever he was, could see the whole game board. All Steel had was bits and pieces of the puzzle. Who was luring these girls to their deaths?

And was he also responsible for the two violent homicides in Silver Falls in the past year that had shaken people up? Those murders had people whispering about a *Chance Creek killer*, but unlike the overdoses, which everyone thought of as accidents, both homicides had involved blunt force trauma. Those victims were male. Not the MO of the man he was hunting, and Steel didn't think they were linked. Neither did Mitch Bolton, which meant he'd assigned those cases to other people.

He had to work harder. Figure out why kids like Rena Klein, a teenaged girl who'd died just a few days ago, and Cecilia Foster, who'd overdosed three months before Rena, kept ending up dead when they seemed to have everything to live for.

He needed to solve this investigation and get it tied off, or he would lose any chance he had with Stella.

If he hadn't lost it already.

Voices sounded closer to him than was comfortable, and he pulled farther back into the shadows, tearing his gaze from Stella. Olivia was back, this time with his brother, Lance—and his aunt Virginia, a termagant of a woman with a sharp tongue and an even sharper-tipped umbrella she liked to carry even when it wasn't raining.

"We need to win," Virginia was saying, and Steel immediately knew the topic of conversation.

The Ridley property—otherwise known as Settler's Ridge—the same piece of abandoned ranch land where he'd tried to grow his pot crop.

Virginia, and everyone else in town, had been obsessed with winning it since the Founder's Prize was announced in the spring. She wanted to add its land to Thorn Hill—and more importantly in these dry times, she wanted control of Pittance Creek, the small stream that ran between the Cooper and Turner ranches. Of course, the Turners wanted it, too.

Whoever contributed the most to Chance Creek would win the long-abandoned ranch. The announcement of the prize had kicked off a hearty competition between his family, the Turners and others in town.

His family launched an improvement plan for Chance Creek High. The Turners countered by renovating the town library and saving the dialysis unit at the local hospital, which had been slated to be shut down. The Lowmans donated a building to house the town history museum, with suitably low rent for the non-profit organization. That left the Turners in the lead.

Virginia was on the warpath.

"At this point all we can do is tie up the contest, Virginia," Lance pointed out. Not too long ago, Lance had been as riled up about beating the Turners as Virginia was. He'd mellowed out significantly after he'd married Maya Turner, and they had both secured scholarships to study history in the coming fall semester. Lance seemed happier than Steel had ever seen him, and Steel was proud of what his brother had made of his life.

"You can do better than that if you put your mind to it. We need to create something spectacular for this town. Something that sweeps the competition."

"What we need is to help the kids around these parts," Olivia countered. "Did you hear about Rena Klein? She overdosed. I think we should raise funds to expand the detox and stabilization units in town. They don't even serve teenagers."

Steel poked his head out, drawn by the content of their conversation, and saw that Jed Turner was heading their way. He pulled back into the shadows as Virginia snapped, "The last thing we need is to associate the Cooper name with anything related to drugs. So come up with a better project than that—fast. You hear me? We can't let those Turners get their mitts on Settler's Ridge."

"Are you forgetting I'm a Turner now?" Olivia teased Virginia. She was married to Noah, after all.

"And so is my wife," Lance pointed out.

"And I hope you don't regret it half as much as I regret having to depend on a bunch of do-nothings to win that land!"

Steel withdrew even more, biting back a smile. Virginia was a scrapper, but he had bigger fish to fry than worrying about the Ridley property. He had a killer to catch—

And he had to do it before he forever lost his chance to woo Stella.

WHERE WAS STEEL Cooper now?

Stella knew she should focus on Eric, who was moving her around to the slow country tune the band was playing, but she found it hard to keep her mind from wandering. The evening was warm, the music good, and a Montana sky's worth of stars shimmered overhead. A romantic setting for sure—

So why couldn't she focus on the man in her arms?

When the Coopers moved back to town three years

ago, Stella had never thought Steel would take up so much of her thoughts, but lately she couldn't shake his face from her mind—or his touch from her dreams.

He'd danced with her on a couple of occasions this summer, each time simply to rile up one of her brothers. Those dances meant nothing, but still she could remember the feel of his hands on her waist, the crispness of his shirt against her cheek and the shivers he'd sent down her spine when he'd whispered in her ear.

"Stella?" Eric's voice broke into her reverie, and she shook off her wayward thoughts. Steel wasn't a suitable match for her, no matter how she reacted when he was near. "What are you thinking about?" Eric pulled her against him, and she shifted to try to get more comfortable. It wasn't fair to him to keep wishing it was Steel's broad shoulders she had her arms wrapped around.

Eric Holden was one of the best men Stella knew. She'd always appreciated his dedication to his job. He was one of the first to get into work in the morning and still there when she clocked off for the day. Several times, driving through town at night, she'd seen his truck in the sheriff's department parking lot, his office light on. He was steadfast, energetic and good-looking, even if he was a bit older than she was. She couldn't say why he didn't rev her up the way Steel did.

"Just… appreciating the music." It was true as far as it went. The band was competent, and dancing with Eric was nice enough. He was a solid man, still muscular despite his forty-three years. Handsome, too, with a strong jaw and green eyes that were easy to get lost in.

She knew other women were watching and envying her, which made it ridiculous that she couldn't keep her mind off Steel.

Daydreaming about the man was wrong in so many ways she couldn't count them. She was a Turner. He was a Cooper. She valued honesty, forthrightness and good citizenship, all characteristics Eric possessed in spades. Who knew what Steel valued? She worked for the sheriff's department as a receptionist—and hoped to move into a different position soon. Steel skirted the law like his father had—and maybe outright broke it.

She needed a man like Eric. A sheriff's deputy, like she hoped to be one day. A good, forthright, caring man she'd always be able to depend on. She'd never have to wonder what Eric was up to; she could read him like an open book. He loved his work, his baseball team and his country. There weren't any layers to him—or secrets. He wasn't like Steel, slipping in and out of her life in disconcerting ways, never making it clear if he thought of her as date material or just the girl next door.

If he thought of her at all.

Besides, she had too much on her plate to worry about men very much. The next intake for deputy training was coming up fast. First she had to pass the entrance exams, including a physical fitness test. That meant getting into better shape.

"I've been thinking a lot about you." Eric broke into her thoughts, drawing her closer.

"Really?"

"Really." He bent to brush a kiss over her forehead.

Stella's heart sank. He'd been thinking about sex with her, clearly. Did he ever consider her intellect, sense of humor or achievements?

Of course he did, she told herself, but they were at a wedding. The whole evening had been romantic. Could she blame Eric for being in a romantic mood—even if she wasn't?

The truth was, she felt torn about her single status. On the one hand, everyone around her was getting married, and she felt left behind. On the other hand, she wasn't sure she was ready for a relationship with anyone. She had things to do—changes to make in her life. She had a feeling Eric was the kind of guy who liked things to stay the same.

Steel probably relished a challenge. He struck her as the kind of man who could wake up one morning and change everything about himself.

Which didn't make him boyfriend material, she reminded herself severely. Eric was far more appropriate. He ticked off all the right boxes as a potential mate, and she liked him. Admired him.

But she never found herself daydreaming about him—not the way she daydreamed about Steel.

When Eric bent down again, angling for her mouth this time, Stella pulled back. "I'm going to try to be a deputy," she blurted. "And I need to pass the physical fitness test. Do you want to train with me sometime?"

He blinked. Pulled back, wary at this sudden change in conversation. "Well, I… sure, Stella, if that's what you want." It was obvious his mind had been on an entirely different activity they could do together.

"Well, you passed it, right?" she barrelled on. "I mean I know it was a long time ago, and maybe you don't even remember the test, but…" Oh, this wasn't going well at all.

She was pretty sure Eric sighed. "I'm not ancient. I do remember the agility test."

Had she hurt his feelings?

"I know you're not ancient." She tried again. "That wasn't what I meant at all. I meant maybe you're too busy for something like that." Over his shoulder she spotted her uncle Jed talking with Steel's aunt Virginia. Those two were known to get into heated arguments, so she knew she'd better keep an eye on them, but they were chatting amicably enough for now.

"I'm never too busy for you." Eric tugged her closer again. "But are you sure you've thought this through? Being a deputy isn't a walk in the park."

Stella straightened. Did he think she couldn't handle the job? There weren't too many female deputies in town, but it wasn't like she'd have to break new ground.

"I work at the station, remember? I have a fair idea what it's like." At the refreshments table, Jed offered Virginia a piece of cake. Virginia stabbed a finger at a plate piled high with cookies, and he added several of them to the dish and handed it to her. Stella bit back a smile. She was fairly certain Jed had a crush on Virginia, despite the way they fought.

"You're not exactly brawny." Eric spanned her waist with his hands as a visual demonstration, pulling her back to their conversation. "I'm not sure you know what you're getting yourself into."

"Well, I'm sure," Stella said crisply. So much for romance. Now she was good and annoyed. She didn't need him talking down to her like that. She was a strong woman, not some debutante in a hoop skirt.

Eric must have sensed her anger. "Heck, Stella, sorry—that was out of line. You're a smart lady, and I'm sure you know your capabilities. I'd be glad to help anytime."

Stella relaxed a little and let him move her around the dance floor again. "I do know my capabilities," she said. Now Virginia was supervising while Jed loaded up a plate of desserts for himself. She could see her giving him a lot of advice. He reached for something, and Virginia swatted his hand away. Her shrill voice carried over the music. "That cake's filling has cream in it, and it's sat out for far too long!"

Eric frowned. "You can't blame me for worrying about you. I'm a man. Guess I like to think of myself as the protector in this relationship. If you're a deputy, too…"

"Then maybe I'll be the one doing the protecting," she quipped. "Welcome to the twenty-first century, Eric. I'll be fine."

He growled in a playful way. "Every time I turn around something's changing. Guess I'll have to change, too."

"Guess so." She spotted her younger sister, Maya, heading over to the refreshment table. Was she doing refills or beginning to pack things away? "I'd better go help out a little. Maya's looking for me." She spotted her mother, Mary, and Enid Cooper coming to join her sister. They'd done a lot to help set up the wedding, and Stella was happy that the two of them had rekindled their old friendship. She hadn't exactly patched things up with her mother, but she supposed she'd get there someday.

"Do you have to?" He made no move to let her go.

"I have to. See you around, Eric." She disengaged herself from his arms, not giving him time to try to kiss her again or ask what she was doing later.

"Everything all right?" Maya asked when she joined her.

"Everything's fine." But as her gaze traveled over the assembled guests, Stella realized she was looking for Steel even though she knew he wasn't there. Everything wasn't fine. She was too smart to be pining for an unsuitable man. Steel was as much a thief as his father was rumored to have been.

And he'd run off with her heart.

STEEL SLIPPED AWAY between the trees, satisfied that his sister was safely married and would be cared for by the man she loved. He would have liked to tell her how happy he was for her, but it would be a long time before he could talk openly with his family again. He'd worked too hard to get to this point in his investigation. People needed to place him firmly in the camp of the bad guys in their minds. That way the bad guys might finally see him as one of them.

It took him a long time to make his way across several ranches to the place where he'd hidden his truck. In the morning he'd get back to work searching for answers. Meanwhile, he'd drive back to Silver Falls, to his new base of operations.

Shortly before midnight, he was sitting in the doorway of the ramshackle trailer he'd recently purchased for a song, lost in thought, trying to calm his mind in preparation for sleep, when the wind shifted and a cool breeze ruffled his hair.

Steel straightened, but it took him a moment to realize what had roused him.

A smell. A certain heaviness to the air.

He looked to the sky again—to the west where clouds already obscured the stars. A storm was gathering. He watched it come his way.

And smiled as the first drops of rain began to fall.

GUESTS HAD ALREADY begun to head for home when the rain started, stopping all of them in their tracks. All around Stella, people tilted their heads back to feel the pitter-patter of drops hitting their skin, such a familiar feeling but one they'd missed for far too long.

Tears pricked Stella's eyes, and she swallowed in a throat that suddenly ached—with gratitude. Finally, this crazy drought would end. It had been a long hot summer that had left the ground as hard and dry as concrete and everyone's tempers stretched to the limits. Their crops had struggled. Their morale, too. Rain was just what the doctor ordered. She hadn't realized how much the constant worry had affected her these past few months until the muscles at the back of her neck relaxed. She blinked back the sudden rush of emotion that welled inside her as the raindrops fell, but glancing around, she realized she wasn't the only one affected this way. Jo Reed had stretched out her arms and was slowly twirling. Lisa Matheson looked like she was praying. Paul Hornsley, one of the oldest men still ranching in the county, kept swallowing, his Adam's apple bobbing up and down.

Someone started to clap. Zane Hall cheered. Soon everyone joined in, giving the rain a standing ovation, as if the curtain had just fallen on some Shakespearian play.

As the breeze picked up and the rain began to fall more swiftly, however, a murmur ran around the remaining guests. Stella woke from her joyful reverie and realized there was food to pack, tablecloths to fold, beer and liquor to carry away—

In a minute this beautiful outdoor venue was going to be a mess.

All around her people gathered up whatever they could and raced for the main house, some distance away. Stella grabbed a platter of desserts and hurried across the parched lawn. Men were stacking chairs. Women flocked around her, laden with whatever food and drinks they could carry.

Stella burst through the back door into the kitchen, set the platter on the large table and began taking the plates and trays from the other women's hands. She shoved drinks into the refrigerator or coolers that a few cowboys had lugged up to the house, stacked table linens and cutlery on the counters to deal with in the morning. A half hour later, everything was indoors and most of the guests were gone, and Stella, exhausted but happy, went outdoors again, stepped into the yard and let the rain pour over her skin.

She'd been as parched as the ground.

Was Steel watching the rain fall, too?

Silly question. If he was, what did that have to do with her? Just because she couldn't quite get an image out of her mind of him joining her out here, pulling her as close as Eric had earlier in the evening, the heat of his body keeping her warm despite the cool rain, didn't mean—

"That's a good way to catch your death of cold," Jed said from behind her.

Stella yelped, caught herself and spun to find him sitting on one of the wicker chairs on the back porch. How long had he been there?

She hoped like hell he couldn't read her mind.

"I'll go dry off in a minute now that I can finally relax," she assured him, quickly crossing the grass and running lightly up the stairs to the porch.

"Don't relax too hard." Jed stood slowly, using his cane to steady himself. "You've still got work to do— and I'm not talking about cleaning all this up."

"I don't need any extra jobs right now, thank you very much," Stella said pertly. She had a sinking feeling she knew exactly where this was going.

She was right.

"I infiltrated the Coopers tonight. Heard their plans."

"What plans?" she made herself ask, although the last thing she wanted was to have this conversation. Her guests had helped with storing away food and washing some of the dishes, but there was plenty more to do.

"Their plans to expand the detox and stabilization unit in town to serve teens and win the Founder's Prize once and for all."

The damn Founder's Prize. It was all she'd heard about all summer. Stella opened the kitchen door and faced the mess inside. If Jed was going to talk, she might as well stay up and tackle some of this now. She grabbed a hand towel and wiped off her hands and face. It had been so hot all day, the dampness of her dress felt good, and she figured it would dry soon enough. "It's not even possible for them to win. All they can do is tie with us," she pointed out as she pulled on an apron, crossed to the sink and began to fill it with water.

"Aren't you going to change out of those wet things?" Jed demanded. "Everyone's concerned about the drug issue," he added. "Especially with those overdoses in Silver Falls. If the Coopers pull this off, they could still win."

Stella couldn't wait until the contest was over. All it did was bury them in extra work.

"What do you want me to do about it?" She added dish soap to the water and put the first stack of plates in to soak.

"Come up with a plan. Do something to get this family back on track." He kept going toward the interior of the house.

"I am doing something. I'm going to become a deputy."

Jed waved that off. "That's not going to help matters any. We've been in law enforcement for generations, and it never got us a free ranch. Come up with something else." He paused in the entryway to the hall. "I'm off to bed. Don't stay up too late. Plenty of time for dishes in the morning."

"I won't." She waited until she was alone and dipped her hands into the water, washing the first dish. Her brothers must have retired with their wives, too, everyone assuming they could finish cleaning up tomorrow.

She wasn't ready for sleep yet, though. She liked hearing the rain.

Liked being by herself.

She let her imagination run free again. Dreamed of a life in which it would be okay for a woman like her to fall for a man like Steel.

If Jed wanted to win the Ridley property, he could do it himself.

Chapter Two

"**L**OOK OUT, GUYS, ghost man walking," Ned Haverstock said, elbowing one of the other Silver Falls deputies.

"Steel, what are you doing here? It's daylight, for Christ's sake, you might melt," Daniel Ortiz joked.

"You forget no one's supposed to know about you?" Alan Crisp asked.

"Meeting with the boss." Steel pushed past the knot of men gathered in the hallway outside Sheriff Bolton's office. It was Monday morning, and everyone was in that post-weekend state where they weren't quite ready to start the work week again. He was used to the jokes, but it made him uneasy that anyone except Bolton knew about his true reason for being in Silver Falls. Loose lips sank ships and all that. One slip of the tongue and his cover could be blown.

He envied the other men. They got to do their jobs openly. Wear their uniforms. Drive in marked cruisers and receive the respect of the populace. Once upon a time, Steel had found the idea of undercover work exciting. Now its restrictions pressed down on him until he could barely breathe. Unbidden, an image of Stella in

Eric's arms settled itself firmly in his mind and refused to budge when he mentally tried to shove it aside. What were the chances she'd wait around for a man like him when she could be with a pillar of the community like Eric?

Maybe he should make more of an effort to befriend the jovial deputies he'd just passed, he thought, but every instinct in him told Steel not to. It would be only natural for one of them to slip up and mention his name to a wife here, a girlfriend there. The more time he spent around them, the more his name would become part of their vocabulary—and the more easily they might slip and spill his secret to someone else, a mistake that could be deadly to him—and the people around him. At least back in Washington he'd been part of a cadre who worked undercover. He'd never felt as isolated there as he did here.

"Come in," Sheriff Bolton called out when Steel knocked.

Mitch Bolton was a man who was getting stout as his years accumulated and desk work took its toll, but he'd once been a cross country medalist and the pride of the county. He took his job seriously, and as far as Steel was concerned he was the best of what the place had to offer.

"Wedding go okay last night?" Bolton asked.

"Yep."

"Anyone see you?"

Bolton knew him too well. "Nope."

"Good."

"Any more information come in about Rena Klein?" That was his reason for stopping in. He hadn't heard back yet about what they'd found at the scene of her death.

"There's nothing to indicate her death was anything more than an overdose."

Not surprising. It had been the same with Cecilia Foster and all the other girls before her.

"No immediate evidence," Steel corrected him. "You're focusing too narrowly. Look at Klein's life as a whole. Teenage girls from good families don't go from perfectly clean to overdosing overnight."

"Sheltered girls who have no idea what they're doing might, by accident," Mitch shot back.

"This isn't just about drugs."

"I know you think it isn't, but I think your focus isn't narrow enough; stop the drugs and you'll stop the deaths. Isn't that good enough for you?"

Steel shook his head. You couldn't stop the flow of drugs when they were available everywhere. "I'd like to see Rena's file again."

Bolton found it for him among a pile on his desk and handed it over.

With a sigh, Steel opened it to see the face of a young woman staring back at him. Blonde. Pretty enough. Seventeen years old.

When he noticed he was crumpling the folder between his fingers, Steel forced himself to relax. He was going to figure out what was behind all these overdoses—or who. It was just a matter of time.

"You going to the pit today?" Bolton asked him.

"Of course," Steel said automatically, reading through updated information. The pit was a vacant lot in Silver Falls where an old colliery had stood for over a hundred years before it was declared unsafe, knocked down and the rubble mostly cleared away. Its broken foundation still stood surrounded by weeds, tangled bushes—and a motley collection of disaffected youth. Outside the center of the small town but close enough to the main strip for easy access to the liquor store and pizza joint, it attracted drug users, runaways and malcontents of every stripe. At least once a night the Silver Falls sheriffs rousted everyone out of there. An hour later they were all back.

"I think it's time Cab Johnson knew about you," Bolton said.

Steel was already shaking his head. "I disagree. Respectfully, of course."

"Of course." Mitch leaned back in his chair. "Cab's a good guy, Steel."

"He's tied to every family in Chance Creek, including mine," Steel said. "No way he'd keep that secret."

"He's a professional."

"He's also human. The minute anyone suspects that Cab is tiptoeing around me, which he would once he understood what I was up to, the game is over. In order for this to work, he's got to be as suspicious of me as anyone else." He lifted the folder in his hand. "What are we missing about her?"

"Nothing, far as I can tell. Good student. Churchgoer. Family is intact. Started acting out a few months back. Cutting class. Staying out late. Refusing to say where she'd been. Changed her sleeping habits, stopped eating. Her family did what they could: grounded her. Tried to get her more involved with the youth group at church. Offered to take her on a trip if she got her grades up. Nothing worked."

"Because someone got to her. Convinced her there was something more exciting to do than all that."

Bolton frowned. "Or like a million other teenagers she decided to get high *just once* and couldn't stop."

"I think it's more than that."

"I know you do, but you need to stay focused. Don't let your past chew you up and spit you out. Got it?"

"Yes, sir." But it was too late for that.

"I THINK YOU'D make a great deputy," Maya said over breakfast, waving a piece of bacon to emphasize her point. "You've worked at the station for years. Cab thinks the sun rises and sets with you. What are you worried about?"

Stella was happy her sister had joined her and Mary for breakfast today, even if she and Lance usually ate at the small cabin on the Flying W where they'd moved after the wedding. Jed wouldn't be down for another hour. Everything was back to shipshape in the sunny kitchen after hours of work the previous day. Liam and Tory, who were to take up residence in the house with Stella, were gone on their honeymoon to Colorado

Springs. Lance was probably already doing chores. Maya had come early and helped whip up a meal.

"Passing the physical agility test." Stella slid a fried egg onto her plate, added some hash browns and crossed to sit at the table with the rest of the family.

"You're in great shape," Maya scoffed.

"I don't know why you want to be a deputy anyway," Mary said primly from her place at the head of the table. Dressed today in a neat sundress and sandals, she looked more prepared for a day in town than one spent at the ranch, but Mary had never liked country living that much. Stella was still surprised that Mary seemed home to stay. "Bad enough your father wasted his life with all that."

"I don't think he wasted his life, even if he made some poor choices at the end of it."

"Still can't believe Dad was growing pot." Maya frowned at her food. They'd learned about their father's indiscretions recently, and all of them were having trouble grappling with the implications.

"You shouldn't believe it," Mary said. "I doubt it's true."

"But you believed he was cheating on you," Stella said tartly.

"So did you," Mary pointed out. Both of them had seen Enid Cooper with William one night thirteen years ago and jumped to the wrong conclusion. It had been the last straw for Mary and William's marriage, but Stella knew now that her parents would have split up no matter what.

"What do you have to do to prepare for the test?" Maya broke in. She always tried to deflect problems, Stella mused. Family dynamics didn't change much over the years.

"I watched a video of the test online, and it's kind of like an obstacle course."

"Like the one the guys at Crescent Hall have?"

"Not nearly as complicated as that one," Stella said with a smile. "Although I suppose if I got good on theirs I could handle the physical agility test no problem."

"Maybe you should ask them if you can try it out."

"Maybe," Stella said, "but I want to set up one here that's more like what I'll actually have to do to pass the test. I figure that way I can get to it several times a day instead of only once in a while, the way it would be if I was trying to use the Halls' course."

"Makes sense."

"I don't think any of this makes sense," Mary said tartly. "What's wrong with the career you already have?"

"What's wrong with yours in Ohio?" Stella countered. "You're trying something new with Enid and Leslie, right? Why can't I change things?" Mary, Enid Cooper and Leslie Falk, who'd been fast friends in high school before a falling out, had patched things up recently and become inseparable. They'd been discussing any number of ventures they could embark on together. At the moment they seemed to favor opening some type of spa. Stella wasn't sure who'd make use of such a thing in this small town, but she wasn't about to rain on anyone's parade. She didn't think she'd ever seen her mother as content as she was these days.

"Why do you have to become a deputy? Can't you choose something else?" Mary gathered her dishes, took them to the sink and left them there. "I'll be out the rest of the day," she said with a sniff and kept going before Stella could answer.

"What's eating her?" Stella asked.

"Maybe she spent so much time worrying about Dad she doesn't want to worry about you, too."

Stella supposed Maya could be right. "What about Noah?"

"Noah's a man—and he's a parole officer, not a deputy," Maya pointed out. "Like I said before, I think you'd do great at the job, but do you really want to be one? I imagine things can get pretty rough. You'll deal with drunks, family disturbances, criminals…"

"It's what I've always wanted to do," Stella said. "I just finally got up the courage to say so."

"Then I'll do whatever I can to help, and I'm sure Noah will, too. What does Eric think about the idea?" Maya stood and began to pack away the food.

"He said he'd help me train for the fitness test," she admitted and didn't know why Steel popped into her head just then. She supposed it would be fun to chase him around an obstacle course. Just thinking about it made her smile. Steel was fit in an entirely different way than Eric. Muscular and quick, with a smile and a way of teasing her that melted her from the inside out.

"I knew it. You and Eric are an item, aren't you?"

Maya asked, misinterpreting her expression.

"No, we're not," Stella said quickly. Despite what he seemed to think.

"You will be if you ask him for help with your training. Give him a call." Maya moved onto stacking the dishes and taking them to the sink as Stella kept eating. "Can I leave these for you?"

"Sure." She had time before her shift started. When Maya left, Stella finished her own meal more slowly, then got to work cleaning up, her mind still on Steel and Eric.

Why wasn't she giving Eric a fair shake? He was a much better candidate than Steel could ever be. He shared her interests, her values and her need to live a life she could be proud of. Steel was… Steel. Very likely he was involved in things that were far from legal. If she was going to be a deputy, she had to give him up.

Stella dried her hands, reached for her phone determinedly and called Eric.

"Stella," he answered before the second ring. "Good to hear from you. Can we meet for dinner or a drink soon?"

She closed her eyes. Dinner and a drink meant more kisses—which was good, she lectured herself. She needed to give Eric a chance. Surely if she spent more time with him she'd learn to like him that way.

"I was thinking about the physical agility test," she said firmly, not quite ready to go there yet. "Last night you said you'd help me train."

There was a long pause, and she could almost hear

him sigh. Was she asking too much of a man who worked so hard already? It was clear what he really wanted was to do something fun with her, and really, could she blame him?

"Sure," he said finally. "What do you have in mind?"

She was beginning to wish she'd never brought it up. It occurred to her that if Eric wasn't into the enterprise, it wasn't going to be very enjoyable for her, either. "Well," she began, "I looked online and saw the obstacle course I'll need to complete for the test. What I want to do is recreate it as best I can here at home. Could you come by after work and help me figure it out? I could feed you dinner afterward."

"Dinner sounds good." His voice deepened to the tone of a man appreciating being waited on by a woman. Stella squashed a rush of irritation. Eric didn't mean anything by it; he was flattered, that was all. "I can't make it tonight, though," he went on. "I could do it day after tomorrow."

Relief washed over her, which made her sigh. She shouldn't have invited Eric at all if she didn't want him to come. "That's okay," she made herself say brightly.

"Meanwhile, how about lunch tomorrow? Can you join me in Silver Falls?"

Damn it, he'd done an end-run around her plan to keep things light. Although lunch was light, she told herself. "Why Silver Falls?" she asked curiously.

"I have an appointment out that way. Do you have something planned already?" he pressed when she didn't answer right away.

Unable to lie, Stella said, "No, but—"

"Top Spot Café," he said. "Noon."

"Okay," she said reluctantly. "See you at work."

"See y—"

She cut the call before he'd finished his answer, disgusted with herself for falling into this trap. No, not trap. She couldn't think of another word for it. Eric liked her, plain and simple. He wasn't interested in training with her. Didn't care whether she became a deputy. He simply wanted to be her boyfriend. She had no doubt he'd be the perfect companion at the movies or dinner or on a moonlit walk. He'd probably be a considerate and capable lover, too. He wasn't looking for a colleague, however. He was looking for a woman who would let him be a man.

That wasn't what she was looking for at all—so why had she even called him in the first place?

Stella took a deep breath and tried to calm her whirling thoughts. It was just a lunch date. Eric wouldn't push her to do anything she didn't want to do. She was so buried in her own ambitions these days she was having trouble seeing the good in him. He was a nice guy—the kind of guy she should want. He certainly wanted her. What was wrong with that?

What was wrong was that even now, all she could think about was Steel's hands on her waist as she'd danced with him weeks ago. The earthy, male smell of him when she'd breathed him in. The way her pulse had leaped when his breath feathered over her cheek—

Stella put her phone away and plunged her hands into the soapy water again. This was the last time she'd take relationship advice from Maya.

"WHAT DO YOU want, creeper?" the girl said, giving Steel the kind of scathing once-over only a teenager can pull off. Lily Barnes was blonde. Maybe seventeen. Dressed in cut-off jean shorts and a clingy top she must have bought in a mall in Billings or Bozeman. Steel knew her family from around Chance Creek but had never spoken to her before and wondered why she and two of her friends would choose to kill time at the pit.

"The question is, what do you want?" He didn't blame her for her caution. He was doing his best to act like the kind of guy who sold illicit drugs to little kids. Not the kind of person any self-respecting young woman would want around her. Why a self-respecting young woman was hanging out in the pit at all was anyone's guess.

"I doubt you've got anything I'd be interested in."

Lily was pretending to be tough, but Steel knew she lived in one of the nicer houses in Chance Creek. Her father was a dentist. Her mother volunteered at their church. Lily should have been prepping to head to Montana State, not hanging out with a bunch of losers in a vacant lot. Her companions, Lara Whidby and Sue Hill, were from similar circumstances.

Steel understood when some of the more disaffected youth from Chance Creek slipped through the cracks, but these weren't girls sidelined by poverty or social awkwardness or anything like that. Healthy, pretty, privileged girls from good families. What were they doing here?

In fact, why hang out in Silver Falls at all?

"You like to party?" he made himself ask.

Lily rolled her eyes. "Get lost, creeper; we're busy."

"Yeah, get lost," Lara echoed.

Lily looked up at the sky as if there was nothing worth seeing around here, but Sue was watching the street.

"I've got connections," Steel ventured.

"For God's sake, don't you understand English?" Lily said. "Get. Lost."

"What are you looking for? I can help you find it."

Before Lily could answer, Lara straightened, focusing on something behind Steel—a vehicle that was approaching. Lara's shoulders tensed, and she glanced at Steel. "Lily," she said warningly.

Lily caught sight of it, too. "Shit," she said disgustedly. "Damn it, creeper, get the hell away from us."

Sue just smiled, as if she knew something entertaining was about to happen.

"Go." Lily waved her hands at Steel as if she could waft him away like an unpleasant odor. When he didn't move, she rolled her eyes again. "It's a cop," she said.

"A Chance Creek cop," Lara echoed.

Sue stayed where she was, that smile playing about her lips. It was the smile of a rich girl who knew she wouldn't get in trouble but someone else might.

Someone like him.

They had to be wrong, though. That wasn't a cruiser, and even if it was a cop—or deputy, rather; there weren't any police here—it would be a Silver Falls deputy, not one from Chance Creek. He turned to confirm this and stiffened when he recognized Eric Holden climbing out of his fire-engine red Ford F-250.

Hell.

"Better stay away from us, creeper," Lily hissed at Steel, "or I'll tell the nice cop all about you."

Steel wished he was far away from them already. Since Eric worked for the Chance Creek sheriff's department, he had no idea Steel worked undercover for Silver Falls. From his point of view Steel was a thirty-something-year-old creep hitting on a bunch of teenage girls.

If that didn't establish his reputation as a bad guy, he didn't know what would.

"Eric?" a woman's voice called out from somewhere across the street. "I thought we were meeting at the Top Spot Café!"

Oh, hell, Steel thought when Stella came into view around another parked pickup truck. This got worse and worse. What was she doing in Silver Falls?

Meeting Eric?

Were they an item now?

"What's she doing here?" Lily echoed and turned to her friends. "I know that lady. This is lame; let's get out of here."

"I'm not going anywhere," Sue said.

"You'd better. That's Stella Turner. She works for

the sheriff's department, too. You want her all over us? Calling our folks?"

Sue pouted, fiddling with her long brown hair, but Lily's words must have hit home. "I guess not." She stood up.

"Come on." Lily grabbed Lara's arm and tugged her along. Sue followed unhappily, all of them moving quickly down the block.

Steel got moving in the opposite direction, but when Stella called out, "Steel? Is that you?" he stopped in his tracks. She'd made it to his side of the street, and her gaze followed the young girls hurrying away from him toward the center of town. "What... are you doing?" she asked uncertainly.

"Yeah, Cooper? What the hell *are* you doing?" Eric moved to Stella's side protectively. Steel burned to shove him away and take his place. He'd known Stella since they were kids, and when he'd moved back to town, he'd immediately been attracted to the woman she'd grown into. What right did Eric have to claim her?

"Minding my own goddamn business," Steel growled at him. He had to get out of here before his temper got the better of him. Like it or not, he had to maintain his cover, even if he'd like to explain everything to Stella so she'd stop looking at him like that.

He would have liked to see where the girls went, but he couldn't follow them with Stella and Eric watching, so he stepped onto the sidewalk, prepared to cross the street.

Stella moved closer to Eric, and regret twisted

Steel's gut. Was she afraid of him? She never had been before.

"Why were you talking to those girls?" she asked.

Because he had a job to do. He couldn't say that, though. "What's wrong with talking to some pretty girls?" he forced himself to ask as if he was the low-life she clearly thought he was at the moment.

Stella's mouth dropped open, then she snapped it shut into a tight frown.

"You'd better keep away from those minors," Eric warned him, stepping in front of her protectively. Stella's frown deepened, and Steel knew her well enough to see she wanted to assert her ability to protect herself but also wasn't sure she should.

The whole situation would have been funny if it wasn't so damn awful.

"I will if they keep away from me." Steel headed for the truck he'd parked some blocks away, knowing he'd done enough damage to tarnish himself in Stella's eyes for a lifetime. The morning had been a bust. He was no closer to answering the question of why girls like Lily and her friends were frequenting the pit and why they kept turning up dead.

Time to go home, if he could call his stupid trailer that.

"Hold it right there, Cooper," a voice called out behind him. Not Eric's—or Stella's, thank God—but almost as bad. Ned Haverstock was walking toward him, Daniel Ortiz right behind them.

Oh, fuck me, Steel thought. He spotted their cruiser

down the block. How long had they been watching this action unfold? Were they afraid Eric would discover what he was doing if they left the situation alone? Had someone called the Silver Falls sheriff's department to report him loitering around?

He allowed himself a look back and affirmed Eric and Stella were still watching.

"Heard you were bothering some little girls," Ned said loudly. "A concerned citizen called it in." He was enjoying this, Steel thought. The man marched right up to him and now was trying to tower over him—which didn't quite work seeing they were of a similar height. Steel had no doubt Ned meant to have a good laugh about this later at the sheriff's department.

"Like hell," Steel growled.

"You like them young, huh?" Daniel pressed him, leaning in, too.

"Fuck you," Steel said.

"Don't talk to an officer of the law like that," Daniel said.

"I'll talk to you dumb shits however I want to." To them this was all a game, wasn't it? He'd heard them talking before when they thought he wasn't around. Speculating on the real reason the boss kept him around. It wasn't like his undercover work had turned up much yet.

"That's it, I'm taking you down to the station," Ned said. "Turn around. Hands behind your back."

"Are you serious?" Steel asked him. He lowered his voice. "Just shove me around a little and let me go. I've got stuff to do."

"Holden's watching," Ned murmured back. "Play it up a little. Let's give him a show. He'll go back to Chance Creek and tell everyone what a hardened criminal you are." He shoved Steel against the sheriff's cruiser they'd driven up in. "Resisting just makes this harder," he said aloud.

Steel thought he heard Stella protesting. The last thing he needed was her coming to try to help, so he went limp. Allowed Ned to handcuff him and lead him to the back door of the cruiser. He swore when Ned shoved him in, managing to hit his head—hard—on the car's frame as he did so.

"You're an ass," Steel told him when the cruiser was on the move, leaving Stella and Eric far behind.

"All part of the job," Ned said. "How about we get some takeout on the way to the station. We did good back there, right? They'll never guess you're working with us."

"Yeah, you did good," Steel forced himself to say, although he was fuming inside. "What the hell. Let's go get takeout. I'm not going to accomplish anything else today."

"THOSE GIRLS' FAMILIES might as well throw in the towel right now," Eric said when he and Stella were eating at a corner table at the Top Spot Café, a depressing little restaurant that couldn't get a side salad right, let alone serve a decent bowl of soup, she quickly discovered. "Once they get a taste of the wild side, they just go to hell."

"That seems harsh." She toyed with a forkful of lettuce, her appetite nonexistent. She couldn't believe what she'd seen back at the pit. What had Steel been doing with those girls? Why had the Silver Falls deputies arrested him? Sure, he'd been mouthy, but he hadn't committed a crime.

Had he?

She hadn't gotten a good look at the girls as they'd scurried away toward town, but she'd been pretty sure one of them was Lara Whidby. She made a mental note to tell Lara's mother where she'd seen her—she doubted Kim Whidby would want her daughter to hang out at the pit.

"You want to be a deputy? Get used to harsh," Eric said, then seemed to remember who he was talking to and relented. "Look, I know you want to believe people can be saved. We all do at the beginning. Then you work the job a few years and see that people are who they are. Those girls look like any others from nice families, but they're not. They're already on the long slide down into self-destruction."

"Not all of them."

"Everyone knows about the pit. They know it's where kids go to get drugs. Those girls have made their choice."

"That doesn't mean they can't be saved."

He pointed his fork at her. "You've got to grow up, Turner, if you want to be a deputy. You can't save people who have given up on themselves."

"Maybe we need to expand the detox and stabilization programs so they can cater to teens," she said slowly, thinking about what Jed had said he'd overheard the Coopers talking about. As far as she knew, there weren't any local treatment programs for teens. "If it wasn't for the drugs, they wouldn't act out like that, right?"

"I don't know. I think some girls like running wild," Eric said. "You going to eat those fries?"

"Go ahead." She watched him take her fries and dig into them the way he'd wolfed down the rest of the meal. She didn't like his cynicism on the subject, but she couldn't pretend she hadn't heard other deputies speaking like him.

Was she setting herself up to end up like them? When she was a deputy, would she feel so jaded she could talk about young girls overdosing on drugs while inhaling a cheap meal?

Maybe Eric was right; maybe she wasn't cut out for the job.

Or maybe Chance Creek needed people like her who cared enough to want to help people who were veering into trouble. Maybe she could stop young women from making bad choices.

"I've got to run to an appointment before I head back to work." Eric stood up. Threw some bills on the table. Stella stood up, too, grateful the meal was over. He caught sight of her expression and stopped. "A lot of stuff goes on in the world that isn't pretty and doesn't have a neat solution. You're a smart woman,

Stella. A good woman. I'm not going to lie. If you become a deputy, it's going to be hard for me to watch while you come face to face with the ugliness."

"I'm not a child," she said.

"I know you aren't. See you soon." He leaned in and pressed a kiss on her mouth that was as unwelcome as the taste of his meal on her lips. Stella pulled back, but Eric didn't seem to notice. He was already halfway across the room.

She reached out to steady herself on the top rung of her wooden chair. That was the second time he'd kissed her as if he had the right to do so. Did Eric think they were together now? He'd never asked if she wanted to be.

She'd let him take her to lunch, though. Let him think she was interested. Since when was she wishy-washy enough to give such mixed signals to a man? That wasn't like her.

She grabbed her purse and walked slowly toward the door. Was it because Noah, Liam and Maya had all gotten married this summer? Was she feeling left behind?

The answer was yes, and it was worse because Maya was her younger sister. She'd always supposed she'd be the first to marry, and if she was honest, she'd thought she'd beat her brothers to the altar, too.

When she neared the door, she realized a steady drizzle had started outside. She was going to get wet walking the couple of blocks to her truck.

"Can you believe this weather?" a woman asked,

rushing through the front door, damp but clearly delighted. Her smile grew with recognition. "Stella Turner? Is that you?"

It took Stella a moment to place her. "Mrs. Hunt?"

"Call me Monica," the woman laughed. "I guess the last time we met you were just a girl, but you haven't changed. You're still lovely."

"Thank you." The praise embarrassed Stella. "I didn't know you were back in town. I've missed Runaway Lodge while you were gone. I always loved coming to swim at your beach on hometown days."

"It's certainly been a long time." Monica shook her head. "I shouldn't have stayed away so long. The lodge is in sorry shape. It'll take a lot of work to fix it up."

"You're going to stay?"

"We'll see," Monica said. "Silver Falls seems like it could use a renovation as much as my lodge can. It was always a little hard on its luck, but these days it seems downright festering."

"Have you seen the pit?" Stella asked her, thinking of her run-in with Steel earlier.

"Not an improvement over the old colliery," Monica said dispiritedly. "I guess I'm lucky all those kids aren't hanging out at my place, though. Good thing the lodge is just far enough away from the heart of town it's not attractive to them." She peered into Stella's face. "Everything all right with you?"

Stella thought about lying but found herself saying, "Someone I know is mixed up with the people who hang out at the pit. I just saw him there. Couldn't believe it, although I've heard the rumors."

"We like to think people will stay the way we think they should be," Monica said. "Doesn't always work out that way, though. Sometimes people show you their true colors and you have to let them go."

"I suppose." Stella sighed. "What about those boys of yours? They ever coming home?"

"Yes, they are," Monica said. "They just don't know it yet."

THE FOLLOWING MORNING Steel figured things had to go better than they'd gone the previous day. He went through his usual routine of sit-ups, push-ups, dips on the pull-up bar he'd installed in the doorway between his trailer's small living room and hallway and the rest of the workout he'd performed every day since he was fifteen. He poured himself a bowl of cereal, splashed some milk on it and dug in while he scanned his phone for the latest local news. Nothing much had happened overnight.

Which suited him just fine.

He was heading out to his truck through a fine misting of rain when a woman's voice cut through the quiet morning. Steel sighed. He'd hoped to avoid this, but by now he ought to know there was no getting past Marion Wheeler's eagle eyes.

Marion had been a fixture in the trailer park for as long as there'd been a trailer park. Longer, maybe. It was rumored she'd settled her single wide on a vacant lot in the seventies and the park had grown up organically around her. It was only recently that Silver Falls had any kind of bylaws. For most of its existence it had been the wild west—people doing what they wanted, when and where they wanted, and damn the consequences.

The consequences of Marion's presence at the Mountain Rise park was that no one could come or go without her noticing and commenting.

"Out causing trouble early today, huh, Cooper?" she called out. She was sitting on a tiny porch that jutted out from her trailer. At one time the trailer's siding must have been powder blue, but it had faded mostly to a silvery gray. The porch had been cobbled together from scrap wood. Steel wondered how it held together, but Marion was a bony, hawk-nosed woman who looked like a puff of wind might blow her away. Only her voice was heavy—grating, even. It followed him as he unlocked his truck. "Someone oughtta call the law on you. Heard you were hitting on minors at the pit yesterday. Shame on you."

He held his tongue through sheer force of will, every inch of him wanting to turn around and tell her he *was* the law, not that it was any of her damn business. How did she know what he'd been up to yesterday, anyway? It wasn't like she ever left that damn porch.

"You should go back to Chance Creek, where riff-raff like you belong," she was calling after him when he drove away.

That was rich. Steel doubted anyone in Chance Creek thought of their town as a step down from Silver

Falls. Chance Creek had its struggles, but Silver Falls was barely holding on these days.

As he drove through the winding streets that led to the town center, he considered her words. Maybe Marion was right—maybe he was from the wrong side of the tracks, if there could be such a designation in a town without a railway running through it—but the kids who frequented the pit these days weren't. Something was wrong with this situation, and while he'd already fingered a dealer or two, allowing Bolton and his deputies to catch them in the act, the girls like Lara and her friends needed help he couldn't give.

He took a right turn, away from the center of Silver Falls, drove about ten miles and turned into a short dirt driveway that led into the woods. When he was sure he was out of view of the road, he gave Bolton a call and waited. He'd already stopped at the station once this week. It wasn't good practice for that to happen very often.

Twenty minutes later the sheriff parked his cruiser behind him, got out and slid into the passenger seat of Steel's truck. "What's up?"

"We need counselors. For those girls hanging out at the pit. Some kind of female liaison officer who can get out there and talk to them in a way I can't."

"You're supposed to be our eyes and ears on the ground." Bolton's tone made it clear he didn't appreciate being dragged from the office for this kind of thing.

"I get close to them, and they think I'm hitting on them." It didn't feel good to him, either. Steel had to do a lot of things during his undercover work he didn't like but nothing that had made him feel so uneasy.

Bolton considered this. "Yeah, that's a problem."

"The problem is that nice young women are ending up dead," Steel pointed out. He couldn't get his mind off Rena. If he'd been doing his job more effectively, maybe she'd still be alive. During the last couple of months, he'd been more concerned about a pair of sisters—runaways he'd finally convinced to go home. He was proud he'd helped negotiate a reconciliation, but he'd missed the signs that Rena was a target. He'd seen her at the pit a few times in the past. Caught sight of her loitering on the corner near the convenience store once or twice. He'd never seen her buy anything from one of the small-time dealers in town, though.

So where'd she get the drugs to overdose?

"Here's the thing," Bolton went on. "If we send a counselor out there, one, what are the chances those girls will even talk to her, and two, that won't lead to us finding the pipeline for all those pills coming into town."

"I'm working on that. But it's like questioning where the water in a rainstorm originates." Steel pointed to the gray clouds filling the sky overhead. The mist had stopped, but more rain was threatening. "There's local distributors and dealers, sure, but you can order this stuff online, too."

"Keep asking around."

"What about a female liaison officer?"

"We don't have the budget for that. You know it as

well as I do." Bolton opened the passenger side door. "Get in there, do your thing and unravel the connections. We need a bust. A big one. That will deter people. Make parents keep tighter tabs on their kids."

Maybe, Steel thought. Maybe not. He knew Bolton was a good guy. Knew, too, that the small Silver Falls sheriff's department was overwhelmed, just like most departments in the country.

"Stop complicating things," Bolton said, swinging himself out the door. He paused there, one hand on the roof of the truck, peering back in at Steel. "It's the drugs killing those girls in the end. Stop the drugs, and you'll stop the deaths. Nice and simple."

Steel watched him go. Nothing was simple about this situation, as far as he was concerned—and that old-fashioned thinking wasn't going to work in a changing world.

"JUSTIN AND LIZ will be here by dinnertime on Saturday. I'm serving a nice roast and baked potatoes. You'll be home, right?" Mary cornered Stella just as she was heading out the door to work.

"Uh... sure," Stella said. Of course she wanted to be there to welcome her stepsiblings to the ranch, but she wasn't sure how she felt about them coming to live here. It was still strange to have her mother back, acting like the head of the household—as if she hadn't walked out on her family when Stella was fourteen.

On the one hand, she appreciated the chance to get to know her mother. On the other hand, she was finding it difficult to let go of the pain she'd felt when Mary left. Suddenly Stella had become the mother-figure in the family. She'd had to take on all Mary's chores and responsibilities just as she entered high school. Hadn't had anyone to turn to with her questions about growing up. It hadn't been easy trying to parent her younger sister, either, when she was barely a teen herself.

Those had been hard, lonely years, with a father whose moods swung wildly, two older brothers who faced challenges of their own and a load of hurt in her heart she'd had no idea what to do with.

A question had always hung at the back of her mind, one she tried never to voice but that persisted nonetheless: What did it mean when your own mother walked out on you?

Now Mary was back, which left Stella just as confused. Had she and her siblings risen in her mother's estimation? Or was Mary merely nursing wounds inflicted by her second husband? He'd been arrested recently for embezzlement.

Stella supposed she should be grateful she ranked higher in Mary's mind than a crook.

She sighed. She was being childish, and she was old enough to know that life was far more complicated than children could understand. Mary had been drowning in unfulfilled dreams when she left Chance Creek. She'd made bad choices and paid for them. If her mother was finding her footing here, especially in her friendships with Enid Cooper and Leslie Falk, that was a good thing.

She didn't have to trust Mary fully, but she didn't have to go looking for reasons to dislike her, either.

Mary was being practical. With her husband serving time in jail, her stepchildren needed someplace to go. Stella had no idea where their biological mother was, and she supposed it was good of Mary to take on their care, but the whole situation was uncomfortable.

She had just reached her truck when her phone rang. Seeing Eric's name on the screen, she nearly didn't answer it but decided not to be a coward. She would be straight with him.

"Hey, Stella—you up for dinner tonight? I've got a baseball game. We could get some takeout on the way, and you can watch."

Watch?

Stella supposed if she really cared for a man, she might enjoy such an evening. She had nothing against the sport and liked hanging out with a crowd cheering on the home team. So why did Eric's offer grate on her? After all, if she joined a team, wouldn't she appreciate her partner cheering her on?

When had she become so judgmental about everyone else? First her mother, now Eric. What else did she have to do tonight, anyway? She'd been so focused on becoming a deputy that she'd lost her sense of humor—and stopped having any fun at all.

She shifted the phone to her other hand. She couldn't picture a future with Eric, but she didn't have anything else to do tonight—or any night for that matter. She hadn't dated anyone in some time, and now all her siblings were married. Meanwhile, she'd been mooning around over Steel Cooper, who thought it was perfectly acceptable to hit on teenagers. Ever since she'd seen it with her own eyes, she'd found herself searching for excuses for his behavior, which was even worse.

"I know it's not the most exciting thing in the world watching an old man play ball," Eric said dispiritedly. "Bet you have something way more fun lined up."

"No, I don't," Stella said truthfully. Hell, now she was bringing Eric down. And for what—because she'd prefer a reprobate like Steel? What was wrong with her? "I'd love to come."

"Really?" There was no mistaking the pleasure in Eric's voice. "That's great!"

When they'd hung up, Stella drove up the long lane, but when she reached the main road, she found herself turning her vehicle not toward town but toward the Ridley property, which bordered the Flying W. The abandoned ranch had been everyone's focus this summer, and now it seemed inextricably linked to everything that had gone wrong—and right—this year. Was it really worth taking on a whole new project to try to win?

Soon she parked and got out of her truck. She surveyed the recent damage to the ranch. A large burnt area swept from where she stood down to Pittance Creek and beyond. Most of the structures had been reduced to rubble. The fire had been edging on Thorn Hill when it was finally put out. She'd never forget the day she and her family—and the Coopers—had battled the blaze, cutting fire break after fire break, stamping out embers as the strong winds blew them forward.

It had been terrifying. Some nights she still dreamed about it—and woke calling out for Steel, who had been bound and helpless inside one of the buildings that had eventually burned down. Only quick thinking on the part of Liam and Tory had gotten him out of there alive.

Stella shivered just thinking about it. She allowed her thoughts to stray there only at times like this, when she was alone, because every time she did, her throat ached with unshed tears. Steel could have burned alive in that fire—and she didn't think she could have borne it.

That night, when their families had gathered together in the hospital waiting room, she'd prayed in a way she hadn't in years. She'd bargained with God, pleaded with him to do whatever it took to bring Steel back to full health. And then he'd disappeared in the night—walked straight out of the hospital without a word to anyone.

The Coopers had accepted the situation with shrugs and sighs—their brother always came and went mysteriously. Stella had a harder time calming her fears. What if he'd breathed in too much smoke and succumbed to it with no one around to notice? For days she'd found herself imagining every possible catastrophe, until she'd caught sight of him driving through Chance Creek one night, apparently without a care in the world.

Still, sometimes her thoughts slipped back to the fire and the awful moment when they'd all realized someone was trapped in that shed, surrounded by flames. She'd known immediately it was Steel. Some thread of awareness connected her to that man even though there was no explanation for such a thing. It was as if he was a puzzle meant for her alone to solve.

What would have happened if Tory hadn't seen the white rag he'd waved to catch their attention through the shed's window? Could she have gone on living in a world in which Steel had died in that fire?

Of course she could, she told herself fiercely. Steel was a sick, twisted individual who hit on teenagers.

But somehow she couldn't believe that, no matter what proof she'd seen with her own eyes.

"Stella?"

A man's voice penetrated her thoughts.

Steel's voice. She shivered again but this time for a completely different reason.

STEEL WASN'T SURE what had brought him to the scene of his near-demise. He'd thought he was a goner when he'd found himself tied up and trapped in a shed with a fire raging all around him. It had been close, that was for sure.

Too close.

An experience like that made a man question a lot of things, including his choice to live undercover on the margins of society. Sometimes he wondered what would happen when he set down the mask he'd been wearing for so long. Who would he be then?

Now he was face to face with the one woman he

wanted to show his real self to, and she was looking at him like something that had gone rotten in her refrigerator. He couldn't blame her, but God, it hurt not to be able to explain.

"Returning to the scene of the crime?" Stella asked lightly, but there was an edge to her voice that had never been there before when she'd spoken to him.

"Something like that."

"They didn't catch the people who set the fire—and tried to kill you," she added.

"Nope." He doubted they ever would, either.

"You think it's the same person who set the fire at Runaway Lodge?"

He shook his head. "Rod Malcolm? No. I think whoever did it hopes we'll think so, though. Last I heard, Rod was cooperating with the fire marshal. His fingerprints were all over that blaze but not this one. Sounds like he'll pay some sort of restitution to Monica Hunt. Maybe do a little time."

"Tory said she saw him at the lodge right before the fire started. He was mean to her in town beforehand."

Steel nodded. "There's old trouble between him and Dale."

"He knew your dad?" Stella shook her head. "I don't know why I'm surprised; everyone knows everyone around here. You know our fathers were growing a pot crop together, right?"

Steel swallowed hard. He hadn't expected her to bring that up. "Yep."

She surveyed him. "That's all you're going to say? It

was supposedly right out here—same place you were growing one."

Hell, he shouldn't have come here. He couldn't answer the questions she was trying to ask.

"Anyone ever tell you you're too smart for your own good?" he said lightly.

Overhead, the sun slipped behind the clouds.

"Do you think it's going to—" Stella laughed when the first fat drops of rain began to fall, her serious expression relaxing into something more like he remembered from when they were kids. "I guess that answers my question. After all those months of drought, the rain keeps surprising me. Sure has been a stormy week."

"Quick. This way." Steel led the way to a stand of trees that hadn't been burnt and gave a quiet laugh when a dilapidated structure came into view high among them. He'd forgotten all about this. "Up here." He tested the boards that were nailed into the tree trunk as a makeshift ladder. They held his weight. He clambered up them and onto the small platform high among the branches. Stella made it up after him a moment later.

"I have to get to work," she said absently. "I had no idea this was here, though."

"Olivia and Maya built it years ago. They used to come and hang out here. Which is how they spotted the pot crop."

"And set off a chain of events that upended everything. What would have happened if they hadn't seen it?" She moved to the edge of the platform and peered down.

"Dad and William would have harvested it. Dad would have become a petty dealer, he'd have made the kind of connections they needed to find—" Hell, he couldn't talk about that.

"To find what?" She turned, and when he didn't answer, she came nearer. "Liam told me our fathers were working together for some reason and that you said it wasn't just for money. So what were they doing?"

He wished he could tell her. Instead, he only shrugged.

"You know what it was, right? Don't lie to me." She folded her arms over her chest.

He didn't want to lie. "Yeah, I know what it was."

"They're both dead. Why keep it a secret anymore?"

"Because… it isn't over. What they were doing." And he was telling her far too much, but Stella's direct gaze made it hard to stop. She surveyed him for a long moment.

"Are you… still after whatever it was they were trying to accomplish?" she asked slowly. When he didn't answer, her brows raised. "You are, aren't you? How did you get mixed up in this—whatever it is?"

Her suspicious tone made it clear she wasn't convinced of his motives. What had she seen of him so far? He skulked around town, hung out with ne'er-do-wells, flirted with teenage girls. He made himself sick. "I've always been involved," he admitted, not knowing what else to say. He wanted her to understand. "Since Dad went to jail, anyway."

"What happened to the pot crop? And the money you earned from selling it?"

He was already shaking his head. "I didn't sell it. I burned it."

"You expect me to believe that? You'd just throw away all that money when your family always struggled to make ends meet? Why? Why would you do such a thing?"

"To save your father's ass!" Steel blazed, then immediately wished he'd held his tongue. He moved away from her, jamming his fists in his pockets. "Your father was just as much a part of it as Dale was. He started the whole thing."

"Why?" This time her question was anguished. "Why would my father be involved in something like that? I can't understand it."

Of course she couldn't. Not without knowing it all, and he couldn't tell her everything without putting her in possession of a secret she might not be able to keep.

A memory surfaced unbidden in his mind, and he had to smile. Maybe she could understand what he was doing—without knowing all his secrets.

"What?" Stella demanded.

"You were always the girl next door when I was growing up. Never paid much attention to you until the day you knocked out Leon Warner."

Stella pulled back. "Hell, Steel, that's ancient history. We're talking about now."

"We were all riding home from school on the bus. Always did hate that. The minute I got my license I bought a beat-up truck just so I would never have to ride that damn bus again."

"I know what you mean."

Steel took heart from her expression of distaste. "That day everyone was a bit crazy. Mr. Sanders wasn't even paying much attention."

"Did he ever?" Stella asked. "God, the things that went on while he was driving."

"You were sitting with Laura Gibbs, both of you the picture of utter decorum."

"That's an exaggeration."

Not much of one. Back then he'd thought the Turners were a bit prissy, Stella most of all with her perfectly matched clothes and neat ponytails.

"Laura was doing her math, getting her homework done before we even made it home from school. Most kids didn't bother doing it at all."

"I did," Stella said pertly.

"I know you did."

"Leon Warner grabbed Laura's textbook." Stella picked up the story. "Her work went everywhere and everyone was laughing—it made me so mad. Why do people pick on the ones who actually do their work? Seems like it's the ones who don't who should get made fun of."

"Spoken like a teacher's pet," Steel said.

"No one did anything. Mr. Sanders certainly didn't."

"He kind of did, though." Steel figured she didn't know this part of the story. Couldn't know it—she'd been too busy attacking Leon. "You jumped up onto your seat, grabbed the book away from Leon, gripped it in two hands and bam! Crashed it down on his head."

Stella covered her eyes with her hands. "It's the worst thing I ever did. I can't believe I didn't get suspended. Guess it was a good thing Mr. Sanders didn't see it."

"Oh, he saw it all right."

Stella looked up. "No, he didn't. He couldn't have—he didn't even stop the bus!"

"He was definitely looking back when you hit Leon. I saw his eyes in the rearview mirror. Then he snapped his gaze to the road as if he'd been looking that way the whole time."

"You mean—he condoned it?" She shook her head, but she was fighting a smile. "Leon yelled like a stuck pig. Some bully he turned out to be."

"You picked up Laura's things, gave them to her, and everybody behaved themselves the rest of the way home. That's when I became your number one fan."

She smiled at the memory, but then she sobered. "What does that have to do with what our fathers did—what you're doing today?"

"You think your dad didn't know selling pot was illegal?"

"Of course he knew."

"You think I go around flirting with little girls for kicks?"

She just looked at him. "I know what I saw—and heard."

He bit back a sigh. "That day on the bus you did

something you wouldn't normally do because the ends justified the means. All I'm saying is maybe you could give me the benefit of the doubt. Go on the assumption that maybe what you saw at the pit goes along the same lines."

"You want me to believe you were flirting with teenage girls for the greater good? You know girls like them are dying of overdoses, don't you?"

Hell. She wasn't supposed to make that connection. "I absolutely know they're dying of overdoses," he heard himself say. He couldn't help himself. He hated the idea of her thinking he was some degenerate.

"And yet here you were growing pot—just like my dad was thirteen years ago. Maybe pot doesn't kill anyone, but you can use it to get kids started down the wrong path. You want me to believe you did that for some mysterious beneficial purpose?"

"That's right."

"What was my dad doing, Steel?"

"You've got to trust me a little here."

"I don't trust you."

He couldn't blame her, but he wasn't prepared for what she said next.

"I… like you, though. I don't know why, but I do, and it's killing me to know you're adding to our town's misery."

Shame reared up like a tidal wave and swamped him. Adding to Chance Creek's sorrow was the last thing he wanted to do. The long drought had turned this into a miserable summer for everyone. The overdose deaths in

Silver Falls were the poisonous icing on the cake.

"That's not my intention." God, he wanted her to believe him. He wanted her to know how much it was killing him not to share with her who he really was.

"Isn't it?" When he didn't answer, she moved even closer to him. Now he had a good look at those hazel eyes of hers. "How about trusting me, Steel? What's really going on here? I'm not as fragile as I look, you know," she added caustically. "I'm going to be a deputy. It'll be my job to uphold the law." She was almost daring him to admit he was breaking it.

Her disclosure took him aback. "A deputy?" That put a whole new spin on this conversation. Much as he'd like to be open with Stella, he really had to watch what he said. She was working for the Chance Creek department. If he told her anything, they'd all know about it—and so would everyone else in town.

Her chin lifted. "I guess you don't think I can handle the job?"

He nearly smiled, but he figured she'd take that the wrong way. Still, as far as she knew he was a criminal. Didn't she see the humor in wanting him to approve of her career switch?

"I think you can handle anything you put your mind to," he said truthfully. "Just didn't expect it."

"And I didn't expect to find you selling drugs," she said shortly.

"I haven't sold any—yet. But I might have to do all sorts of things before this is all over. Might even have to bash a bad guy over the head with a textbook while the

66

bus driver isn't looking."

"You're saying you're doing something good—even if it looks bad?"

He was walking too close to the line here, but he couldn't stop. He nodded once.

"Steel—do you mean that?"

"Yeah," he said roughly, her insistence on knowing catching him off guard. Hell, he had to get out of here before he told her everything. "I mean that—but I can't say anything more, honey, so please don't ask."

Her face changed at the endearment. Softened. He saw the echo of his own desire in her eyes. Steel found himself still talking. "I'm trying to do right. Remember that even if you hear the worst about me. Even if you need to move on and make a life for yourself with some ass like Eric Holden. Just know—" He broke off and tried again, catching the flare of surprise in her eyes when he mentioned Eric. "Know I wouldn't hurt you—or anyone—if I could help it."

"Steel." His name tore from her like she was pleading with him. He told himself to stay where he was, but despite that, he reached for her, and she stepped into his arms, threaded hers around his neck and met his kiss with her own. It was a long time before either of them pulled away. When they did, her cheeks were flushed, her lips bruised. Steel was hard and hungry. He'd only made things worse.

"Gotta go," he said desperately, moved to the edge of the platform and began to climb down.

"When will I see you again?" She followed him,

peering over the edge.

"You won't. Not if I can help it. Not until this is all over."

"I could help." She watched him maneuver down to one of the planks nailed into the tree trunk.

"No, you can't. Whatever else you do, stay away. If you hear about me, or see me—"

"I'm stronger than you think," she insisted.

"So am I." He climbed down easily and stared up at her from the ground. "I don't need help. I need you safe. Don't wait for me, you hear? I'm not worth it."

But she was.

God, she was worth anything he was able to do.

HAD ANY OF that really happened? Stella gave Steel the time he so obviously wanted to leave the property without further discussion, then climbed down from the treehouse and surveyed the soggy, blackened land in front of her, as bleak as her mood now Steel was gone. At the end of October, someone would win this land. Maybe even her own family. Would that make up for the emotional roller-coaster they'd all ridden this summer?

And what did Steel mean he was trying to right a wrong—and that William had been trying to do so, too, when he and Dale grew a pot crop years ago? The only explanation she'd ever believed for that aberrant behavior on her father's part was that he'd been desperate for money. It was never easy to keep a ranch in the black. He'd paired up with Dale, a known criminal.

Could she have misunderstood their motives so badly?

Stella walked slowly back to her vehicle, turning it all over in her mind.

Steel had grown a pot crop. Had nearly gotten killed over it. He had been hanging out at the pit the other day. Chatting with teenage girls.

What would he have hoped to gain by engaging them in conversation?

Pot—the pit—teenage girls—

It was teenage girls overdosing. Ending up dead. A rash of them, just like there'd been the year her parents split up. She remembered everyone talking about it, remembered the adults' hushed voices when they discussed it and the gossip at school. Everyone knew those girls were trouble. More than one person had said they'd gotten what they deserved.

This time around a different class of girls were getting in trouble. She recognized the family names in the paper. Rena Klein. Cecilia Holmes.

History was repeating itself but with a twist.

Why had her father and Dale been growing a pot crop the last time it happened? Why had William conceived of the plan and gotten Dale involved? Because Dale would know how to sell the pot? What had her father hoped to gain by it if not money?

Connections?

Stella paused by the door to her truck. It took connections to distribute drugs, right? Even pot? And if you teased out those connections, maybe you'd learn who was selling the other kinds of drugs in town.

Was her father trying to solve the mystery of the overdoses?

Had there even been a mystery?

Chills tingled down her spine as she opened the door and climbed in. Could she be right? Suddenly she burned to know. She put a call through to Angie Higgins, one of the other dispatchers, a woman who'd been with the Chance Creek sheriff's department for decades.

"Angie, it's Stella."

"Hi, doll. You coming in today?"

"On my way. Just had a question. Remember all those overdoses that happened about thirteen years ago—those young women?"

"The prostitutes? Yeah, I remember. What a summer. Every time you turned around, one ended up dead."

"Were they all prostitutes?" Stella was a little taken aback by Angie's matter-of-fact description.

"Not all of them. Rough customers, though, from what I remember. Young but already on the wrong road."

"They were accidental deaths, right? Not murders."

There was a long pause. "You been gossiping with the deputies?"

"No. Why?"

"You're not the only one talking about that summer. Hard not to bring it up with what's going on out in Silver Falls."

"So people did suspect a murderer was behind it?"

"Your dad did," Angie answered slowly. "People thought he was off his rocker, and that's still the general consensus today when anyone brings it up. Fentanyl is everywhere, you know. Kids don't know how much they're taking—they end up dead."

"Is that what you think?"

Angie paused again. "Always thought your father was smart. Got a call coming in. See you soon."

She clicked off. Stella pocketed her phone and started up the truck, thinking it over.

Her father had thought someone was killing those young women thirteen years ago. He'd enlisted Dale to try to infiltrate the drug community.

And then Maya and Olivia had seen their pot crop. Maya had been too young to recognize the plants for what they were, but Olivia, not so gently raised, had known right away. She'd dragged Maya back to Thorn Hill to get her away from the crop and taken her to play in her family's barn, even though the Turners and Coopers were always fighting and Maya wasn't allowed on Cooper property.

She might not have recognized the pot plants, but she'd definitely recognized the hides she'd seen curing there. She'd ended up telling the sheriff about them, who'd used Dale's out-of-season hunting as an excuse to search his properties, including the hunting cabin where he'd stored firearms he'd planned to run over the border and sell in Canada.

Dale had ended up in jail, but he'd never ratted out William, Stella mused. Her father had gone back to his life as if nothing had happened. Dale had died behind bars.

No wonder her father had kept Thorn Hill solvent all those years—and made sure Steel and his siblings got their inheritance even if it strained her family's finances.

Stella sat in the idling truck as the rain began to fall in earnest.

Now girls were overdosing again. Everyone was blaming fentanyl. But Steel had been growing a pot crop—was he trying to forge connections with the local dealers, just like his father had? Trying to discover who was giving those girls the drugs—

Or killing them?

Another shiver ran down her spine as she pictured Steel alone against an entire county's worth of trouble-makers. Some of them would resent his intrusion into their territory. Some of them would have secrets they wanted to keep hidden.

And one of them would want to silence him forever.

Chapter Three

"IT'S BAD FOR business," Troy Melkin said when Steel caught up with him at the pit later that morning. Troy was a two-bit dealer who used far too much of his own merchandise to make it very far up the food chain, but he was chatty and sometimes let a bit of useful information slip when they hung out.

The warm sun was making the soaked ground steam. Steel had seen a junkie duck out of sight around the corner of one of the taller foundation walls, probably getting his fix. Otherwise, he and Troy were the only ones around.

"All these girls dying. Someone oughtta tell them to stay home if they're going to be stupid like that."

"Lot a girls coming to buy from you?" Steel asked, nudging a broken piece of concrete half-trapped in the dirt with his foot.

"To me? Nah. That's not my clientele." Troy grinned at the fancy word, showing off a mouthful of rotten teeth. "Wouldn't mind, though."

"Guess not."

"How about you?"

Steel shook his head. "Lost my crop. No one's giving me work." He shrugged. "Maybe those girls aren't getting it around here."

"They aren't." Troy sniffed. "Not from any of the dealers, anyway. Maybe someone else is giving it to them."

Steel forced himself not to give away his surprise. "Who would give it to them?"

"Someone who wants something else from them." Troy tapped his temple. "What any guy wants from a pretty young girl."

"And then kills them? That's pretty sick."

"Heard someone tried to kill you. Seems like you're not getting the message."

Steel poked the bit of concrete again with the toe of his boot. "What's the message?"

"The same thing the message always is. Stop asking questions." Troy sniffed again. "Man, you ain't ever going to get anywhere in this business if you can't figure that out." He eyed Steel. "But you aren't really trying to get anywhere, are you?"

"What the hell is that supposed to mean?" Steel knew he had to end this line of inquiry fast or he'd lose all the ground he'd gained so far.

"It means no one's going to tell you what you want to know, because no one's got a death wish. Just open your eyes, man. This ain't some outside job. It's an inside job, if anything."

"Wait—" Steel said when Troy got up. "I don't get—"

"That's right, and you ain't going to get it from me.

I'm just a junkie, man. I don't know anything. Don't even know what I just said to you." He stuffed his hands in the pockets of his ragged black hoodie and strode away.

An inside job.

What the hell did that mean?

STEEL'S WORDS WERE still on Stella's mind at lunchtime, when she grabbed her purse and headed for the door. She'd planned to order some takeout and eat in her vehicle down by Chance Creek, but it occurred to her she could do one better. After doing some research on her phone while standing in line at the Burger Shack, she drove straight to Silver Falls and turned down the road leading to Runaway Lodge.

As she'd hoped, she found Monica Hunt there cleaning up the lodge, which had been closed for so long. She'd thrown open all the windows and propped the door with a large rock. Inside, she was scrubbing kitchen cabinets.

"Hi, Stella, nice to see you," Monica called out as soon as she spotted her.

"Just popping by for a few minutes. I'm on my lunch break. Want to come sit with me outside?"

"Gladly. I've got a salad in the fridge, so I'll grab it and join you. I'm glad the rain stopped for a minute. Heard we're supposed to get more later."

She joined Stella at the beach, where they each perched on log rounds by the large bonfire circle and bent over their lunches. In her fifties, Monica was an energetic-looking woman dressed in khaki shorts, a yellow T-shirt and flip-flops. All she needed was a whistle on a string around her neck to complete her camp counselor ensemble, Stella thought.

"I used to love it here," Stella told her. "We came every year when you opened the lake to the public, and I'd swim all day, then gorge myself on s'mores at night."

"I think everyone did." Monica smiled at the memory. "Those were the days. Sunshine, swimming and flowers galore. And then winter would roll around again." She made a face.

"Any word from those boys of yours?"

"Not yet. I'm still planning my attack. Gotta hit them just right to lure them home from their exciting lives."

"I'm sure you'll figure out a way." Stella wondered what the Hunt brothers were like now. In their early thirties, she thought. A lot of the boys from around here in that age group had ended up in the military. Now they were coming home, bringing new life first to Chance Creek and, if Monica had her way, to Silver Falls, too.

"What brings you out here?" Monica asked in turn.

"Besides the lovely view?" The rain from that morning had cleared, leaving a tremulously blue sky. "Just an idea. You know I work at the sheriff's office, right?"

Monica nodded.

"A lot of young people are getting in trouble with drugs these days, some quite seriously. It's the opioids that are the worst, I think. Anyway, I checked, and it turns out Chance Creek's rehab center lacks any support for teens, and I think that needs to change. I would like to hold a fundraising event to get things going. I'm just in the starting stages of thinking it through, but I wondered if we could hire Runaway Lodge as our venue. People would love to come here for a beach day."

"That's a good idea." Monica nodded thoughtfully. "I would love a way to reintroduce myself to the people around here and let them know sooner or later we'll be back in business. I'm all for supporting the community, too. I'm not sure a day of swimming will be exciting enough to draw a crowd, though. You'd need to make it more interesting."

"I thought we could have food—and maybe some entertainment," Stella said uncertainly.

"Of course, but I think to get the numbers you're talking about, you'd need something more. Don't you?"

"Maybe. But what?" Stella asked.

Monica took a bite of her food, and Stella followed suit, racking her brain for an idea.

"My boys always liked competing," Monica mused when she'd swallowed. "Maybe there could be some kind of contest people could participate in? Swimming or boating…?"

"A water Olympics," Stella blurted out. "A whole day of events. People could sign up ahead of time and train for them. There could be silly prizes. A podium for the first, second and third place winners to stand on. We could have a photographer—"

"I love it," Monica exclaimed. "We could do opening and closing ceremonies," she improvised. "Maybe fireworks?"

Stella considered this. "Maybe, now that we've gotten some rain. But only if we get enough between now and then. The last thing we need is another fire." She bit her lip. She'd forgotten who she was speaking to.

"I know what you mean," Monica said dryly, then smiled to soften her words. "And I think this is a great idea. It gives me a reason to get moving with fixing up the lodge and a reason to tell my sons about my plans. Thank you, Stella."

"Thank you. And don't worry; I'll gather lots of willing hands to help."

"When should we get started? The swimming season's just about over," Monica pointed out. "Besides, the Founder's Prize will be handed out soon."

Stella laughed to hide her chagrin. "Am I that transparent? I really do want to help the teens in town, but I have to admit my uncle has been pestering me to do something to try to win the prize."

Monica waved her off. "I understand, and I'm all for it. Why don't we get together tomorrow night to flesh out a plan—unless you have a hot date."

"No hot date," Stella said. "Besides, I'd rather work on this. Remember to think what you'll charge us for the venue. No, don't wave me away. It's important, and you can use the funds to get ready to reopen. Fixing up all your cottages and treehouses won't be cheap."

"That'll be my sons' problem," Monica said.

"GREAT. THE CREEPER'S back," Lily said loudly when Steel ambled into the pit again midafternoon. He'd hoped to see Troy, but something told him the man would be elusive for a while. He'd taken a risk talking to Steel at all, and Steel wondered if he was a spokesman for the other dealers. Maybe all of them were feeling the heat because of the overdose deaths.

"You're kind of creepy yourself always hanging around here," Steel shot back. He needed to find a way to talk to these girls if he was going to protect them. Maybe he'd been too reserved before. Maybe he should lighten up. Try to be more like them. Now that Troy had confirmed that other people were asking questions about why girls were dying, he felt like he'd been vindicated in that, at least. He wasn't the only one who thought there was a killer.

An inside job.

"Whatever." Lily turned to her friends, and once again, Steel got the feeling the trio of them were watching for someone. Someone who wasn't turning up, if their irritation was anything to go by. As Steel took a seat on a chunk of concrete from the old colliery foundation, carefully keeping his face turned away, as if he had nothing better to do than watch a spider weave a web between nearby weeds, he heard them talking about the time and whether to leave or stay.

"He'll come," Sue said loudly.

"Not if *he's* still here," Lily hissed.

Were they talking about him? Steel tried another gambit. "A girl like you turned up dead a few days back.

Is she one of your friends? Rena Klein."

Sue groaned but didn't look up from the phone she held in her hand. "Rena Klein, Rena Klein—that's all anyone talks about these days."

"Maybe because she was fooling around with things she shouldn't have and overdosed. Maybe people don't want it happening to someone else—like you three. You should find somewhere else to hang out."

Lily turned on him. "Are you really going to hand out life advice, creeper? You're a fucking dealer, right?"

Steel just shrugged. *Don't admit anything*, that was his motto.

"Besides, life's cheap. You gotta die sometime."

Spoken like a hard case, but Lily wasn't some street kid. Those shoes she was scuffing in the rubble of the pit had cost a pretty penny.

Sue was still looking at her phone. Had she even heard the conversation? Lily was watching the street. Lara was watching Lily.

"Do you know where Rena got her drugs?" Steel asked. It was a gamble, but he'd been getting nowhere with them, and his conversations with Stella and Troy had lit a fire under him.

Lily's mouth formed an O of surprise, but then her expression hardened into that fake tough veneer she liked to sport. Lara blinked but kept watching Lily, obviously waiting to take her cue from her friend.

"Why do you care about a dumb addict like her, anyway?" Lily asked.

"You never hung out with her?"

Lily shrugged, surprising him. He'd only wanted to verify that Rena hadn't been one of their friends, but that shrug seemed to suggest something else.

"You had a falling out with her recently?"

"I didn't drug her to death, if that's what you mean." Lily stood up. "We should go," she said to Lara and Sue. Sue waved her away, typing rapidly on her phone.

"Who's texting you?" Lara asked her, leaning over the screen. Sue yanked it away.

"None of your business!" She stood, too. "I've gotta go. Mom's coming to pick me up."

"Your mom—here?" Lily asked, surprised enough she dropped the tough act and looked like the teenager she was.

"Couple blocks from here. See you." Sue rushed away, leaving her friends staring after her.

"That was weird," Lara said. "We'd better go. My mom was pissed last time."

"That *was* weird," Lily echoed, but she didn't move. She frowned when she noticed Steel was still there. "Get out of here, creeper."

"So you used to be friends with Rena," he pressed. "I heard she was a good kid. Nice girl." He shrugged as if to say, *How did she end up here?*

Lily barked out a bitter laugh. "You don't know anything about her. Or us."

"What should I know?"

For one split second he thought she might tell him something real. Then she looked after the diminishing figure of her friend striding away and shook her head.

"Nothing. Come on, Lara."

Steel watched them go, thinking that even if Lily hadn't spilled her guts, she'd let some information slip. She, Lara and Sue knew Rena, which made sense since Chance Creek was such a small place. Once upon a time, they'd been friends, but at some point, Lily had begun to see Rena as an adversary. Or maybe a rival? Weren't girls always jockeying for position among their groups of friends?

Steel thought about that for a while. Rena and Lily were frenemies of some kind, but Rena had started coming to Silver Falls. Doing drugs. She'd overdosed. Now here was Lily, following in her footsteps.

All this time he'd concentrated on the drugs in this drama, but now he wondered if there was something more going on. Lily's reaction to Rena's name had been telling; instead of feeling sorry for the dead girl, it was as if she felt Rena had betrayed her in some way. Then there was her reaction to the way Sue had suddenly left. Lily didn't trust the girls around her—even her friends.

Were girls always so suspicious of each other? Or was something else going on?

Steel sat back. If these girls had known Rena, had Rena known Cecilia, who'd died several months ago? Had Cecilia known any of the prior victims? Did some connection run from girl to girl that only the killer could see?

Was he pitting his victims against each other?

Would Lily end up dead next?

He needed to scare her and her friends away from Silver Falls—and he needed to get more information from them. Doing both would require him to walk a fine line. Should he follow them?

No—they were already heading home.

But he'd keep an eye out for them from here on in.

"STELLA?"

Eric seemed as surprised as Stella was when she bumped into him at Thoughtful Coffee, where she'd popped in before driving back to work from Runaway Lake.

"What are you doing here?" Stella asked. "Aren't you working?"

"Just heading back from a break. You?"

"Same. Had lunch with a friend."

Eric ordered his coffee, and she put in her order, too. While they waited, Eric picked up the conversation. "What friend?"

Was that a touch of jealousy she heard in his voice? "Monica Hunt," she said. She explained her idea to raise money to expand the rehab center so it could accommodate teenagers. "Seems like drugs are a problem everywhere these days."

"I guess." He didn't seem convinced the expansion would do much good. "Water Olympics, huh? Guess that could be fun if you like that sort of thing."

"I think so." She was a little put off by his lack of enthusiasm. Eric seemed to realize this and touched her arm.

"Hey, sorry. Just stuff on my mind. How about I help you—and meantime, we start training? We can combine the two—train for your deputy test and for the Olympic competition. What do you say?"

When he smiled, she relaxed a little. She couldn't fault a man with a job like Eric's for being gruff once in a while. "When do you want to train?"

"How about tomorrow morning?"

"Sure." She didn't know why Steel's face slipped into her mind. He wasn't going to train for the agility test with her. Nor would he be around to support her fundraiser. Not that he would anyway, most likely, given this was an attempt to win the Founder's Prize for her family once and for all.

"Looking forward to it—and to tonight, too. Should be a good game," Eric said with more conviction than he had earlier. "It'll be fun." He brushed her cheek with his lips and grinned. "Don't you think?"

"Uh… sure," Stella said. But it would be a whole lot more fun if it was Steel who'd kissed her.

Chapter Four

"**S**TEEL COOPER! LOOK at you all grown up."

Steel straightened and put away his phone. It was too early in the morning to catch anyone doing anything nefarious, but he hadn't been able to sleep, turning over his lack of progress in his mind all night—and thinking about Stella, too, if he was honest. Now that they'd talked—and kissed—she was on his mind constantly.

He'd been hanging around on a bench in front of Silver Falls' convenience store, keeping an eye out for any sign of Lily and her friends, who hadn't been at the pit since lunchtime the previous day. He turned to find a middle-aged woman smiling at him. It took a minute for him to place her. "Mrs. Hunt."

She rolled her eyes. "Monica, please. You're not a boy anymore." She craned her neck to look up at him as he stood and came to greet her. "You sure turned out handsome."

He couldn't help the smile that tugged at his mouth. "Nice of you to say."

"Save the aw shucks routine." She laughed. "You know darn well you turn heads. I can see it in your swagger."

He laughed, too, but then remembered who he was supposed to be. Steel Cooper, petty criminal. Not the kind of man Mrs. Hunt—Monica—should be hanging around.

"Heard you were home," he said, scanning the area to see who might be watching them. The street was largely empty at this time of day. One or two older women heading into the coffee shop across the street. A couple of kids fooling around as they walked home from somewhere.

"I am—for now."

"And your boys?"

"Doing well. They're all grown up, too. In the military for the time being."

"You thinking about calling them home?"

"You always were a smart one. People used to speculate you'd use those smarts to get yourself into trouble."

"People were right." He kept his tone light, but it was important she believe it.

Monica cocked her head. "Really? What kind of trouble are you getting into?"

He shrugged. "A little of this, a little of that. Like my dad."

Her eyebrow went up. "Like your dad, huh?"

Why had she said it like that? Steel shifted uneasily. "Yeah. What of it?"

"Dale was a man of many talents, as I recall." Monica smiled again. "He was great in the senior play in high school, you know."

"Senior play?" He supposed he shouldn't be surprised she was in school with his dad. Silver Falls kids had always attended Chance Creek High since their town wasn't big enough to support a school of its own. But she'd caught him off guard, and he was sure she'd noticed it.

"Wasn't even the understudy, but when Chris Brooks got sick the night of the show, Dale stepped in and played his part perfectly. Knew all the lines, the gestures, where to stand, what to do."

"My dad?"

"Your dad," she confirmed. "The thing to remember when you're playing a part is that you're *playing a part*. Which means at some point you have to exit the stage and get back to real life."

Steel could only stare at her. Was she still talking about Dale—or something else entirely?

"I've heard Silver Falls has gotten a bit rough around the edges since I left," Monica went on. "Good thing it has such a fine sheriff's department, don't you think?"

"I... guess."

She was already walking away. "Good to see you again, Steel. Hope you'll come to the fundraiser for the Chance Creek rehab center expansion. There'll be posters up all over the place soon. Sorry I have to rush off, but I'm late."

"Rehab center expansion? You been talking to Olivia?" he called after her. Last he'd heard that was her idea.

"No, I've been talking to your neighbor, Stella Turner. Nice girl. Know her well?" she tossed over her shoulder as she kept walking.

Not nearly well enough, apparently.

"ON YOUR MARK, get set—go!"

Eric exploded off the starting line at the Chance Creek High track, and Stella did her best to follow him. Within steps his lead expanded. She redoubled her efforts, pumping her arms, increasing her pace, but he hit the finish line with enough time to turn and watch her pass it.

"Beat you again," he crowed, coming over to raise his hand in a high five. "You're going to have to do better than that." It seemed a bit strange for him to ask her to celebrate his win when she was his adversary, Stella thought, but Eric seemed to think it was perfectly natural that she acknowledge his superiority, and as she'd seen last night at his baseball game, he was highly competitive. "Aw, come on," he laughed at her. "I'm a middle-aged man fading away from my youthful prowess. Don't I get to crow about beating a twenty-seven-year-old?"

She smiled at that. She supposed she couldn't begrudge him a victory or two. She'd been relieved his team had won last night, because by the end of the game it had become clear that he'd take a loss badly. Men were like that, though, she'd told herself. Liam had always been a bear during his football days when

Chance Creek High wasn't doing well.

"We need to do obstacles," she said when she regained her breath. "That's what the agility test is all about. That's why I wanted to practice at home—so we can build some."

"First we need to increase your speed. I'll time you, and we'll see if we can start shaving seconds off."

Stella checked her phone to hide her impatience. She was jogging every morning—she'd gotten up early to do so today before coming out here. "Unfortunately, I've got to get going if I'm going to shower before work," she told him.

"What about tonight?"

"Sorry, I'm busy." She moved to her gear where she'd left it on the grass near the track and snagged the handles of her workout tote.

"With what?"

There was that jealous tone again. "Fundraising planning. For the rehab center, like I told you. Monica Hunt and I are getting together to iron out a few things."

"I said I'd help, too."

"Later, when we've got the basic plan in place," she assured him. She wasn't going to invite him to their preliminary meeting. Eric was the type to dominate everything he was involved in, and this had to be her family's work if it was to count for them winning the Founder's Prize.

"You know, maybe you should look into something like that," he added.

"Something like what?"

"Counseling—at a rehab center. Girls are good at stuff like that. Helping people."

Stella nearly dropped the bag she'd just picked up. "I'm going to be a deputy, remember? That's what I'm training for." Anger straightened her spine. She wasn't a girl. She was a grown woman.

"Right. Just saying it's an alternative. If the deputy thing doesn't work out." He lifted his hands to ward her off. "Just a suggestion. Easy there, tiger! You are really going to have to toughen up if you're going to be a deputy, Turner."

Why was he suddenly using her last name when he'd always called her Stella before? Was he threatened by her desire to be his equal? Or angry she hadn't invited him to come along tonight?

"Whatever." She was past even pretending she wasn't furious. And why should she try to keep the peace? Eric wasn't right for her—he'd made that obvious. "See you around."

"Stella—hey, I wasn't—Stella!"

She kept walking.

STEEL WAS SO deep in thought about his earlier conversation with Monica Hunt he barely glanced at the figure who turned the corner of Main and Dairy Street just as he was preparing to cross it later that morning, but at the last minute he glanced up and caught sight of a familiar face.

Sue Hill.

A very downcast Sue Hill.

She noticed him at about the same time. Her eyes widened, and he could see her considering whether to change directions, but in the end she lifted her chin and kept coming toward him. He waited on the corner for her, concerned by the change he saw in her. The last time he'd seen her she'd been almost arrogant in the way she'd thrown off her friends and gone racing down the street—to meet her mother. At the time he'd been sure she was lying and thought Lily seemed suspicious, too. Sue had seemed far too excited to be meeting a parent who surely wouldn't be happy to find her daughter at the pit.

Now she slouched along, hands buried in the pockets of her jacket, and if he wasn't mistaken those were tears dried on her face.

"Did you lose your friends?" Steel joked as she approached, not knowing what else to say to a tear-stricken teenager.

"What friends?" She walked straight past him.

"You have a fight with Lily and Lara?" He caught up and fell into step with her, sweeping the sidewalk ahead of them to see who might be catching sight of this conversation. Someone had called him in for talking to the girls at the pit, after all. There were a lot of stores on this street. A lot of prying eyes.

"Those two? They're just kids. Who cares what they do?"

Interesting.

"So who are you hanging with these days?"

"None of your business!"

"I could get you something—whatever you need. You and your new friends."

She huffed out an annoyed breath. "Me and my new friend don't need anything, thank you very much. We've got that covered, so get lost, or I'll scream."

Steel stopped and let Sue keep going.

Friend. She'd said "my new friend" rather than "my new friends." He hurried to catch up again.

"So you threw Lily and Lara over for a man?" He wanted to say boy, but he figured that would rile her all over again. She seemed determined to be treated like an adult even if she was acting like a kid.

This time Sue stopped, turning a wide-eyed, desperate look on him that threw him off. "What do you know about it?"

"Nothing. Sounds like you don't need them anymore now that you've got what you really want."

Sue's face crumpled. "I don't have anyone," she wailed. "Get away from me!" she added, her voice rising.

Hell. Steel turned sharply and ducked down the narrow alley between two shops, then emerged on the other side of the block and kept going. He'd make tracks now, but he'd be back to get more answers. Maybe Sue and her friends were in the middle of a teenage quarrel, and maybe it was something else entirely.

"LET ME MAKE it up to you," the card read. "Tonight at

the Dancing Boot. I'll be a gentleman, I promise. And I'll try to keep my foot out of my mouth."

Stella stared at the huge bouquet that was making it difficult to see anyone coming into the Chance Creek sheriff's department. It sat in a glass vase on the edge of her desk, blocking half her view. She'd been up late the last two nights coming up with a preliminary plan with Monica and woken early each morning to do her daily run. They'd looked at a calendar and realized they had to fast-track their plans. Summers cooled quickly into fall weather. If they wanted people to come to a water-based event, it had to be soon.

"Those are some flowers," Angie commented on her way past. "Someone must have messed up pretty bad."

Eric had messed up, she thought tiredly, but at least he'd realized it. She didn't fancy another round of his boasting, but the truth was she'd been out of sorts all day, and she wouldn't mind a night out. A drink or two. Some dancing. Maybe a game of pool. She'd see friends—everyone ended up at the Boot on a Friday night. She'd have plenty of time to go home after work, shower, change and head out again.

She pulled out her phone and accepted Eric's invitation. *No shop talk,* she added.

Got it, he texted back immediately.

By the time she made it to the Boot that evening, her anger had mostly passed away. Now when she thought about his need to beat her in every race and his not-so-subtle attempts to dissuade her from becoming a deputy, it was kind of funny. Funny in a pathetic kind of way, but humorous nonetheless.

Eric was intimidated by her. There was no other explanation for his actions. He was afraid she might not only get into the deputy training program but also excel at the work. What if she did better than he did?

His fragile male ego couldn't handle that.

Too bad. She wasn't pulling any punches, and if Eric couldn't deal with a woman with ambition, he could find someone else to be with. Tonight was just fun. Getting out there. Blowing off a little steam.

The evening started out just as she'd hoped. Eric bought her a beer, steered her to one of the tables at the side of the room where they could leave their things and soon joined her on the dance floor. The live band was rocking, the room was filled with dancers and Stella let all her cares wash away as she danced. She'd kept her outfit casual, but she'd taken enough time with her hair and makeup to feel like she was having a real night out. It had been too long since she'd cut loose a little.

When Eric excused himself to take a call, she kept dancing, joining a couple of friends from school who were out as a group. Eric came and went, dancing for a while, then fielding texts and calls, moving back and forth from the table to the floor where she stayed with the others. If it had been anyone else, she would have been angry, but she was having more fun than she'd expected with her friends and didn't miss him.

"Everything all right?" she asked when he finished his latest call.

"Everything's great. Just work." He waggled his beer bottle at her. "A hero's job is never done."

Fifteen minutes later when Eric took another call, Stella headed for the ladies' room, thinking maybe it was time to head home. She had chores in the morning even if she wasn't working—plus her morning run…

"Hey, there," someone said in her ear.

"Steel?" She sucked in a quick breath, all her senses tingling at his proximity. He'd been leaning against the bar, taking a pull from a beer. She hadn't seen him come in—not that she'd been looking for him, she told herself.

"Off to the ladies'?" he asked.

"Yeah."

"Grab me on your way back for a quick dance before he notices." He jutted his chin at Eric huddled over his phone across the room.

"You got it." Stella hurried on her way, telling herself that if Eric had ended his call by the time she got out, she'd head right back to him, but when she returned to the bar, he was still talking on his phone, his back turned to them.

"You're safe; he isn't even looking this way," Steel asserted. He took her hand and led her back to the dance floor. The band had just started a slow song, and he drew her in close. Steel was wearing a black Stetson, and he kept his head bent to obscure his face from most people's view. A glance told her Eric was still occupied. Like Steel said, he hadn't even noticed she was gone.

"Wearing a hat indoors?" she teased him. "Bad

form."

"Couldn't care less," he said, his low voice thrumming through her. "Couldn't miss my chance to be with you."

"I really shouldn't." But she didn't pull away. Steel kept his arms around her.

"It's just a dance, not a commitment. Although maybe someday..." He let the sentence trail off, but the whisper of his breath against her neck made her shiver.

"I'm not going to be with a criminal," she made herself say. She knew how Steel's touch could make her lose all sense. "I'm going to be a deputy, after all."

"I remember. Have you been training for your test?"

"A little. Not as much as I'd like," she admitted. "I've been running every morning."

"That's good. The real challenge is the obstacles, though."

"What do you know about deputy training?"

"Nothing." Steel looked away. "I was kind of into track and field in school, that's all."

He looked like she'd caught him off-balance, which was new. Steel was always so self-assured. Was he embarrassed about having extracurricular activities? Maybe he figured being seen participating in anything didn't fit with his bad boy persona.

"Anyway, I trained a bit with obstacles. Mostly low hurdles and steps," he continued.

Stella nodded. That was most of what she would have to contend with during her test.

"The obstacles themselves aren't hard to get over,

but you'd be surprised how they destroy your momen-
tum if you're not used to them, which wrecks your time.
You have to practice; there's no substitute."

"I thought so," Stella said, feeling vindicated. "I
wanted to set up something like that at my ranch, but—"
But Eric hadn't been any help. "I guess I haven't found
the time."

"Make the time—you've got to go after what you
want."

And then he kissed her.

His mouth moving over hers elicited a wave of desire so strong Stella found herself clinging to him, her
fingers twisting in the white cotton of his shirt. It went
on and on, but each passing moment only increased her
desire rather than slaking it.

She wanted more.

When he snuggled her in a little closer, something
kindled deep inside her. This night could get a whole lot
more fun if she was going home with Steel—

"Hell," Steel said, peering out from under his hat.
"We've got company. Gotta go." He snatched one last
kiss. "By the way, heard you stole Olivia's idea for a teen
detox program. Who's the criminal now?"

And he was gone.

"Who the hell was that?" Eric demanded when he
reached her.

"No one," Stella said.

She had the feeling Eric meant to make a thing of it,
but his phone shrilled loudly, and he reached to pull it
out. When his expression changed, she nearly laughed.

"Damn it. Deputy business. Gotta go." Eric looked up. "See? You'd hate this line of work. Always getting interrupted just when you're having fun." He stole a kiss even though Stella tried to pull back. "See you tomorrow."

That was two men gone—and it wasn't even ten. Some Friday night.

Time to get herself home as well, Stella figured.

Chapter Five

WHAT WAS HE playing at?

It was past midnight when Steel made for home. He'd stopped for a burger, then driven out to Thorn Hill to spy on his family's home before finally turning his truck toward Silver Falls, taking the long way there. The last thing he wanted to do was spend another night alone in his damn trailer.

As he drove through the rain, Steel kicked himself for dancing with Stella in public like that. Now he was hot and bothered, and he knew he'd struggle to sleep later. He could still feel her mouth under his, the curve of her hips under his hands. He wanted to undress Stella. To spend the night exploring her body.

He'd always struggled with impulse control, and there were times he figured he understood exactly why his father had run so close to the law so much of his life. Dale must have had the same kind of struggles. Possibly worse ones. He shouldn't even have come to town.

He'd driven around Silver Falls earlier this evening looking for Sue or Lily or Lara, determined to get more answers about their relationship to Rena, but he hadn't seen any of the girls at the usual spots and the light drizzle had turned to real rain. He doubted they'd be out on a night like this.

He kept thinking back to the day he'd chatted with the three of them at the pit. The way Lily had been so watchful—the way Sue had run off so happily, Lily watching her go with suspicion.

Sue's devastation when he'd seen her again.

High school crushes and jealousies. Every time he thought of their behavior, that was how it read to him. But what boy or boys would be dropping them off or picking them up at the pit?

Or what *man*?

The same one who killed Rena? When Sue had wailed, "I don't have anyone," she hadn't sounded like she was talking about a dealer; she'd sounded like she was talking about a boyfriend.

Again he wondered if the killer was playing them against each other. Maybe he and Bolton had been wrong from the start, and the girls weren't drawn in by the drugs—maybe they were drawn in by a man who preyed on their desire to be wanted.

To be loved.

Was some man enticing young women with the promise of a grown-up relationship? Were the drugs just a side game? Did he start them off slow with party drugs that put them in the mood—made them easier to seduce?

What turned the game deadly?

Those questions haunted him as he'd cruised around

Silver Falls, until finally he'd driven back to Chance Creek, needing to be close to home even if he couldn't return to Thorn Hill. He'd ended up at the Dancing Boot and decided to go in for one beer. Be around people. He figured he'd stick to himself, and most folks would let him be.

Then he'd seen Stella.

He should have left right then, but he couldn't seem to make himself move from his seat at the bar. He'd watched Eric take one call, then another… and another until he built up a head of steam about the way the man was ignoring his date. Stella didn't deserve to be treated like that. If something was blowing up at the Chance Creek's sheriff's department, Eric ought to apologize to Stella and go to work. If it was anything else, surely it could wait until he took her home.

When Stella had come his way, Steel had taken the opportunity to show the man how it was done.

It had felt good to draw Stella near. To breathe her in. Somehow Stella always smelled of sunshine. The ocean. He'd been to the ocean several times when he lived out west, and he'd once thought he'd give up undercover work and spend his time beach-bumming it up and down the west coast.

Maybe he should.

He wasn't sure what good he was doing here. He wasn't any closer to figuring out why the girls of Chance Creek were overdosing, and he wasn't doing Stella any favors, either.

His fingers tightened on the steering wheel as the

road curved through fields and began to rise beneath him. The rain was falling harder now, making it difficult to see the edge of the road in the dark. He didn't think Silver Falls—or the dilapidated trailer he lived in— would ever feel like home. He wasn't a mountain man. He was a rancher, no matter what direction his life had taken since he was eighteen. Someday he hoped he could get back to the work. Back to himself. Stop hiding in the shadows all the time. Be someone a woman like Stella could be proud of.

Steel navigated another turn, the road rising more sharply now. Scrub gave way to real forest around him as he neared Silver Falls. He passed a swaybacked barn sinking into the woods growing up around it. A house that hadn't been painted in years, its clapboard siding a silvery gray in the darkness. Sometimes he thought the forest would swallow Silver Falls whole, reclaiming everything men had carved out of it a hundred years or so ago. It had never prospered to quite the same extent Chance Creek had in its heyday, but for a while, in the 1940s and 50s, it was a busy summer retreat for people from all around. While Runaway Lake was the biggest body of water in the region, several other small ponds and lakes had once hosted busy campgrounds and day trippers. There'd been excursions to nearby lookouts. A small but thriving artists' community that held an annual show. People had picnicked at the falls.

Now they avoided the area.

He clicked the windshield wipers into a higher gear as the rain fell harder. This wasn't a shower anymore—

it was more like a deluge. As he peered through the wipers at the curving road ahead of him, he hoped Stella had gotten home all right. There would be accidents tonight. The creeks would rise fast, too. The ground was so dry it wouldn't absorb much moisture, and the fast-flowing water could get dangerous.

Right on cue, his sheriff's department radio sputtered to life. "Steel, you there?"

It was Bolton.

"What's up?"

"We got another overdose," the sheriff said.

"Who?" Damn it, another one?

"Sue Hill. Just in the last hour."

Steel swore. Punched a fist against the steering wheel once. Twice.

"Pull it together!" Bolton called through the phone. "You driving?"

"Yeah," Steel growled and pulled over even before being told, flipping on his hazard lights. Last thing he needed was to be hit.

"I take it you know the girl."

"I know her," Steel said. "I've talked to her before. She was upset." He scowled. "The killer did this."

"We don't know that. If she was upset, maybe she did herself in," Bolton said, but he sounded less certain than usual. Was he thinking the same thing as Steel— that they could have saved Sue, if only they'd been quicker to act?

"Where was she found?"

Bolton hesitated. "At the pit," he admitted.

Steel cursed himself again. He should have stayed in Silver Falls.

He and Bolton both knew what it meant she was found there. If a girl like Sue had wanted to kill herself, she would have decked herself out and done it at home so as to be discovered in a way to drive the knife home through her parents' hearts. If she was found at the pit, someone else had put her there.

"I need to talk to her friends. Lily and Lara. Sounded to me like they had some kind of falling out recently. Sue had some new friend she was going on about—a friend who hurt her feelings earlier today." Steel had a new thought. "What's on her phone?"

"No phone that we can find."

"Any word from her parents?"

"Just that she's been moody lately. Been depressed for several days. Locked herself in her room tonight after barely eating dinner. Parents didn't even know she was gone until they got the call."

"Hell, how'd she get past them?"

"I don't have that yet. They're in shock, Steel. They're not ready to answer those kinds of questions."

All the information they needed would be on Sue's phone. Steel remembered the way her fingers had flown over the keys the other day. It was all in there—the name of the killer. His plans.

"You need to get those phone records."

"I know."

Steel doubted that was true, though. No phone records had turned up in the other cases. If the killer communicated with his victims, he did it some other way. Maybe he was wrong; maybe Sue had been texting with her mother, after all.

They'd have to wait and see.

"THERE SHE IS." Monica waved a woman in her thirties over to the table Stella was sharing with her at Thoughtful Coffee. She'd spent the morning catching up on chores at home, then drove to Silver Falls to meet Monica and her friend. The newcomer had sandy-brown hair in a pixie cut that accented her expressive brown eyes and wide smile. She brightened when she spotted Monica and threaded her way through the coffee shop to join them. "Joan, meet Stella Turner. Stella, this is Joan Wexler. She works for Chance Creek Social Services." She turned back to Joan as the woman took her seat. "Stella is organizing a fundraiser in the hopes that Chance Creek's detox and stabilization program can be expanded to support teenagers. I really wanted you two to meet."

Joan looked at Stella curiously. "I think that's a wonderful idea. You really think you can raise those kinds of funds?"

Stella swallowed. She'd known ever since Monica broached the idea of her meeting Joan that the woman would probably have questions she couldn't answer. She'd hoped to be able to field one or two before they got to the hard ones, though.

"I'm not sure, honestly. All I know is that people are dying—kids are dying."

"Don't I know it. Another one last night." Joan shook her head.

"Another one? Who?" Stella asked.

"Sue Hill. A Chance Creek girl."

"I know her—by sight," Stella said, shocked to the core. Had she been one of the girls at the pit with Lara Whidby? Now that she thought about it, it seemed possible.

She flashed to Steel talking to them, and her stomach sunk.

"Her parents must be devastated," Monica said. "Does the sheriff have any leads?"

"I haven't heard," Joan said. "Rumor has it she overdosed."

"Just like Rena Klein," Stella said.

"And Cecilia Foster before her."

"We need to do something to help these kids." She wondered what Steel knew about the girl's death. Was she naive to hope he knew nothing at all?

"A worthy sentiment," Joan said. "But it will take a lot of practical work to get it done. There's a reason Chance Creek's facility caters only to adult clients. There simply isn't enough money to offer services to younger people. We just nearly lost the dialysis program at the hospital because of budget cuts."

"I know, but there must be something we can do. I looked into it, and teens have to travel to either Billings or Bozeman to get a bed at a detox or stabilization program, and often they have to wait weeks. We need something local to fill in the gaps until they can get into those programs."

"I'm not sure that would have helped Sue. It didn't seem to me like she was involved in the culture for all that long. I'm not sure she would have accessed any programs," Joan said.

"She was making bad choices, though. Hanging out at the pit. I think I saw her there," Stella said, finding herself closer to tears than she cared to admit. She'd spoken to Lara's mom, who hadn't been pleased to hear where her daughter had been. It had been an awkward conversation. Should she have pressed Kim to ask Lara who she was with? Should she have pursued the information herself?

"Disaffection is a problem that seems small but is actually devastating," Joan said. "I think the question we should be asking is why these girls are craving a thrill so badly they'll put their lives on the line. What has unmoored them from their lives?"

"Hormones?" Stella suggested distractedly. "Aren't teenagers just kind of crazy?"

"Hormones certainly can contribute," Joan conceded, "but I'm wondering about connections. Are these kids losing their connection to the community, to their families—to something bigger than themselves? Is this the white flag they're running up to show how much that hurts?"

"Why would it be a bigger problem now than at other times?" Stella asked.

"Times have been tough lately," Monica pointed out. "Since I've been home, I've noticed how everyone is struggling. With parents working harder to make ends meet, there's less time for family events. Then the drought hit… Kids pick up on despair. Maybe this is their way of expressing their fear that there's nothing that can be done to help."

Stella thought this through. "So they need to feel like problems have solutions?"

"And that they can help with those solutions, ideally," Joan said.

"I knew this was a good idea," Monica said smugly. "Put two smart women in a room together and they'll save the world."

"I'm not sure what this has to do with raising money to expand services for teens," Stella said.

"I do," Monica said. "We enlist Chance Creek's teenagers to help with the water Olympics—I always used the lodge as an excuse to keep my boys busy and out of trouble. They had chores every day. Between that and their sports and part-time jobs, there wasn't much time for anything else."

"Do you think you can convince teenagers to volunteer?" Joan asked.

"We can try," Stella said firmly. "We'll spread the word all around."

"I'd like to help, too," Joan said.

"Of course."

When their coffee date was over and Joan had headed off, Stella hung back to talk to Monica.

"Thank you," she began. "I'm really glad to have met Joan."

"I thought the two of you would get along. You still coming to the lodge with me for another planning session?"

"If you've still got the time." More than ever it seemed important to do something to help Chance Creek's teens.

"Of course."

Monica pushed the restaurant's door open and stepped outside, then halted at the sight of the rain falling.

"I've got an umbrella. Let me walk you to your truck." Stella took it out and raised it. "This rain is going to make all the difference. Especially when you add it to last night's downpour."

"I hope it slows down a little," Monica said as they hurried down the sidewalk.

"I hope it doesn't," Stella said ruefully. "We need all of it we can get."

Later that night when she was home from her planning session with Monica, she was still thinking about her conversation with Monica and Joan. Up at the lodge, they had finally finished a huge to-do list that could now be broken out and shared with volunteers, come up with a plan for the water Olympics, and formed a general idea of how much help they'd need. She'd start calling around now and see who else they could get on board, and she vowed to get to it as soon as possible, but when she stood in the front hall of her family's home, shaking water from her umbrella and leaving it on the porch, the sound of young voices stopped her.

Footsteps approached, and Mary came into view. "Stella, there you are! Come right in to dinner. Justin and Liz are here."

STEEL SLAMMED THE brakes of his truck a hundred yards from his trailer. It was dinnertime, he was exhausted after a night and day of consulting with Bolton and the other deputies, going over all the facts and evidence they'd gathered so far about Sue's death, but even more exhausted by what they didn't know. None of them were going to take the weekend off when there was so much to do.

Sue's parents had confirmed what he'd seen: that Sue had come home early in the afternoon in tears several days prior to her death but hadn't confided any details to them. They'd chalked it up to hormones and a fight with her friends; they'd noticed she wasn't hanging out with Lily and Lara anymore.

On Friday she went to her room after dinner and never came out again. Her parents, tired of her sulking, left her there. They were just about to go to bed when they got the call from the sheriff's department.

Sue's bedroom was on the first floor, so it hadn't been particularly difficult for her to climb out a window and leave. Neither Lily nor Lara had seen Sue that day. They admitted they'd been fighting, but they both claimed it was because Sue had been lording it over them the past week or so. That she had a boyfriend and they didn't. Typical girl stuff.

It wasn't typical, though. Not when neither girl would admit who that boyfriend was. They claimed Sue had never told them his name, and neither of them buckled under close questioning.

Steel was sure they were lying.

All Steel wanted now was a hot shower and his bed, but as soon as he pulled into the trailer park, he knew something wasn't right.

He let the truck's engine idle, scanning his temporary home, trying to spot the difference the reptile portion of his brain had instantly noticed. The trailer looked peaceful enough. The front door was closed, although of course he couldn't tell from here if it had been forced open and then shut again. The tiny front porch was empty. Although his garbage cans might overflow, he deliberately kept the porch clean so he could come and go as quietly as possible. His work took him out at all hours, and he didn't want his movements tracked by his neighbors, though he doubted anything went unnoticed by Marion.

His gaze shifted to her trailer. It was dark, for once, not a sliver of light escaping the windows, the curtains all closed.

Strange. Normally at this hour Marion was still ensconced on her porch, mug of coffee in her hand. He swore she lived on the stuff. Had a pot plugged in outside somewhere. He never saw her re-enter her trailer for a refill.

He looked back at his trailer and stiffened. His own living room blinds had been drawn tight yesterday when he'd left, to thwart any curious peeping Toms—or peeping Marions, more to the point. Today one of them was askew, not quite covering one corner of the living room window.

Someone had been inside.

A normal man might question whether he had been careless when he drew the blinds closed the previous day. Not Steel. Years of working in dangerous circumstances had taught him to watch for details like this.

Someone had definitely been inside his trailer. The question was: Were they still there?

He put the truck in Reverse and backed out of the trailer court slowly, spinning his steering wheel when he got to the end of the lane and turning toward the entrance. Back on the road, he drove a quarter mile, parked and headed overland through the woods that rimmed the park, coming at his trailer from a different angle.

When he reached the back of it, all was still inside, and it would have been easy to assume the perpetrators were long gone. Steel acted from an abundance of caution, working his way up the side of the trailer, listening for telltale signs that someone was inside, checking each window in turn.

His bedroom at the rear of the trailer, which looked out into the woods, lacked any shades at all, an oversight he'd been meaning to fix, but the room was dark and he couldn't see anyone inside it when he stepped up on a stump a few feet away and peeked in. He jumped down lightly and inched along the side of the trailer.

The bathroom window was open, as usual. It was too small for him to easily climb into—high up, too. He kept going. When he reached the front porch, Steel came to a decision, drew his pistol from his shoulder holster, hidden under the shirt he wore, and stepped cautiously toward the front door.

With his back to the wall, he reached out a hand and slowly tested the doorknob. Like he'd suspected, it turned and opened. Someone had jimmied the lock.

He peeked around the jamb cautiously—and stopped.

"Marion? What the fuck?"

"Get your ass in here and explain yourself, Cooper," Marion said caustically. She was sitting in the threadbare easy chair he'd rescued from a thrift store, the only piece of furniture in his living room except the television set sitting on a wooden crate. In her lap she had a binder.

Steel swore. She'd found his case notes—all the information he'd gathered about the overdose deaths that stretched back to thirteen years ago.

He pulled back, gathered his thoughts and peeked again. Marion didn't look armed. She was definitely dangerous to his peace of mind, though. With a sigh he stepped into the small room, shut the door behind him and holstered his pistol, making sure she got a good look at it.

"Don't think you're scaring me, Cooper," she said. "I've been dead a long time; my body just hasn't caught up to my soul yet. You put a bullet in me, you'd be doing me a favor."

"Why are you in my house?"

"Why are you photographing dead girls?" she countered, holding up the binder.

"I'm not photographing dead girls." He wouldn't be spurred into letting any information slip, but his gut had knotted up good. The information in that binder wouldn't help his image.

"Girls who ended up dead, then," Marion said. She flipped through the photocopied pages. "Beth Wright, Lori Means, Cecilia Foster, Rena Klein." She raised an eyebrow at him, her lined face hard with contempt. "Bet the sheriff would be interested to know about this. Were you the one who lured Sue Hill to her death? Did you give her the drugs she overdosed on? Were they tainted?"

"Ask me the real question you want to ask." He could see it in her eyes, a disgust that went beyond the general contempt she'd show a drug dealer.

"Did you kill her?" she spat out.

"No. And I didn't kill any of the others, either." Steel came to a decision, one he'd hoped never to have to make. Once one civilian knew about him, it was only a matter of time before everyone else did, but he had a hunch about Marion. She knew everything. He had no doubt she disseminated as many rumors as she soaked up, but something was keeping her on her porch.

What?

"I don't believe you," Marion said. "I remember your father; he was just like you. Always hanging around. Meeting people on the sly. Offering them things."

"You were here when my dad was alive?" He knew she was, but he wanted to keep her talking.

"Right here. Place was different then," she said.

"Different how?"

"Full of nice people. Respectable families. Maybe we didn't have much, but we didn't live in squalor." She waved a hand at his empty living room. A couple of pizza cartons he hadn't taken out to the trash. He wasn't the neatest man in the world, but you could hardly call this squalor. Marion was still talking, though.

"It was safe here. Silver Falls was a good town. People were happy. Healthy. Girls grew up, got work where they could. Married and had families. And then it all went to hell."

Steel wasn't sure what made him ask, "Did you know a girl who died—thirteen years ago, the last time this happened?"

Her lips parted in surprise, and suddenly Marion looked every one of her seventy-plus years. "My... granddaughter. Abigail. You don't have her photo."

"Abigail." Steel racked his brain, but he hadn't seen any information about a victim with that name. "When did she die?"

Marion named a year that was too early to have been included in the cluster that Dale and William had been investigating. Of course, back then they were the only ones who thought the deaths were anything but random overdoses.

"She overdosed?" he asked.

"Not on purpose," Marion hissed. "She wouldn't have. She was far too smart for that. She got involved in a little trouble, that was all. Then someone did her in."

Steel made a note to look for outlier cases. Marion could be exaggerating the details. When a string of other girls died, she might have lumped those cases with Abigail's in her mind even if they weren't related, but Steel wondered if there were other cases they'd missed. Maybe the killer had been operating over a longer timespan than they thought.

"Your father did her in," Marion hissed.

"No." Steel shook his head. "Not my father. Look, I'm going to tell you something no one else knows."

An avaricious gleam came into Marion's eyes. She traded in secrets, and she couldn't help herself, he supposed. He was taking a huge risk trusting her like this, but he didn't know what else he could do. If Marion made trouble for him and the press got wind of it, he'd lose any possibility of making progress.

"I'm a sheriff's deputy." He reached into his pocket, drew out his wallet and showed Marion his identification. He was gratified at the little squeak of surprise she uttered. "I'm working on the cases of Beth, Lori, Cecilia, Rena—and Sue."

"You're finding the dealer who's giving them bad drugs?" Marion was still looking over his identification.

"I think we both know there's more going on than that," Steel said. She looked up, and he went on. "There's a serial killer out there. Someone who's luring women to their deaths. The drugs are a part of it. He's using overdoses to cover his tracks, but this isn't about the drugs. It's about power over these young women who are so desperate for his attention. That's his high."

Marion made another noise, like an old wound had just been torn open. Her mouth worked as if she was trying to speak, but no words came.

"I'm going to say it all, so we don't have to say it again," Steel said gently. "Thirteen years ago he wasn't as bold as he's being today. He found his victims on the fringes—girls already in trouble, like you said your granddaughter was. I think he strung them along a bit. Maybe let them think he'd help them. Then he killed them, disguising each crime as an accident."

"What's he doing now?" She was struggling to sound calm, but her hands were shaking.

He hadn't spoken his theories out loud, but he might as well do so now. Maybe Marion would point out the holes in them.

"He's gotten bolder. Now his victims live right in town. Good girls who are maybe a little bored. A little ready for an adventure. A little insecure about something. He flirts with them, makes them feel special— asks them out." He remembered Sue's secret smile at the pit. The eager way she'd been texting. The way she'd hurried off to meet someone. "When they say yes, he drives them around, maybe he gives them little gifts. Maybe they fool around a little." He was making this up as he went along, but it was plausible.

Marion was shaking her head, but Steel kept going.

"At some point the drugs come into it. Maybe he starts with some kind of party drug that gets them high—teaches them there's a whole world out there they don't know about. I think he sleeps with them, too. There'd been evidence of that in previous cases. It's all fun and games and a big fuck you to all the other adults in their lives who still treat them like children. But then things start going awry."

"In what way?"

"He plays on their insecurities. Their jealousy. I'm not sure about this part yet, but some of the victims knew each other. I'm wondering if he tells them to invite a friend or two along next time. Says they'll party together. When his current mark goes along with the suggestion, thinking she'll finally get to show off her secret boyfriend, he gets them all high—and hits on one of her friends. Maybe he tries for a threesome. I don't know." Rena and Sue had known each other. Lily had been jealous of Rena—and suspicious of Sue. Sue had run off from the pit thrilled to be picked up. Days later she'd been devastated.

He noticed the distress in Marion's eyes.

"Girl number one gets mad," he went on. "They fight. He drops her off. Girl number two sticks around. Now he's got her hooked on the drugs—and the drama."

"Where does the killing come in?"

"Our man likes the feeling of two girls fighting over him, but he knows there's a limit. If girl number one gets too angry—and tells her parents..."

"Then he's in trouble."

"So he pushes it to the brink, gets high on the danger he's causing by his own actions, but when he senses girl number one is about to break, he texts her again. Tells her he's sorry. Asks her out again—she's the one he's always wanted."

"And he gets her high one last time," Marion said slowly.

"And watches her die."

"Why don't any of the girls report him?" Her voice was thin. Hardly audible. Steel understood her pain.

"Because now girl number two is caught up in the story. She's the special one now. The girl who came before her was too dumb for her own good. Took too many drugs and overdosed. Girl number two thinks she's too smart for that."

"Until it's too late," Marion said.

"This guy, whoever he is, is reckless, but he's not stupid. He knows he's getting to the end of the line. If we don't catch him soon, we won't catch him at all. He'll go underground again, just like he did last time." He wasn't sure how he knew that, but he did. As the details of Sue's death got out and combined with what people knew about Rena and the others, it would be clear the killer had a type, which would make it harder for him to find more victims.

A tear slid down Marion's weathered face. Steel could only imagine the pain of thinking about her granddaughter's last days. Could only imagine what else had gone on in her family that Abigail had slipped into the fringes of society even before the killer got to her. Did Marion blame herself for some part of what happened? Steel figured it was all too easy for those left behind to do so.

"You were living in Chance Creek at the time? When your granddaughter was killed?" That was where the first cluster of deaths had occurred.

She shook her head. "Livingston."

Steel straightened. Livingston was west of Chance Creek and had never been mentioned in the investigation. "We never looked at deaths in Livingston," he admitted to Marion.

"I told Abigail's mother to go to the Chance Creek sheriff when girls started dying there thirteen years ago. I told her those deaths were related to Abigail's."

"Where is Abigail's mother now?" Steel wished he didn't have to ask.

"Dead. Didn't take care of herself once Abigail was gone." More tears ran down Marion's face. He crossed to the kitchen, found the end of a roll of paper towels and brought it back to her.

"Sorry. All I have."

She took the paper towels and tried to mop her face with them, but her grief got the best of her, and she sobbed into her hands. Steel let her cry it out. He knew she wouldn't want him to touch her. Knew she'd hate herself for showing weakness like this.

"It's the same man back at his old tricks, with a few new twists. I'm sure of it. I'm trying to track him down, Marion. I'm undercover asking questions, gathering information, doing everything I can to find the connections and bring him in."

She wiped her eyes. "I thought you were just another Cooper. Another criminal."

"Like my father? You're right—Dale broke some laws in his time. But he was trying to help at the end, too. If you saw him hanging around Silver Falls, it was because he traced the killer here."

"Dale was tracking the killer?" she repeated.

"Trying to," Steel said.

Marion's fingers pleated the soggy paper towels in her lap. "And he's still here. Abigail's killer is still here—walking around scot free."

"That's right. You want to help me catch him?" Steel said, inspiration striking.

Marion went very still. "Help how?"

"Doing what you do best."

WHEN STELLA TOOK her seat at the dining room table, she found Noah, Olivia, Maya and Lance had joined them. Mary had placed herself at one end of the table and Jed at the other, as usual. Each couple sat across from each other, with Stella the odd woman out next to Maya on one side. Justin and Liz sat to the right and left of Mary. The twins had turned fifteen recently. Justin was tall but hadn't filled in yet. His dark hair hung in his eyes in a rather endearing way. Liz was somewhat shorter, her shoulder-length locks dyed an unfortunate shade of blonde that did nothing for her coloring.

"Hi, Justin, hi, Liz," Stella said, bowing her head as

her mother said a quick grace. She and her siblings hadn't kept up with the tradition much these past few years, but she figured she had a lot to be thankful for—especially the rain.

"Hi, Stella," Justin said brightly, helping himself to a large spoonful of mashed potatoes when Mary's prayer was done. "What have you been doing today?"

Stella smiled at his good manners. "Planning a fundraising event," she said. "How about you? What time did you get in?"

"Right after lunch. I got to help with the horses a little. Maya took me to see them. I wanted to ride one, but it was raining too hard."

"We'll have you riding in no time," Maya assured him.

"I don't want to ride," Liz said. She didn't lift her gaze from her plate, and when Mary passed her the platter of chicken, she passed it right along. She did take a small amount of salad, an even smaller dollop of potatoes and some green beans.

"You don't have to if you don't want to," Stella said. "Are you a vegetarian?"

"Nope." Liz didn't elaborate, and Stella decided not to push her.

"Liz has always liked my chicken in the past," Mary said. "I guess she's not hungry tonight."

"Teenagers are always hungry," Jed declared.

"Don't talk about me like I'm not here."

Stella met Mary's gaze. Mary rolled her eyes and shrugged. Stella figured this wasn't the first time she'd locked horns with her stepdaughter.

"What would you like to do, Liz?" Olivia asked kindly. "Are you an outdoorsy person or an artistic person?"

"I like to be left alone."

"Liz," Mary reproved.

"It's okay," Olivia said. "When my mom moved me halfway across the country, I wasn't too happy, either."

Stella held her breath, hoping Liz wouldn't take this opportunity to deny that Mary was her mom. She knew her mother wasn't trying to take Liz's mother's place, but she also knew it would hurt her feelings. Jed looked like he had plenty to say, but thankfully he was too busy eating to say it.

Liz shot a suspicious look Olivia's way. "Why'd she move you?"

"Because my dad went to jail and she was too embarrassed to stick around in Chance Creek. We went to Idaho."

"Idaho? That's even worse than Montana," Liz said.

"It's not exactly halfway across the country, though," Mary said reprovingly.

"Felt like it," Olivia said with a conspiratorial wink at Liz. "I loved Montana," she told her. "All my friends were here. Of course, I was embarrassed, too, so it was a push-pull situation, but I settled down in time. Came back here after my father died. Took me a while to find my place again, but eventually I did."

"I already like it here, too," Justin said. "Way better than the city. You should draw the horses if you don't want to ride them," he said to his sister. "You always draw animals."

"Oh, you're an artist?" Stella said. "Then I know a few people in town you should get to know."

Liz scooped up a forkful of potatoes and ate it, and Stella thought they'd made a good beginning, at least. After dinner, she stepped out onto the porch to take a call from Megan Lawrence, a local realtor.

"I heard a rumor you're spearheading a fundraiser."

"Yes, to make detox and stabilization available to teenagers in Chance Creek. We're planning to hold a water Olympics at Runaway Lodge and invite everyone in the area to come and participate." Stella was glad word was getting out. She'd posted the information to a few friends but needed to do more.

"That sounds great. I think it's a good cause, especially with all these overdoses, and the water Olympics is a fun idea, but…" Megan trailed off. "Are you sure you want to hold the fundraiser in Silver Falls after what happened to Sue Hill? I swear that town is getting creepier by the day."

"Silver Falls is a little rough," Stella admitted, "but Runaway Lake is wonderful, don't you think?"

"I guess." Megan sounded unsure. "Speaking of a little rough." She lowered her voice. "I saw you dancing with Steel Cooper the other night. Are you two an item?"

"No. Definitely not an item." Stella knew she should never have let him guide her around the floor. People had already linked their names together. Was this the real reason for Megan's call? Was she digging for gossip?

"Did you know he lives in Silver Falls now?"

"I thought he lived at Thorn Hill with his family."

"He's got a place in the Mountain Rise trailer park. A single wide. Nothing fancy. I just thought that was strange."

"He's a grown man. Maybe he wants a little privacy." Steel had never mentioned a trailer to her, but he had said he meant to stay away from his family until he'd finished whatever he was working on. She couldn't help wonder where he was now. What had his reaction been to Sue's death? If he'd been talking to her only days before, had he known she was in danger?

Was he the one who'd put her there?

She really didn't know Steel, after all, despite their conversation in Maya and Olivia's old treehouse. She wanted to believe he was tracking the real killer, but there was no reason to believe he was anything but a criminal himself.

"Maybe. He does have a dangerous reputation." Megan faltered. "Sorry. I shouldn't say that."

"Why not? He does. Whether or not he deserves it, I don't really know." Until she did, she needed to stay away from him. "We're not an item," she asserted again and hung up.

"You and who aren't an item?"

Stella whirled, surprised to see Olivia standing behind her on the porch. "None of your business." Olivia was the last person she wanted to talk to about Steel.

Olivia shrugged. "Fair enough. I'm more interested in your scheming, honestly."

Stella's mouth dropped open. "Scheming?"

"You were talking about fundraising to make the rehab center available to teens, weren't you?" Olivia gestured to the phone in Stella's hand. "One of my friends let me know your plans. That was my idea. What gives you the right to steal it?"

She'd been caught red-handed, and Stella didn't have a good answer. "I guess I thought the important thing was helping those kids—especially now. Who cares who gets credit?" But even as she said it she knew it did matter. Maybe the drought had ended, but it had been a long, hard summer for both families, and the future still looked uncertain. Whoever won the Founder's Prize would win a valuable ranch. "Look, I'm sorry. Uncle Jed cornered me, and I couldn't think of anything else," she admitted.

"Your family already has two good deeds under your belts. We only have one. The least you could do is come up with your own idea. I had no clue you were so cutthroat." Olivia's cheeks were flushed, and Stella felt rotten. Olivia was right; what she'd done was really unfair.

"I'm not. I don't even care about the Ridley property; it's Jed who's up in arms."

"Give it back."

"Give what back?"

"My idea. If you really don't care, then you won't mind letting me run the water Olympics."

"But... the water Olympics was *my* idea!"

"Too bad! What do you think is going to happen when you win and Jed gains control of the Ridley property—on both sides of Pittance Creek?"

Stella shrugged, but she knew what Olivia was trying to say. There'd be trouble between their families, no doubt. Jed might even try to alter the course of the creek—or at the very least divert more of the water than was their family's share. There'd already been incidents on both sides this summer during the drought.

Olivia waited for an answer, and finally Stella said, "You really want me to just hand over the whole fundraiser to you? What if Monica Hunt doesn't want to work with you?"

Olivia laughed. "I know Monica as well as you do. My family went to all the hometown days at Runaway Lake."

"Then go ahead. Take it." Stella turned to go, fighting back tears although she wasn't sure why. She really didn't care all that much about winning the Founder's Prize, but she did care about helping girls like Sue.

"Stella, wait. Hey—" Olivia caught up to her before she reached the steps. "I don't want to fight with you. Look, this is my fault, too. I let Virginia talk me out of the idea when I knew it was a good one. That woman has the uncanny ability to make me feel about two feet tall."

Stella stopped. She knew what Olivia meant. "Jed's pretty good at that, too. I meant what I said; I don't care who gets the credit, and you're right, it was your idea. I shouldn't have stolen it like that."

"I'm married to your brother. Lance and Tory are married to Maya and Liam, but if your family sweeps the Founder's Prize, there will be all kinds of hurt feelings. None of us needs that. Don't you think it would be better for the Turners and Coopers to tie?"

Stella thought that over. "What do you think the Founder's Prize committee will do if that happens—split the Ridley property in half?"

"Maybe. Or maybe by then it won't matter."

"What do you mean?"

Olivia smiled. "Come on, Stella. Noah and me, Liam and Tory, Lance and Maya…"

"What are you trying to say?"

"It would only take one more wedding to make the Turner/Cooper feud truly a family affair—and probably a thing of the past."

"You mean if I marry Steel?" Stella couldn't believe her ears. "Did he send you to play matchmaker?"

Olivia grinned. "Nope. But I have a feeling he wouldn't mind."

Chapter Six

WHEN STEEL SPOTTED the blonde teenager ambling up the street toward the pit, his stomach sank. He'd been heartened by the fact the place had been empty the last week or so since Sue's death and was about ready to head to town to grab something to eat. The Chance Creek kids were staying away and so were the petty dealers and other local riffraff. This girl was young. Fourteen or fifteen, he figured. He didn't recognize her, and she didn't seem to be in a hurry. She poked along the street, shoes scuffing on the sidewalk, her expression surly enough he'd bet she'd fought with her parents or her boyfriend in the last twenty-four hours.

Sometimes his sisters had looked like that in their teen years, not that teenage boys were any better. Still, girls' resentment and repressed anger seemed more dangerous to him sometimes. Probably because he didn't understand it. Boys took their fury and channeled it into sports, fistfights and insults. Girls seemed to turn it back on themselves.

This girl was looking for trouble, whether she knew it or not, and if she kept coming around here, she was going to find it.

When she spotted him, her footsteps faltered a moment, then she picked up speed and marched determinedly past him. Steel relaxed against the broken foundation section he was leaning on. The road extended only a few more blocks in the direction she was going before it hit the woods. She'd have to make a left turn, then there were only a few blocks that way before the road ended. She'd eventually circle back to the heart of town where she'd come from.

Nothing was happening here, so he might as well make his way out, too. He'd given Marion instructions to keep her ear to the ground and report any information she heard, whether or not she thought it was important. He didn't know her sources, and he didn't need to. Better to let her get on with it and stay out of her way. So far she'd given him bits and pieces of information about the daily habits of men and women he'd already met. Marion seemed to track the comings and goings of dealers and customers about as well as he did. She hadn't told him anything he didn't already know, however.

"No one can know about me," he'd told her. "You have to pretend you still hate me."

"Got it covered," she'd said succinctly. The prospect of helping track down her granddaughter's killer had revitalized her. Steel wasn't sure if he believed she could keep a secret, but there wasn't much he could do about it now.

"I always knew it wasn't an accident," she'd told

him several more times since then. "I knew someone had it in for her."

Now that someone else had bought into his theory, his own doubts were creeping in. If he was wrong, he'd given Marion false hope and was wasting everyone's time—including his own.

"WHERE DID LIZ get to? She's still not back," Mary asked. She and Stella were in the Top Spot Café, much to Stella's chagrin, where they'd met for a quick lunch with the twins. Mary had been taking them everywhere she could think of, trying to entertain them during the summer holidays since they hadn't made any friends here yet. Stella had suggested they check out Runaway Lake.

Now that Olivia had taken on the responsibility for the fundraiser, she had taken a backup role. Monica had accepted the change with equanimity and seemed to find the whole Turner/Cooper feud over the Founder's Prize funny. After a couple of days had passed, and Olivia's cheerful questions and praise over the work she'd already done had smoothed Stella's feathers, she found it possible to participate and enjoy herself again. In fact, she was enjoying herself more now that all the responsibility for the event wasn't on her shoulders.

She had to admit Olivia had a knack for organizing things. For her part, Stella was enjoying contacting school teachers, church groups and more to come up with a list of teenagers who might volunteer on the day of the Olympics. She hoped Liz and Justin might get involved, and Monica had been more than happy to have Mary bring them to visit and take a dip, and she'd even let the twins take out a canoe for a paddle. Even Liz seemed slightly more cheerful when they met to eat. Justin was over the moon about the treehouse cabins and the idea that one day they'd be fixed up enough for him to explore.

"I guess Liz is still at the corner store," Stella told her mother now. Justin was out on the sidewalk waiting for them. She had just settled the bill, and as they made their way out of the restaurant, she looked up and down the street but didn't see any sign of her stepsister, who'd asked to run and grab a bag of chips for later. "Let's go meet her. She's certainly taking her time."

"Maybe she can't decide what kind to get," Mary said. "Don't you have to get back to work?"

"I still have a minute or two." Stella glanced at her phone.

"I'll go find Liz." Justin loped off down the road. Two minutes later he was back—without his sister. "She's not there," he said and shrugged.

Mary sighed. "Where could she have gotten to?"

"I'll try texting her." Justin was already fumbling with his phone. They were waiting for a reply when Stella spotted Steel rounding the corner.

He saw her about the same time and slowed his steps. She had a feeling he was deciding whether to approach or walk the other way, which she understood completely given recent circumstances. After all, she'd seen him chatting with Sue and her friends just days before her death. He'd hinted he was trying to fix things in Silver Falls, but she had no way of knowing if he was lying. Still, Steel was her neighbor growing up. She'd known him all her life, and she'd never seen him hurt anyone. She took matters into her own hands. "Steel— have you seen a teenage girl with dyed blonde hair? I'm looking for my stepsister."

He hesitated. "About five foot five?" he guessed. "Blue shirt?"

"That's right." Stella's heart thumped in relief. "Where is she?"

He shook his head. "I'd better take you to her. Come on." He took off in a half jog similar to Justin's gait when he'd headed to the corner store to find Liz. Stella followed suit, glad she was dressed casually. She kept up easily with the pace he'd set, and soon she spotted Liz ahead of them.

"Liz," she shouted.

Her stepsister stopped and reluctantly waited for them to catch up.

"Mom's about frantic waiting for you. Why'd you take off like that?" She ushered Liz back the way they'd come, Steel following behind them.

"Just looking around."

"Thank goodness Steel saw you."

"Whatever."

They reached Mary and Justin a few minutes later.

"Where'd you go, Liz?" Mary asked. "You gave us a scare."

"Thought these small towns were supposed to be so

safe. That's what you told the judge in Ohio," Liz retorted.

"For the most part, they are," Stella said, "but you're new here. You don't know your way around. What if you got lost?"

"I'm not going to get lost in a town with one stoplight."

"You need to worry about more than getting lost," Steel put in. "There's a serial killer working these parts, and more than one teenage girl has wound up dead."

"A serial killer?" Liz repeated. "You're putting me on."

"No, I'm not."

She waved him off. "Grown-ups always try to scare you when they want to control you."

"You want to head down to the morgue for a look at the last victim?"

"Steel!" Stella caught his gaze and held it. She couldn't believe he'd even brought it up. He shook his head.

"Sorry. I'd better go. Glad your sister turned up safe."

They all watched him walk away.

"What a loon," Liz said, loud enough he probably heard, but he kept going. Stella squashed the urge to give the girl a good dressing down. That was Mary's job, not hers. Besides, Steel had definitely gone beyond the bounds of good manners. He'd tempered her concerns about him, though; surely he wouldn't make such a fuss about the serial killer if it was him.

"I'd better get to work," she said instead.

STEEL WAS STANDING in line at the Burger Shack to grab a late lunch, thumbing through a social media feed on his phone when he got a text from Olivia forwarding a post asking for volunteers to help with a fundraiser at Runaway Lake Lodge. Curious, he clicked on it and read more. Last he'd heard, Stella was the one raising money for a detox and recovery program for teenagers. What was Olivia's part in this?

"Please join us tonight to help make our Water Olympics Day at Runaway Lake Lodge a success," the post read. "We need people to run contests, lifeguards, food preparation, set up and clean crews and more."

Sounded like it was going to be a great time—and as usual he'd be stuck on the outside looking in. Would Stella still be involved somehow? She hadn't been happy with him for telling Liz about the killer, but to his way of thinking he'd done her a favor. Maybe he'd scared Liz away from making the kinds of mistakes Sue Hill had.

Still, that wasn't the way he wanted to leave things between them. He hadn't made any progress investigating Sue's death. It was like everything in Silver Falls remained in suspended animation. Dealers were laying low. The pit was empty most of the time. Maybe that would be the last of the killings.

Somehow Steel doubted it.

"Rehab for teens? What a crock of shit," a man's voice said close by. Steel turned and craned his neck to see Eric Holden in one of the booths with a man he didn't know. "Those kids don't need a recovery program; they need a good ass-whupping. That'd set them straight in a hurry."

This was the man who kept trying to date Stella? Eric had always been an arrogant prick to Steel's way of thinking. He shuffled forward with the line, but there were two people ahead of him, and he kept an ear cocked toward where the deputy was pontificating about kids, drugs and getting what they deserved.

This wasn't the first time Steel had run into an attitude like Eric's. Law enforcement could make the best man callous and the worst man a downright power junkie. He hoped Eric wouldn't go down that road.

"Yeah, I'll go," Eric said in response to a question the other man asked. "Stella's involved with it. I could care less about raising money for a bunch of parasites, though."

Steel forced himself to relax. Eric was spouting off, trying to impress his friend with his hard-ass attitude, no doubt. At least he was going to help Stella with her fundraiser.

If it still was her fundraiser.

You should come, Olivia texted, right on cue.

Who's running this event—you or Stella?

Me, now. She nearly got away with stealing it, but I was too quick for her. She added a smile emoji.

Look at you, facing off with the enemy.

I've seen you dancing with the enemy more than once, she texted back.

Hell. She had him there.

I still think you should come, she added. *Stella's helping me, actually. No hard feelings.*

Maybe I will.

More and more lately, Steel had been thinking about what his life would look like after all this was over. If he could put it all behind him and go back to normal ranching life with the rest of his family. Lance, Tory and Olivia could use his help with Thorn Hill, especially after the strain the drought had put on their finances this summer. From what he could gather, the Turners were struggling, too. They put on a good facade, but Steel knew they weren't any better off financially than his family.

Whatever it takes to win the Ridley property, he added.

No worries there; we'll win it one way or the other, she replied back.

How do you figure that?

Olivia answered his text swiftly. *Do the math, big brother. When you marry Stella, what's theirs is ours and what's ours is theirs.*

Steel guffawed, but a shot of desire coursed through him at the thought of marrying Stella—standing up in front of their families. Pledging himself to her. Whisking her away for their wedding night.

He shoved his phone in his pocket when he realized it was his turn to order. A few minutes later, he was back on the street without Eric having seen him, which was probably good. He was crossing the parking lot to his truck, still chuckling over Olivia's text, when he spotted a girl slouched against a lamppost, her shoulders drawn in as if she was trying to make herself invisible.

Lily Barnes.

Steel slowed down, all thought of lunch, Olivia and Stella erased from his mind. Lily had to know who Sue was with when she died, even if she'd refused to tell the deputies who'd questioned her.

He approached her cautiously. She was so hunched in on herself he didn't think she'd seen him.

"Hey—you all right?" he asked softly when he drew near.

Lily jumped, scrambling away from him. "Don't touch me!"

"Hey, hey, I'm not anywhere near you, okay? You just looked a little rough. You need a ride somewhere?"

She laughed, a bitter and utterly humorless sound. "I'm not stupid, you know. I'm not going anywhere with anyone."

"Why are you hanging around a parking lot, then?"

"I'm waiting for my mom."

"Exactly what Sue said last time you were with her," Steel pointed out.

Lily's eyes flared wide. "I'm telling the truth. I just came to tell Lara not to go back to the pit. She's not answering my calls, but her brother posted a photo— they were here earlier getting lunch. I didn't get here fast enough to catch her."

"Why isn't Lara answering your calls?"

"I don't know." She looked down. "She thinks it's my fault that—"

"That your friend died?" he finished for her.

She looked at him like he'd lost his mind. "Friend?"

"Sue Hill," he clarified.

"Sue wasn't my *friend*. She went behind my back—" Lily bit off her words. Started again. "If you think she's innocent, she's not." She was blinking fast, holding back tears, her bravado slipping to reveal a very frightened girl.

"Look, Lily," he began, but she shook her head.

"I'm done. I'm not going back there. You'll never see me again. I don't want to talk to you or anyone— and Lara shouldn't, either."

"Do you think Lara is in danger?"

"I don't know!" Lily cried. She kept backing up.

"Who got to Sue?" he asked. "Give me a name, Lily."

Her mouth dropped open in shock, and she shook her head.

"Lily—"

She turned and sprinted away. Steel considered going after her, but—

"You bothering that girl, Steel?"

Hell. Steel stiffened and slowly turned around. It was Eric, and he'd seen Lily run away from him. "I'm not bothering anyone," he snarled and backtracked to his truck, Eric watching him every step of the way. Damn it; he'd been so close to getting an answer.

Would Eric report what he'd seen to Stella? Probably.

Steel wanted to find Stella and tell her the truth of the matter, but instead he made himself get into his truck and drive away. He should have headed for Silver Falls, but at the last minute he turned and went the other way, taking a familiar road toward the last place he should be going. He couldn't explain himself to Stella, couldn't stop Eric from blackening his name, but maybe he could show her who he was in a different way.

"ALL SET FOR this?" Monica asked Olivia and Stella that evening.

"I think so." Stella surveyed the folding tables and chairs they'd set up in Runaway Lodge's cavernous interior. It was a little musty in here, devoid of the furniture she remembered from her youth. Monica had told her she'd sold most things when she'd shuttered the place over a decade ago. "I wonder how many people will show up?"

"I expect more than you think out of sheer curiosity. You two aren't the only ones who've told me they remember coming here when they were younger. I wish it was in better shape." Monica made a face. "Can't help feeling like maybe I was hasty getting rid of all the old things we used to have. A lot of it had seen better days, though. I figured I'd sell the place and the new owner would want to spiff it up."

"But you didn't sell it," Olivia pointed out.

"I meant to. Just never could make myself do it. Keeping up the lodge was always something of a labor of love. I got a large settlement when James's plane went down just after the boys were born; that's what I've lived on for the most part, but even though Runaway Lodge isn't a money machine, it was a solid business in its day. Parts of this place date back over a hundred years. I wanted to preserve it for my boys. Then they grew up and left, and I—well, I guess I needed a break." The older woman squared her shoulders. "But the past is the past. Now we're talking about the future. How's your training going for the agility test, Stella?"

"Not as well as I'd hoped." It was Stella's turn to sit a little straighter. "I've been waiting for someone to help me, and now I've decided I'm going to help myself. I need to set up an obstacle course at home that's as much like the one I'll be tested on as possible and practice. It can't be that hard."

"Like they say, if you want something done right, do it yourself." Monica looked off into the distance, and Stella wondered what she was thinking about. Her sons, maybe? Was she afraid they wouldn't come through to fix up the lodge? Or maybe wouldn't come home at all?

"That'll be the first of the volunteers," Monica said, snapping out of her reverie when the sound of an approaching vehicle reached them. She stood up and crossed to the door, Olivia close behind her. Stella hung back, letting Olivia be the face of the operation. As people filed into the lodge, however, soon she was greeting old friends and acquaintances from Chance Creek—and a few from Silver Falls, too.

Twenty minutes later Olivia stood in front of a small crowd of people sitting around the tables while Stella handed out cans of pop and plates of finger food.

"I'm so happy to see everyone here today," Olivia said. "As you all know, Chance Creek has had a high incidence of overdose deaths recently, and we aren't the only ones facing this problem. Opiates have flooded the country and are much too accessible to everyone—including our youth. I'd like to introduce Joan Wexler. She works at Chance Creek's detox and stabilization program, and she has a few words to say about what they need to help with the problem we're facing."

People shifted in their seats as Joan stepped up to the head of the room, and Stella knew they thought they were going to get a lecture. Monica's idea to serve some food had been a good one. At least that gave people something to do while they listened.

If they expected dry statistics from Joan, they were mistaken, however. Joan probably had enough experience speaking to people about her work to know that was the best way to lose their interest.

"I won't keep you long. You already know there's a problem," she said, gazing from one to the other of them. "And you know Chance Creek's youth are just as much at risk as the adults who live here. More, maybe. You all remember being kids, right? Don't get me wrong, the country is a wonderful place to grow up, but when you're seventeen and you're watching TV, or seeing influencers on social media talking up their exciting big-city lives, you start to feel left out, don't you? You feel like maybe you'll never amount to much while these other people are living the high life."

Heads were nodding around the room.

"When times get tough—when money gets tight or a drought hits—"

Laughter swelled the room as a rumble of thunder sounded outside.

"Or lightning sets your barn on fire," Joan added with a shrug, "it's human nature to look for an easy out from the pain. When you're a teenager and you're getting picked on, or you didn't get asked to prom, maybe you start looking for a way to numb out."

People had stopped eating, Stella noticed. Joan had them hooked.

"I'll be honest with you—addiction is a problem that's far easier to prevent than to cure. First and foremost, the work you'll do volunteering for this fundraiser is prevention work—getting the community together for a good cause. Stella will talk to you about her plan to include teenagers in the volunteering. That's a good start. I hope all of you think of ways to get teens involved and connected. That's the best way to prevent addiction."

"I like that," a woman called out. "We've had a lot of fun events this year because of people going after the Founder's Prize. I hope that doesn't stop happening when it's over."

"I hope so, too," Joan said. "Now, what you're going to raise money for this time is expanding the detox and stabilization program we already have. We need a space that's dedicated to teens; they can't be in with the grown-ups. That's two more rooms for sleeping: one for girls, one for boys. A common space to hang out, have meetings in and speak to counselors. Restrooms. And we need increased staffing, of course." She named a number that would get them started. It was a lot of money, to Stella's way of thinking. "If we can get the program started, it will be easier to get matching state and federal funds," Joan finished. "I'll hand things over to Stella to get into specifics about the day itself."

Just then the door opened and Eric slipped in. He smiled and waved at Stella. She gave a little wave back, gratified that he'd come to help. He'd texted her that he would make it, but he hadn't sought her out after their night at the Boot and she hadn't been sure he'd show up. He took a seat near the back of the room, quietly greeted the others already sitting around him and gave her his attention.

"Well, like I said earlier, this will be the Runaway Lake Olympics, and maybe it will be an annual affair, who knows?" She shrugged. Monica shrugged, too.

"Guess it depends on how fixing up the lodge goes."

"We're going to host an array of events, most in the water but some on land," Olivia went on.

"Is it just for kids?" a man called out.

"No, kids and adults. There will be different age groups so that everyone can participate. That's why we need so many volunteers. I'm going to pass around sheets of paper with the events we've come up with listed. Please sign up for any you'd like to help out with and note down the time period during which you're willing to participate. If you have some ideas of your own, let us know."

Stella passed around the signup sheets, and a buzz of conversation rose around the room. When she got to Eric's table, he got hold of her wrist and playfully tugged her closer.

"I think this is really great. You're going to help the community in a big way." He stroked his thumb over her skin and leaned closer. "Can I take you out after this? Get a drink?"

"Not tonight. I've got work tomorrow, and it's been a busy day getting ready for this."

"Another time, then." He stroked her wrist again. "I've been missing you, you know."

"We see each other all the time at work." She tried to keep it light, but she didn't like the way he was proclaiming their relationship for all to see with his actions, especially since they weren't actually having one.

"Seeing and doing things together are very different, don't you think? Look, I'm sorry training together didn't work out the way you wanted it to. Sorry I've been busy lately, too. I guess I'm a competitive guy, and that's not what you were after in a training partner."

"Not exactly," she admitted, but his awareness of the problem softened her.

"I think I'm better at dancing with a pretty girl than training with her. I've got kind of a one-track mind. I can't be attracted to someone and just be buddies, you know? I can't be doing something competitive and be focused on someone else's performance. So... as much as I hate to say it, maybe find someone else to train with and just go to dinner with me?"

She wasn't sure about dinner, but she didn't want to sort that out here. At least he understood what he'd done wrong, Stella thought. She nodded.

"I'll text you later."

"Sure."

The rain stopped before she drove home, and as she maneuvered along the slick streets, she found herself wondering about Eric. Was there simply too big a difference in their age? Was that why they were never quite in sync? Steel was only four years older than her—

Stella blew out a breath. Always Steel. But where was he today? Eric was the one who'd showed up and was volunteering for her fundraiser. He'd admitted he'd messed up and asked for a second chance. What had Steel done lately?

Nothing but dance with her when he thought he could get away with it.

Steel was never going to be boyfriend material, she told herself as she turned into the lane that led to the Flying W. He'd said someday he'd be done with his mysterious endeavor, but she needed to make sure she didn't waste her life waiting for something that might never happen.

Movement in the pasture closest to the house caught her eye as she pulled in and parked.

Strange.

The cattle weren't anywhere near this enclosure. What had gotten in there?

Darkness had fallen early with the storm, but now

there were breaks in the clouds, revealing starry skies behind them. She peered through the gloom to try to make out what she'd seen moving.

There it was again, a shape lurching along in an ungainly fashion.

Stella got out of the car and shut the door behind her carefully. Whatever it was hadn't been disturbed by her headlights cutting across the field. Was it an animal in trouble?

No—she was pretty sure that was a man. Was Liam or Noah out there doing some chore?

She moved toward the pasture, more curious than fearful. This was her home, after all, and whoever was out there seemed to feel they belonged.

Something about her surroundings bothered her, though. It was still difficult to see anything clearly, but the geography of the space felt wrong. There were fences where there shouldn't be fences.

Sections of fences, actually, standing alone in the middle of the field.

There was the way the man was moving, too. Lurching forward a step at a time.

Was he dragging something?

She moved closer and gasped. That was a body—

With a grunt, the man dropped his load, and the body clattered to the ground.

Stella pulled out her phone and flicked it into flashlight mode, even as the significance of the incongruous sound penetrated her fear. Bodies didn't *clatter* like that.

"Hey!" Steel shielded his face with his hands until

Stella lowered the light and aimed it at his feet, where she took in what seemed to be some sort of dummy.

"Steel, what the hell? You scared me!"

He looked around him, as if surprised to find himself there. "I was thinking about what you said at the Dancing Boot, about how you didn't have a proper course to train on. I remembered that Lance always has a bunch of junk leftover from his projects, so I…acquired some."

Stella eyed him. Did he mean he'd stolen them? "You don't think Lance would have given it to you if you'd asked?"

"He would have. Didn't want him to know I was there, though. Hell, I was hoping you'd never know I was *here*."

"You thought I'd find an obstacle course that sprang up in my field overnight and never question where it came from? You don't know me very well, do you?"

Steel shrugged.

Stella moved her flashlight beyond him, casting the beam from one obstacle to another. He'd done good work. There was a length of chain links strung up between two wooden posts, a solid fence of wooden planks, and a variety of sawhorses and wooden blocks arranged to form high and low hurdles. Finally, she moved the light back to the dummy, which she could use to practice the body-drag portion of the test.

"Lance had a dummy lying around?"

"It was in his shed. I think it's a cast-off from firefighter training. He's friendly with some of those guys."

Stella considered the uncanny approximation of a body sprawled at their feet, limbs stretched out at unnatural angles, then quenched the light and tucked her phone away, leaving them in the starlight. "Why do all this—now?"

He was quiet for a moment before responding. "Because I can't spend the time with you I want to. I can't volunteer for your fundraiser."

"It's not my fundraiser anymore," she said ruefully.

"Olivia said she confronted you."

"And rightly so," Stella said. "I did steal the idea from her, like you said."

"Maybe it's a good thing she's taken it on; it gives you more time to prepare for your test." He gestured at the obstacle course.

"What's it to you?" She crossed her arms over her chest, still finding it hard to believe he'd worked so hard to build this.

"Chance Creek needs a deputy like you."

"You think so?" His words moved her more than she cared to admit. No one else seemed to understand how important this was to her.

"I know so." He moved closer. "I know something else, too."

"What's that?" His proximity awakened her senses. Made her heart beat a little faster.

"I need you, too." He cupped her chin with one hand and bent slowly to kiss her, giving her plenty of time to back away. Stella leaned forward instead, meeting his kiss with her own. She loved the smell of him and the feel of his mouth on hers. As she lifted her arms around his neck, he gathered her closer, his hands sliding to her waist, drawing her in.

They were blessedly alone out here, only the stars as witnesses to their actions, and Stella found herself casting off all care for what was right or wrong— sensible or reckless.

She needed Steel, even if she didn't know what drew them so inexorably together.

In a way she'd always wanted him, she admitted. Ever since they were kids, he'd existed in the periphery of her life, a handsome, cocksure boy who'd turned into a sexy, confidant man.

Stella wondered if he remembered the way he'd come to her rescue once years ago. Until then he was just a neighbor, but that day her awareness of him changed. It was at the county fair. She'd had a rabbit to show, a beautiful Holland Lop she'd fussed over and groomed within an inch of its life. Valiant, as she'd named the little beast, had gotten out of its cage and raced away, minutes before the judges were to arrive.

She'd had no idea what Steel was doing there, but he'd rushed to help her, and they'd spent several long minutes chasing Valiant around while other kids who were waiting to show their rabbits laughed at them. Finally, Steel had scooped Valiant up, cradled the wriggling creature and carried him back to her.

"He's a mess," she'd cried.

"Get your brush. I'll hold him." And he did for five

long minutes while Stella raced to groom the rabbit all over again. She didn't win, but Valiant placed third. He wouldn't even have been in the running if it wasn't for Steel.

Now Steel was holding her. Kissing her. His strong arms creating a safe haven for her, his hands sending delicious shivers through her body.

He was hard, and if she was honest, she wanted him like that. Ached for him.

Had always ached for him.

Steel had been fodder for her dreams since she'd known enough to have dreams about men. Now here he was—and she wanted more of him.

Much more.

When Steel's fingers found the gap between her shirt and jeans, Stella moaned. She wanted him to touch her everywhere.

She tugged at the hem of his shirt, and he got the message, moving away from her just far enough to snag a hand in the fabric of it and pull it up and over his head, breaking off their kiss only long enough to finish the job and toss it away before snagging her mouth with his again.

Stella flattened her hands on his bare chest, loving the feel of his muscles under his skin. When he gently unbuttoned her shirt and eased it over her shoulders, she gladly let it fall to the ground and gasped when he covered her breasts with his hands. He eased them around to undo the clasp of her bra, and she shimmied out of it, tossing it away, too. Her nipples perked up in the cool air, and when he palmed first one and then the other with his warm hands, she swayed toward him, drunk with the feeling of his touch.

"Someone could see us out here," he cautioned, pulling back and sparing a glance at the house.

"No one will see us."

"The ground's pretty wet."

"I don't care. Steel—" Her last word was a plea. She couldn't wait any longer for something she'd wanted half her life.

He got the message, closed the distance between them, wrapped a hand in her hair and kissed her again, hard this time, letting her know exactly how much he wanted her, too. His other hand fell to the waist of her jeans, and he undid her belt, popped open the button and yanked down the fly. When his hand plunged into the confines of her jeans, sliding between her thighs, Stella sighed. God that felt good, but she wanted a lot more than his hand.

"Be patient," he said, the smile on his face echoed in his voice.

"I can't. I've wanted this for so—" She broke off, realizing what she was revealing.

Steel stilled, his fingers still moving in lazy circles against her core, but his gaze was on hers. "You've wanted this?"

"Forever," she told him, no longer able to keep the truth from him. "I've always wanted you."

With a growl she couldn't interpret, Steel pulled his hand out of her jeans, yanked them down unceremoniously and snapped the tiny bands that held her panties together.

"Hey—those were my favorite—"

"I'll buy you a new pair." His mouth covered hers again as he kicked off his boots and shucked off his own jeans. She finished the job getting hers off as well. All the time, their kiss went on and on, and Steel managed to steal a few caresses that left her hot, tingling and wanting him even more.

When they were naked, Steel stepped back and surveyed their surroundings. "Never thought I'd take you in the mud for our first time."

"I don't care where you take me. Just do it already," Stella said. His chuckle had her stepping forward and poking a finger in his chest. "You got me all hot and bothered, cowboy. Now do something about it."

"Like this?" He tugged her close again, slamming her body against his, and slid his hands down to cup her bottom. He snugged her up against his erection.

"Exactly like that."

Stella savored every one of his caresses, glorying in the feel of his body against hers. When he finally laid her down on the ground, she didn't care about the wet dirt pressed against her backside or the mist of rain that had started again even though stars were still visible to the east.

She opened gladly for him, and when he slid inside her, she sighed. Steel hesitated. "You deserve better than this."

"What could be better than this?" she demanded.

"This is honest. You. Me. The sky. The dirt. This is Turner land, but it's becoming Cooper land, too, isn't it? And Cooper land belongs as much to my family as it does to yours. Olivia was right—two families are becoming one. Whatever happens next, this is perfect." She slid her hands down to cup his backside and urge him deeper into her. "I want you, Steel. I want this. Right now."

And when he began to move again, she shut her eyes and gave herself to him utterly.

Chapter Seven

S TEEL HADN'T KNOWN it was possible to feel like this. Joined to a woman so completely that he merged into her, the two of them moving as one toward the same goal—absolute obliteration.

He gave himself over to loving Stella with abandon, no longer worrying about the dirt, the rain or their exposure to prying eyes. He couldn't stop from plunging into her, working both of them toward the climax that was just out of their reach.

Stella moaned beneath him, her fingers digging into his skin, her breasts lifting and falling with their motions. She was hot and slick and tight, and he needed more—

Steel came with an animal sound that tore from his throat, and Stella joined him, her cries pushing him to move faster, plunge deeper and bring them both over the brink. He pulsed within her as she clung to him, her shudders drawing out the last of him, until he was spent and collapsed on top of her, gathering her to him, one arm braced in the mud, the other cradling her.

"Stella—" He couldn't seem to say anything else. What was there to say? His body must have told her everything she needed to know.

Stella lay back, breathing hard, her face damp with the light rain that was falling. "Wow."

He thought that summed things up pretty well. He kissed her softly, savoring the taste of her, still buzzing with the connection. He didn't want this to end. They were still joined, although all he had to do was shift and he'd slide out of her. Stella chuckled as a certain part of his anatomy twitched.

"You want to do it again." It was a statement, not a question. His body had given him away.

"Hell, yeah," he whispered. "Again and again. Every night for the rest of my life."

She stilled, and he realized what he'd said. Steel slid out of her and turned on his side. It wasn't fair of him to be talking of forever when so much stood between them.

"Steel," she began. He silenced her with a kiss.

"No talking about the future. Let's just stay here. Right now. You, me and the mud."

She chuckled again. "Sounds perfect." She turned on her side as well, pushed him over and climbed on top of him. "Your turn in the dirt."

Steel was more than ready for another round, and this time as he eased inside her, he got to watch her moving above him, her breasts swaying as their hips met and parted again, her eyes closing when desire overtook her.

Stella was beautiful in her abandon, and Steel knew she was giving him a precious gift—her trust in him.

What had he done to inspire that trust?

He didn't know, but he swore to himself he would deserve it from now on. Then he stopped thinking at all, too entranced by Stella's beautiful form perched above him, silhouetted against the night sky, the feel of her encompassing him, enticing him to abandon himself.

Their slow, languorous lovemaking built up his need to a crescendo that couldn't be ignored, and as he came again, release breaking from him in waves, Stella's cries rang in his ears again as she shattered against him, Steel's determination grew. He was going to break the case he was working on, prove himself once and for all worthy of this woman.

Then he would marry Stella.

There was no other conclusion he could tolerate.

Later, he walked Stella home across the pasture and made sure she made it safely inside, waiting to see the light in her bedroom window and hear her soft, "Good night," through the screen before heading for home.

He had to laugh when he reached his trailer and surveyed himself in its tiny bathroom. He was covered with mud, which sluiced off him and swirled around the shower drain until he was finally clean.

He woke the next morning to a feeling that all was right with the world before he remembered that was far from true. Lily's concern for Lara stuck with him, and he vowed to check on both girls one way or another.

Stella haunted him, too. As much as he'd enjoyed the previous evening's romp in the mud, he needed to steer clear of her until his job was done. He didn't want to tarnish what they had by involving her with his undercover persona. He needed to catch the killer—now.

No one was hanging out at the pit these days, though. The petty dealers had shifted to other locations. Steel got the feeling parents were keeping a close eye on their kids, which was a good thing, of course, but he knew it couldn't last.

He was still pondering the problem while he drove through Chance Creek a few days later after stopping at the hardware store, where he'd picked up a hinge to replace one on a kitchen cabinet. He'd had no intention of fixing up his trailer when he rented it, but the condition of the place and the long hours he spent alone there had driven him to making small repairs. He caught movement out of the corner of his eye as he drove past the Chance Creek library and quickly pulled over to park when he spotted Lara speaking to another girl. Was this his chance? He needed to wait for her to be alone—

Hell.

Steel leaned in to get a better look. That was Liz, Stella's stepsister, with Lara. How did those two know each other?

They were talking intently, Lara peppering the conversation with hand gestures. She was describing something.

Steel was out of the truck before he realized he'd made a decision, and he strode across the library's lawn to its front steps.

"Hey," he shouted before he even reached them.

"What's going on here?"

The girls jumped apart, but Liz quickly regained her composure.

"What's your problem?" she demanded. He could tell she recognized him from the last time they'd met.

"My problem is I already told you to smarten up. First you hang out at the pit, now you're here with her?" He jabbed a finger at Lara. "You know who she is, right? She used to hang out with Sue Hill—until Sue died."

The blood drained from Lara's face. "Sue was an addict. You can't blame me for that."

"I can blame you for not telling the sheriff who she was with. I know you know."

Liz looked from one to the other of them, avid curiosity shining in her bright eyes. "You knew the girl who died?" she asked Lara. "Was she your friend?"

Lara turned an anguished gaze to Steel. "I didn't know she'd do what she did."

"What did she do?" Liz asked.

"Who was she with?" Steel drew nearer. For one second he thought Lara might answer.

"Steel Cooper?" a new voice called. "What are you doing at the library?"

"Gotta go." Lara slipped away as soon as he turned to face Mary Turner, and he cursed the woman's lousy timing.

"I'm just looking for a book," he lied.

Mary looked him up and down. "Hmph. Doubt it. Liz, why aren't you inside finding something to read?"

"Because reading is boring." Liz was tracing Lara's path down the street, and Steel bit back an urge to shake her. Lara was the last person she should be hanging out with.

"Because she was out here talking to Lara Whidby—Sue Hill's friend," he told Mary. "Better keep a closer watch on this one. She's attracted to trouble."

"Am not!"

"I was your age once," he told her, catching Liz's gaze and holding it. "I know exactly what you are."

Mary laughed, and Steel straightened, surprised.

"Oh, come on," she said to him. "You're still attracted to trouble, even at *your* age."

He supposed she had him there. "Doesn't mean I can't call it out when I see someone else making a mistake."

Mary looked after Lara's receding figure. "You think she was caught up in that stuff? In the drugs?" she clarified. "Like her friend?"

"Yep. And the rest of it."

"Rest of it?"

He shook his head. He didn't want to get more specific in front of Liz, but Mary's raised eyebrow seemed to indicate she understood there was more—and it wasn't good.

"Sometimes girls get jealous of their friends when they're running with a man who's out of their league," he said lightly.

"Running with a *man*," Mary repeated, her jocular tone slipping away. "I see. Liz, come on. If you aren't going to read a book, let's look for a movie you'll like." She put an arm around her stepdaughter's shoulder. "Thank you," she added to Steel. "For putting it plainly."

"Hope you'll spread the word," he said.

"Does the sheriff know about this?"

For one awful second Steel thought he'd given himself away. Then he realized how odd it must look for someone like him to care about any of it. Of course Mary would think the sheriff should be the one handling this kind of information.

"I wouldn't know." He shrugged.

"I'll make sure he does."

Steel struggled to decide whether that would be a good or bad thing. "Just don't mention my name." When Mary narrowed her eyes, he added, "If you want him to believe anything you say."

She nodded. "Right. Well, try to stay out of trouble. And—I'm sorry."

"For what?"

"For any trouble I've caused your family in the past. Your mother worries about you," she added. "It would be nice if you turned out okay in the end."

Steel laughed. "I'm not making any promises."

"I won't give up on you yet."

"THAT'S YOUR BEST time ever," Liam said, holding up his phone to show Stella the timer app on its screen.

"You're doing it, Stella," Justin cheered.

"I need to be faster," Stella said, panting, though she

accepted an enthusiastic high five from Justin. "I want to be able to beat our course with a lot of time to spare to make sure I can beat the real thing."

"My turn," Liam said. "You need to recover before your next attempt."

Stella bit back a smile. Liam had found her practicing the day after Steel built the course. She'd told him she'd built it herself, and while he'd been skeptical, he hadn't pressed the point. Instead, he had cheerfully volunteered to help her train. She'd found he and Justin loved to run it themselves. Did it remind Liam of his old football days? She hadn't asked—she was afraid of spoiling his fun. Ever since he'd arrived home from his honeymoon, he'd been in the best mood she'd ever seen him in. Tory was certainly good for him.

Stella took his phone. "On your mark, get set—go!" Liam took off running, and Stella almost laughed at his obvious enjoyment. When Tory joined her a minute later, she was smiling, too.

"He'll make you try it as soon as he's done," Stella warned her.

"Aren't you the one who's supposed to be training?"

"She needs a rest," Justin said cheerfully as he tracked Liam's progress, eagerly awaiting his own turn. Stella was pretty sure that helping her train wasn't Justin's primary concern, but she didn't begrudge him that. She was happy he was fitting in so well and enjoying his new life on the Flying W and could only hope Liz would one day feel the same.

Stella hit the stop button as Liam raced past them and showed him the time when he came back, panting. "You did pretty good."

"I did better last time," he grumbled. He gave his wife a kiss. "Coming to tell me it's time to leave?"

"That's right. Go clean up and take me to dinner."

"Will do." Liam loped off.

"You're going to do fine," Tory told Stella as Justin raced off down the track. He didn't ask anyone to time him; he just loved running it. "You're in great shape, and you already work for the department. They'd be fools not to hire you."

"Tell that to my mom," Stella said.

"She's just worried for you. That's what I've figured out with people." Tory smiled. "Whenever they wig out at you, they're either scared for you or scared for themselves, and if they really wig out, you've probably uncovered their biggest fear."

"My mom's biggest fear is that she doesn't stack up to everyone else." Stella bit her lip, realizing it was true. "I'd think having a daughter who's a deputy would make her proud."

"Maybe her second biggest fear is losing the people she loves," Tory suggested.

"Maybe."

"That doesn't make it easier when you want their support, does it?"

"No."

"I think we have to go for what we know is right and assume people will come around in the end."

"What if they don't?" Stella asked.

"Then we have to be our own mothers." Justin came racing back, and to Stella's surprise, Tory pulled out her phone. "Go on, get to the starting line. I'll time you."

"Thanks." She stepped to the line feeling a little lighter in spirit than she had before. Maybe Mary wasn't ever going to stand on the sidelines and cheer her on. That didn't mean she didn't have a team of people who would support her.

She was nearly through the course when she spotted Eric standing next to Tory and Justin. She stumbled, caught her balance again and finished as best she could, but she knew this wouldn't be her best time.

Tory confirmed that when she read her the time. "Gotta run," she added. "See you later."

"See you."

Justin hesitated as if unsure what to do. At a pointed look from Eric, he awkwardly trundled after Tory, his shoulders hunched.

Stella wished Eric hadn't sent him away. "What are you doing here?"

"Hi to you, too," he said, surveying the course. "Pretty impressive. Did you do this by yourself?"

"I had help," she said warily. As a seasoned deputy, she thought he would catch an outright lie. He'd probably think she meant Liam or Noah, though.

Eric nodded. Was he realizing he was the one who should have pitched in?

"I stopped by to see if you wanted a lift to the meeting tonight. We could get dinner on the way."

Olivia and Monica were holding another fundraiser meeting, and she was going to help. This week they were going to work with the teenagers who'd volunteered to get them ready for the water Olympics, which was the part of the job she'd taken charge of when Olivia had taken over the event. Many of them wanted to compete as well as help run the events, so there was a lot of coordination and planning to take care of.

"I guess that would work," Stella said.

"You guess?"

"I mean, sure, that sounds nice." She'd planned to train for at least another forty-five minutes, but she supposed she needed to eat, too.

"How about DelMonaco's?"

"Fila's," Stella countered. All the extra exercise gave her a huge appetite, and it was too easy to gorge herself on the wrong food at the country-style steakhouse. At least at Fila's, she could order something light.

She watched as Eric stepped closer to the starting line she'd marked in the grass with two sticks. What was he doing?

"What's your best time?"

She told him, and he nodded.

"Get your phone out." Eric crouched down.

"You're wearing boots," she pointed out. "You can't run in those."

"Watch me. You ready to time me?"

What else could she do but pull out her phone? "On your mark, get set—go!"

Eric erupted out of his crouch and barrelled toward the first obstacle, moving faster than she'd thought possible in a pair of dress cowboy boots. He clattered up and over the first obstacle, a section of chain link fence, and raced for the next one.

"Go, Eric," she called, trying to be a good sport. That's what friends did for each other, right? "Oh!"

He landed funny on one foot after jumping over a low hurdle, careened sideways a few steps before he caught his balance and raced on, but he was limping.

"Don't run on that injury!" she called out, but Eric ignored her. He finished the course, huffing and puffing as he went, his face mottled with color, obviously straining against the pain. When he crossed the finish line, she hit the stop button and hurried to his side. "You need to get that on ice."

"I'm fine."

"Eric—"

"I said, I'm fine!"

Stella stepped back, shocked by his anger. Eric straightened, took a step, winced and swore. "Let's get going. I have a reservation for us."

"At DelMonaco's? I told you I want to go to Fila's." She couldn't believe what she was hearing. He couldn't ignore what had happened; his ankle was going to swell up.

"I can go to dinner without you. I could even bring someone else. Don't think I don't have options," he snapped.

"I never said you didn't have options." She took a

breath. "Look, you're in pain. Is there anything I can do for you?" Why were men so damn touchy when they made mistakes? A woman would never act like this.

"What you can do is get changed and meet me at my truck." He held up a hand when she went to protest. "I'm really fine, Stella. Just... humor me, okay?"

"Okay," she said slowly, even though what she really wanted was to call the whole thing off. The strain on Eric's face stopped her. He was in serious pain, and she hoped if she went with him, she could persuade him to have his ankle looked at after their meal. "I'm going to follow you to town in my truck. I have to stay late after the meeting to help Monica and Olivia clean up and go over a few things. And I'm going to Fila's."

"Fine. See you there." He limped off toward the driveway, and Stella headed to the house. She wasn't bringing her truck because she had to stay late; she was bringing it because in an hour or so, Eric wasn't going to be able to drive, and she was damned if he was going to ruin her night because of his own stubbornness.

Her fears panned out. They got through their dinner in near-silence, Eric answering her polite questions with a single word or two by the end of the meal. His face was drawn with pain, but he even refused her offer of an ibuprofen to take the edge off.

Luckily, a friendlier face appeared as they were finishing their dinner. "It's been too long!" Camila Whitfield, the restaurant's co-owner, said as she embraced Stella. Her pregnancy was showing, but she seemed in good health and spirits.

"We didn't get to talk much at the wedding, did we?" Camila had lived on the Flying W before moving onto her own ranch with her new husband, Carl, and it still felt strange to not see her every day. "How is Laurel Heights treating you?"

"It's great—especially now that it's raining again. You know Carl is working on growing Mexican produce with Sven?"

"I heard something about that." Despite both being retired millionaires, Camila's husband had been joined by his friend a few months ago, and neither seemed capable of simply sitting back and enjoying themselves. Instead, they'd thrown themselves into running the ranch. Last Stella had heard, they were using geothermal something-or-others to provide Camila with fresh ingredients she'd normally need to have shipped in from Mexico.

"The real challenge will be getting the plants to survive through the winter," Camila said, "but the water shortage nearly killed everything before they even got this far. Luckily some of my cousins from Mexico were able to get their paperwork sorted, and they're working on the ranch now. They've worked with chilies and gauyabas and so on their whole lives and were able to keep the plants alive until the rain started again. Anyway, if all goes well, the food here is going to be better than ever!"

"Here's hoping! How about you? Are you feeling okay?" Stella asked, indicating her growing belly.

"Feeling great," Camila said. "Just started my second trimester."

"That's wonderful." Stella finished off a stuffed pepper. If the delicious food Camila served was the poor man's version of what she could cook, then Stella couldn't wait to taste what she could make with better ingredients.

After leaving Fila's, Eric insisted on following Stella in his truck to Runaway Lodge, but he sat in the back of the room, his shoulders rounded, talking to no one as Olivia directed the meeting and Stella worked with the volunteers to schedule them all on the roster of events.

He waited until everyone else had left before he stood. Concerned by the gray tinge to his complexion, Stella hurried to his side. "Are you okay?"

"That's about the fiftieth time you've asked me that tonight."

"Ready to admit you aren't?" she asked.

She thought he'd blow up at her, but instead he heaved a sigh. "Yeah, I guess I am. Damn ankle is so big I don't think I can get my boot off."

"I'll give you a ride to the hospital."

"What about my truck?"

"I don't know," she said honestly. "Guess you'll have to come fetch it another time."

"You don't have much of a bedside manner," he grumbled.

"Not when I'm dealing with someone who brought it all on himself," she agreed. "You were showing off, because for some reason you don't want me to feel like I can achieve the goal I've set myself."

"I told you before; it's a dangerous job…"

"And you want to hog all that danger for yourself. Yeah, I know," she said, holding the door open so he could hobble out. "Bye, Monica, Bye, Olivia," she called over her shoulder.

"Bye!"

"You really are a ball-breaker, aren't you?" Eric said when they made it to her truck.

"Yeah, I am. This is me, Eric, and I'm not going to change. If you don't like me exactly the way I am, then go find someone else."

Something flashed in his eyes, but it was gone a second later. He didn't like being confronted like this, did he? Stella didn't care. She wasn't about to back down.

"Maybe I'm set in my ways," he admitted a moment later. "Maybe I'm having a hard time adjusting to you newfangled women."

"You're not that old, Eric." She got into the truck and waited for him to make his way to the passenger side, knowing he wouldn't take any help from her. When he was settled in, she said, "But you're right; times are changing. You'll have to change with them if you don't want to get left behind."

Eric just grunted, sat back in his seat and was quiet all the way to town.

STEEL HAD MEANT to stay away from Stella's fundraiser, but when the day of it dawned two weeks later, he found he couldn't. He'd done a good job keeping his distance from her, though. He'd texted a time or two, just to let her know he was thinking of her, but made it clear he didn't think it wise for them to be seen together yet.

He'd made no headway in talking to Lily or Lara again, had spent a lot of time with the other petty dealers, talking about the possibility of growing a new pot crop, trying to get them to open up about how drugs were making their way into town—especially the ones responsible for the deaths.

All he'd heard were blanket denials that anyone local was supplying the drugs to a killer. He kept coming across an *honor-among-thieves* mentality among the dealers that made them assert they knew their customers well enough to know they couldn't be killing young women.

It interested Steel to hear that these same dealers believed the overdoses weren't accidental.

"No way all the dead people would be hot young teenage girls," was how one of them summed it up succinctly. "If it was a mix, some old, some young, some guys, some girls, yeah—then I'd believe it, but not this shit. Someone's doing it on purpose."

He knew Bolton had questioned Lily and Lara again, and that both girls had stuck to their story: they'd never seen Sue's boyfriend. Had no idea who he could be.

Something about that didn't sit right with Steel. Sue was dead. Lily and Lara had to know they could just have easily been the victim. Why would they keep secrets?

Steel went over all of it again and again in his head.

But today he needed a break.

He needed to see Stella.

He'd spotted Eric Holden limping a couple of weeks back and heard a rumor that he'd twisted his ankle running an obstacle course. The only obstacle courses he knew of were situated at the Halls' ranch— and Stella's. Had Eric been helping her train?

Have you given up on me? He'd felt like a teenager himself when he'd sent the text to Stella.

Not yet. Hurry up, she'd texted back.

Working on it.

He arrived to find the road down to the bridge that led to Runaway Lodge packed with vehicles, so he parked where he could and walked the rest of the way, carrying swim trunks and a towel. It had been a while since he'd swum in a public place, preferring to find some lonely mountain lake or stream to cool off in the summer instead, but he remembered childhood visits to the lodge and found his mood elevating in anticipation as he approached the little bridge that crossed Runaway River.

They'd lucked out with the weather today. More often than not it had rained these past few weeks, and Pittance Creek, which had almost dried up, now flowed fast and high like all the other streams and rivers in the area. Runaway River was just as high, spinning under the little bridge like a spring torrent.

The trees to either side of it still bore marks from the fire that had scorched them a month or so back. Liam and Tory had driven their truck hellbent for leather through the flames to be able to get to town and report the blaze. He was just thankful they'd survived the experience and so had Runaway Lodge.

Crowds milled around on the beach when he approached, and he ended up in front of a folding table manned by three teenagers taking donations and signing people up for events.

"Hi, welcome to the fundraiser for Chance Creek's detox and stabilization unit," a teenage girl said when it was his turn in front of the table, rattling off a script she must have repeated a hundred times already. "Would you care to donate?"

"Of course." Steel handed over a hundred dollars, knowing some people would view his donation askance. The girl in question seemed unaware of his identity or the rumors that swirled around his family, however. She happily took his money, filled in a receipt for the donation and gave it to him.

"What events would you like to participate in?" She gestured at a bulletin board set up behind her, where a number of activities were listed, including swimming races, diving contests, kayak races and so on.

"What's that?" he asked, pointing to a separate one labelled, "Overall Best."

"If you participate in all the contests, you can compete for the title of best overall athlete," the girl said. "The one with the highest combined score wins."

"I'll do that."

"Great." The girl beamed and began to fill his name in on a form. Since he was to compete in all the contests, it took a while, and the line lengthened behind him, even though the other two teenagers at the booth were signing people up, too. "Here's a schedule of events. Be sure to be at the starting line for each one, or you won't get any score at all for any that you miss."

"Sounds good." In for a penny, in for a pound, Steel decided. Besides, it sounded like fun. He loved a contest.

"What're you doing here?" a man's voice broke into his thoughts as Steel straightened and turned to go. Eric Holden.

Figured, Steel thought. Too much to ask for a day off from all the stress in his life. "I'm competing."

Eric spotted his name on the signup form and bent closer. "You're going for all around best?" He snorted. "Good luck with that."

"I don't need luck."

"You will to beat me." Eric turned to the teenager. "Sign me up, too. For everything."

"You still got a bum leg?" Steel asked him.

"Looking for an advantage? Too bad—my ankle is fine," Eric said.

Steel noticed a bunch of twenty-something cowboys behind them exchange glances of amusement, and he realized this competition could go sideways. Eric had a temper. He was in good shape, but he was also in his forties, and Steel had always been fit. There was no reason either of them should be cocky enough to think they could win this thing; there were plenty of other competitive men in Chance Creek and Silver Falls, but even if he didn't win, Steel figured he had a pretty good chance of besting Eric. He had a feeling the deputy wouldn't like that one bit.

He caught sight of Olivia overseeing the setup of the eating area, awards podium and the large tent where a band would play later. Stella stood in a crowd of teens handing out folders and whistles, prepping them for running the competitions, he figured. If he made Eric mad, it might have negative consequences for her. Should he withdraw and simply leave? He probably shouldn't be here anyway.

Then he caught sight of Lily Barnes standing to one side, near other kids but not among them. He might have a chance to speak to her today. At any rate, he could keep an eye on her, see who she was talking to.

"Better run away while you still can," Eric said.

Steel waved him off and kept going. He spotted his aunt Virginia among the crowd. Seemed like a good opportunity to check in with her. He hadn't talked to her in a couple of weeks, and sometimes lately Virginia seemed a little frail.

When he got closer, however, he realized that Jed Turner was with her, and Steel veered away again, joining a nearby line for lemonade, straining to hear their conversation. The two weren't yelling at each other, which was a good start. Maybe the bright sunshine had mellowed them out.

"There weren't any treehouses back then," Jed was saying. They were talking about Runaway Lodge, Steel realized. He wondered about the first time Jed and Virginia were here. The main lodge had quite a history.

"That's right. There were fewer trees," Virginia said, gesturing to the grove around the lodge.

"I think it was logged in 1940," Jed said. "These trees were saplings back when we came."

"Look at them now," Virginia said.

"Steel."

He was surprised by Stella's touch on his arm and lifted a hand to stop her from saying anything else. He jutted his chin at Virginia and Jed. "They're talking about the old days," he said softly.

"It's been a long time," Jed went on, "but I've never forgotten the first time I brought you here."

"I haven't forgotten it, either," Virginia said tartly. "I retain my full faculties."

"I never doubted that," Jed said.

Steel appreciated Stella's quiet presence by his side. She seemed as interested as he was in their older relatives' conversation. For as long as he'd known his aunt and her uncle, the two had been at each other's throats.

"Do you remember the moon that night?" Jed asked Virginia.

"Some moons you never forget," she said, surprising Steel all over again. He didn't think he'd ever heard his aunt utter a romantic remark before. Something touched his hand, and he felt Stella's fingers tangling with his. She squeezed his hand, and he squeezed hers in reply.

"I remember your bathing suit," Jed said. "You were a knockout."

"Oh, hush." Virginia laughed, an almost girlish sound. "Kids these days would find it hilarious, but at the time I felt pretty daring."

"I thought you looked like a movie star. When you agreed to go on a canoe ride with me, I thought I'd won the lottery."

Virginia was silent for a long moment. "You had." She lifted her chin and spoke in a brusquer tone. "But then you found a way to mess it up."

"I made a mistake," Jed said. "One I've regretted ever since. There's a reason I stood you up at the homecoming dance, you know."

"Homecoming dance?" Stella turned a wide-eyed glance Steel's way. This was part of family lore—a mystery no one but Jed and Virginia knew the truth of.

"You were a fool. You didn't know what you had until you lost it, and anyway, you know that topic is off limits." Virginia refused to show it, but Steel thought he read traces of her sorrow there. He'd heard rumors about Jed standing her up at a dance years and years ago, but he didn't know why.

"You're right; I was a fool, but I think it's time to talk about why. It's time, Virginia," he repeated.

Virginia was silent a moment, then gave an almost imperceptible nod of her head. "Maybe it is."

"Thing is, I believed what Foster Crake told me," Jed said earnestly.

"Foster?" Virginia blinked. "That redheaded idiot? You know he asked me to the homecoming dance that year, too. But I saw the way he treated his sister—

pushing her around every chance he got. Making her cry all through school. You know he stole all the money she'd saved up to buy a dress for that dance. Gambled it away. I wanted no part of that."

Jed heaved a sigh. "He told me you were setting me up. Said you'd been seeing Roger Dickons for weeks. That you were going to dump me and waltz into the dance on his arm."

"Why the hell did you believe him?"

Steel exchanged a look with Stella. He wasn't sure he'd ever heard his aunt swear before, but before Jed could answer, Virginia's expression changed and she answered her own question.

"Because I spent every day after school with Roger leading up to the dance. Oh, you stupid oaf, I told you we were studying. He was failing science, Jed—he had to pass to keep his scholarship to Montana State."

"I got jealous," Jed said simply.

"And you stood me up for that? Because Foster Crake whispered lies into your ears? You didn't ask me for the truth of it, Jed?" A half century of pain went into her question. Steel found himself holding Stella's hand. Stella was blinking back tears. Everyone knew Jed and Virginia had been halfway to engaged when they'd split up at the end of high school. No one knew what had happened.

"I tried to talk to you later. You threw things at me—"

"Of course I threw things at you!"

Other people were looking. Jed noticed and touched

Virginia's shoulder. "Maybe we should sort this out—somewhere we can really talk."

For one long, awful moment, Steel thought Virginia would object—or possibly hit him with her umbrella, which she wielded with unswerving accuracy in his experience. When she finally nodded, he let go the breath he hadn't realized he'd been holding.

Virginia walked at a dignified pace around the corner of the lodge. Jed hobbled after her. Everyone else around them had gone back to their own conversations, but Steel followed them, Stella close beside him. When he reached the corner of the lodge and peeked around, he saw Jed and Virginia heading for where he knew the old greenhouses stood. He hesitated a moment, then curled his fingers more firmly in Stella's and led her to the back of the lodge.

"Do you think they'll finally patch things up after all this time?" Stella asked, watching them go.

"I hope so."

"They let a little misunderstanding get between them for so long." She looked away but not before Steel saw her eyes had filled again. "Our whole family is like that—both our families," she asserted. "Holding on to old grudges, old pain. Why can't we get free of the past?"

"I think we're close."

"Do you?"

God, he hoped so. It was why he'd stepped away from his family, why he was working so hard to find Sue's killer.

"I do."

"Where are we going?" Stella asked when he pulled her around another corner, out of sight of anyone else, and stopped. Jed and Virginia were long gone. They were alone.

"I just needed a little of this." He bent down to kiss her. Stella waited until his mouth was just an inch away from hers and closed the gap. As her hands twined around his neck, Steel encircled her waist with his arms. This was what he needed—to be alone with Stella. To be pressed up against her. Kissing her. Drinking in the possibilities of what could be between them.

When they drew apart again some time later, Stella smiled at him, her gaze searching his.

"What?" he asked when he began to feel like she was trying to peer straight into his brain.

"I don't understand why this works so well. You and me," she clarified. "But it does. You're like a drug, Steel. The more I have of you, the more I want." She dropped her gaze. "I probably shouldn't tell you that."

"You can tell me anything." He rested his hands on her hips. "Stella—" He broke off, not knowing what he meant to say. "I wish I was already finished—"

"I know. Me, too. But you said you're working on it, right? Whatever it is you're doing? So someday...?"

"Someday," he agreed. "For now this will have to be enough." He pulled her close and kissed her again.

"That'll never be enough," she complained when he let her go again.

A series of shrill whistles interrupted them, and Stella sighed. "Time for the competitions to start. I've got to go," she explained.

"Go ahead. I'll follow in a minute. Don't want to give people ideas."

"No, we wouldn't want that." She bounced up on her toes to kiss the underside of his chin. "To be continued."

"Definitely." Steel stepped back and watched her walk away. A minute later he followed and came around the front of the lodge to find even more people crowded between the building and the beach—grown-ups, teens and children everywhere, waiting for the water Olympics to start. Something caught his peripheral vision, and he turned to see Eric Holden watching him, his expression grim. The man deliberately shifted his gaze to Stella where she was consulting with her volunteers and back again.

He'd seen them. And he was pissed.

He let his own gaze slide away, and when the whistles blew again, Steel went to join the rest of the competitors who would participate in the first adult contest, a swimming event.

"I still need to change into my suit," he told the teenager in charge.

"Better hurry; contest starts in five," the kid said, pointing to the main entrance to the lodge. "There are change rooms set up in there."

"Thanks."

STELLA CAUGHT SIGHT of Steel hurrying to the lodge,

probably going to change, before another volunteer came hurrying up with questions about the event she was supervising for the kids' division.

"I think I've bitten off more than I can chew," Stella said to Monica when she'd sent the teen back to his position. "We've got events all day, volunteers everywhere, and everyone has questions. What if I can't keep up?"

"You'll keep up." Monica waved a hand to encompass the crowd. "Look at what we've managed to pull together. We're going to raise a lot of money for your cause."

"Olivia's cause," Stella joked. "Just kidding; I'm thrilled with how well it's all going."

Another volunteer rushed up. "One of the parents wants her kid to wear a life vest during the competition. Is that okay?" she asked worriedly. "I'm not sure it's fair."

"I'll take this one," Monica said, allowing the girl to lead her away.

When Stella realized no one else wanted a piece of her, she allowed herself to take a deep breath. Despite the chaos around her, things were really going well. The sun was shining brightly. Everyone looked excited to be here. She shadowed her eyes with her hands and looked for Olivia to see if she needed any help.

"What the hell do you think you're doing?"

Her pulse jumped, and Stella spun to find herself face to face with Eric. A very angry-looking Eric.

"I don't know what you mean."

"I saw you—with Steel Cooper. Slipping away with him. What are you—auctioning yourself off to the highest bidder?"

"What?" Stella drew back, shocked at his implication.

"You're supposed to be with me."

"I'm supposed to be my own woman," she said. "You and I have gone out a few times. That's it."

"Exactly. You're my girlfriend. So what the hell are you doing with another man?"

"Going out and being together are two very different things," Stella told him, his tone making her good and angry. "You want to be my boyfriend, you've got to ask, and you never asked, did you?"

Eric's face darkened. "That's a bunch of bullshit. You knew exactly what you were doing when you let me pay for your dinner at Fila's. Friends don't pay."

Was that his definition of love? "Friends pay all the time," she countered. "I pay for my friends' meals. They pay for mine."

"Quit the innocent act," Eric spit at her, his hands balled into fists. Around them, people were beginning to look their way. This was the last thing Stella needed.

"It's not an act," she hissed at him, "but you're sure putting on a show for everyone. You've even got the sheriff's attention."

Eric's head whipped around, and when he caught Cab Johnson looking their way, he stepped back. "Fine. We'll handle this later."

"There's nothing to handle. I'm not going to be

with a man who yells at me, and I'm certainly not going to be with a man who calls me a whore. This, whatever it was, is over. Now I've got work to do."

She stalked off, shaking, knowing that if it weren't for the crowds—and the sheriff—Eric would undoubtedly follow. She knew he had a temper. How could she not see how controlling he wanted to be? She could sure pick them, couldn't she?

Stella spent the rest of the morning putting out fires. Not real ones, thank goodness, but problems that flared up quickly and had to be quenched just as fast. Eric kept his distance, but instead of leaving, like she'd hoped, he stayed and competed in the contests he'd signed up for—which turned out to be all the adult ones. When she realized that both Steel and Eric were competing for overall best, Stella had to squash the urge to get in her truck and drive away.

This was not going to end well.

Chapter Eight

"**W**HAT ARE YOU doing here?"

Steel had almost reached the beach when Liz confronted him. Clad in a bikini, towel balled in her arms, she looked even younger than her fifteen years.

"Enjoying myself like everyone else." Steel kept going.

"People like you shouldn't be allowed to be here, creeper."

That gave him pause. The name didn't bother him, but it bothered him that Lily's and Lara's words had already become part of Liz's vocabulary. Was she still in touch with Lara? When several people in the vicinity turned to look, Steel forced himself to walk on, telling himself he'd ask Stella to follow up on that. This was what he was going to face even after he'd solved these cases—if he ever did. The climate in Chance Creek and Silver Falls would be toxic for him, and Stella would suffer, too, if they were together.

"Hey, *creeper*, you competing, too?" Ned Haverstock had been following close behind him, and he must have overheard what Liz said. They joined the small crowd gathered for the first swimming competition.

"You know it." He shrugged off Ned's joshing even though it stung.

"Isn't that girl a little young for you?" Daniel Ortiz added, appearing by his other side.

"Fuck off," Steel told the other deputy.

"Heard she was hanging around at the pit," Ned put in.

"When?"

But just then, the teen in charge of their contest blew his whistle, and everyone surged forward to hear his instructions. Steel wondered if Liz had been back to the pit, or if Alan was referring to her first venture there, when he'd collared her and taken her to Mary and Stella.

Steel found himself between Daniel and Eric Holden at the starting line, Ned a little farther down. They were supposed to dash into the water, swim around a buoy positioned far out in the lake and swim back again. The first one out of the water to touch the finish line would win.

"Someone might think you're the one luring these teenage girls to their deaths," Daniel said. Steel knew he was joking—trying to throw him off to get an advantage in the race. They joked all the time at the station. On his other side, however, Eric snapped his head around to look at them.

"What the hell does that mean?" he asked just as the teen in charge blew the whistle again.

"On your mark, get set—go!"

Steel didn't bother to answer Eric or acknowledge

Daniel's tasteless joke. He raced to the water, splashed a few more strides and dove in, coming up to swim with a practiced crawl toward the buoy.

At first trying to swim in the pack of racers was an exercise in warding off stray elbows and kicking feet, but Steel had always been a strong swimmer, and soon he found himself at the start of the pack. He caught a glimpse of Eric's face to his left. A flash of Daniel's orange swim goggles to his right. Steel dug in for all he was worth. He was not going to lose to either of these men in his very first race.

His muscles were screaming by the time he passed the buoy. Heading back to the beach meant swimming with the waves rather than against them. It wasn't that choppy, but every bit helped. Refusing to be distracted by the other swimmers, Steel went for a steady pace rather than a frantic one. When he judged he was halfway back to shore, he glanced around, located his competition and increased his speed. He passed Eric in the last fifteen meters and saw the man had drained his reserves and was barely making headway. Daniel, on the other hand, was still going strong.

Time to dig for all he had, Steel decided. He put his head down and went for it, his motions crisp and precise, drawing on all the years he'd spent swimming in lakes like this. Soon the sandy bottom was under his feet, he raced back out of the water and surged past Daniel to reach the finish line first.

A cheer went up from the crowd, which warmed his heart as Daniel reached the finish line just moments after him. Several other racers joined them before Eric staggered up and crossed it. The look Eric sent him should have struck him dead, and Steel allowed himself to smile back. Eric stiffened. Glowered at him.

Steel turned away and caught Stella's eye. She was talking to yet another volunteer, and he knew he'd be hard-pressed to get another moment alone with her, but she nodded, affirming she'd seen his victory, and flashed him a small thumbs-up. He didn't need to look back at Eric to know the effect that would have on the man.

This was going to be fun.

SOMEONE WAS GOING to get hurt before this day was through.

Stella had to admit to herself it had been humorous at first to see Steel beating the pants off Eric—and everyone else—in the competitions, but as the day went on, and she took in Eric's rising fury, she began to worry. It wasn't like Steel won every event. A Silver Falls deputy, Daniel Ortiz, was giving him a real run for his money, and several of the other cowboys had managed to win some of the competitions.

Not many men had signed up to compete for the all-around award, however. There were plenty of athletic men in these towns. Heck, a number of ex-military men had won handily in the competitions in which they took part. But those were family men who wanted to cheer on their wives and children, too. Only a handful of single guys and one or two married men were in every event.

Meanwhile, she was kept on her toes helping to make sure the contests went off on time, the volunteers knew where they were supposed to be and what they were supposed to be doing and keeping track of a million details in between. Olivia flitted around like a madwoman, trying to keep watch over the food vendors and drink tents, reunite lost children with worried parents and make sure the evening program was ready to go at the end of the day.

Stella was grateful for all the volunteers. So many teens, men and women had donated their time and energy that there always seemed to be a pair of hands to lend some help when she needed it, but still, there was an energy to the day she wasn't entirely comfortable with.

With each of the men's events, a bigger crowd was accumulating. Most of the younger kids' contests had been scheduled early, and those families were now hanging out near the beach on blankets they'd spread, kids playing among them, little ones taking naps in portable cribs in the shade.

The events for teenagers were scheduled through the day, many of them later in the afternoon, since so many teens had been involved in supervising the younger kids' events. Now they were happening one after the other, leaving amorphous clumps of teenagers hanging around in between their events.

The women's events concluded with a diving competition that got a lot of attention, especially since Ella Hall, who used to be a movie star, had taken part. She turned out to be a fantastic diver, and Stella had heard more than one teenage girl talking about wanting to be just like her when they grew up.

Now it was down to the final events for the teens and men.

Stella would have liked to watch them, even though her stomach was knotting in worry about the way it might all turn out, but it was nearing dinnertime, which meant helping Olivia and Monica to supervise the set up of tables and chairs inside the lodge and out. There were several food tents for people to choose from, and they'd wanted to provide a restaurant-like atmosphere with candles on the tables and live music. The band had just arrived.

It was only when a loud cheer burst out from the crowd on shore that Stella realized the final event of the men's competition was about to get underway.

"Come find me if you need anything," she told Olivia, who was talking with the leader of the band, and hurried toward the shore. She'd just take a minute to watch…

She had to push her way through the crowd to reach a place where she could see the competitors, and then she groaned. What had made any of them think this was a good idea?

The men were supposed to race on stand-up pad-dleboards, which was all well and good, except several men were in the water at the starting area, evidently having fallen in. A glance told Stella the men had realized that by rocking back and forth on their own boards they could create waves and knock the other men off theirs. The teenager in charge, a young, rather timid-looking girl named Dierdre, was trying to get them to line up so she could start the race, but the men were too busy knocking each other off the paddleboards to listen.

As she watched, Steel rocked his board furiously, producing waves that upended several other men, including Eric and Daniel. Both men popped up out of the water and climbed furiously on their boards, Daniel quickly, Eric struggling a little before managing to push himself up and on again.

A shrill whistle blew three long blasts. "Get it together, men!"

Stella bit back a smile. It was Cab Johnson, Chance Creek's sheriff, who'd used his own whistle for the cause.

Finally, the men got into a straggling line, and Dierdre was able to call the start. The men dug their paddles into the water and stroked with all their might. Stella bit her lip, remaining silent as everyone cheered around her.

Like many of the other events, this one involved rounding a buoy in the water and paddling back to the start. At the buoy, near as she could tell, Daniel Ortiz held first place. Steel and Eric were neck and neck behind him.

"Eric will pull ahead next," Monica commented beside her. "Daniel will keep up with him, and at the very last minute, Steel will surge ahead of them both. They each have their way of doing things and refuse to change."

"That's men for you," Stella said, but she couldn't stop watching Steel. After Eric's outburst she couldn't even pretend she didn't prefer him.

"There goes Eric," Monica pointed out.

She was right. The older man was paddling for all he was worth, and soon he left Steel behind, passed Daniel and took the lead. The crowd on shore cheered harder. As a Chance Creek deputy, Eric was popular with most of the crowd. Of course, so was Daniel with the Silver Falls people.

"And you're right; Daniel's keeping up," Stella said. The younger man had redoubled his efforts, and now both were paddling like mad.

"Steel keeps to a steady pace," Monica said.

But his strong, even strokes were cutting the distance between him and the others, and as they headed into the home stretch, he kept moving like a machine while the other two faltered. He came abreast of them, and for one awful moment Stella was sure Eric was about to reach over with his paddle and knock Steel off his board. Monica must have thought so, too, because she breathed, "Don't do it!"

His momentary desire for revenge had lost Eric his rhythm, and he fell behind the other two. Daniel, catching sight of his nemesis, bent to paddle even harder, but stroke by stroke, breath by breath, Steel inched forward and left him behind.

The crowd on the beach was going wild. Stella

wasn't even sure who they were cheering for—maybe they were simply cheering for the effort all three men were expending. When Steel reached the finish line, she whooped, unable to contain herself.

"You did it!" she yelled. "He did it!" she said to Monica.

"Yes, he did. And not everyone is all that happy about it."

Eric splashed out of the water red-faced with rage, and Stella knew she had to do something to prevent what was about to happen.

"Here." Monica shoved something into her hand, and Stella recognized it as the portable microphone they'd bought for the event. "It's on—say something," she hissed at Stella.

"Congratulations one and all!" Stella's mouth was much too close to the microphone, and feedback screeched an unholy sound. All around her, the crowd reeled and slapped hands over their ears. Even Eric seemed knocked off-guard by the sudden noise. Stella held the microphone a little farther away and tried again. "Our water Olympics is coming rapidly to an end, but we've still got a few events left in the teen category. I hope everyone will give those contestants the round of applause they deserve."

People clapped politely. There were a few cheers. Eric was still eyeing Steel angrily, but Steel was helping the teen volunteer running the next event to clear the paddleboards away and get set up. As she watched, Stella could tell Eric was running out of steam. His adversary was ignoring him, and he couldn't confront Steel without making an ass out of himself.

"When those events are over," Stella continued, her amplified voice cutting through the noise of the crowd, "I hope you'll make your way to the food tents and enjoy your dinner at our indoor or outdoor seating areas." She went into a spiel about making sure to recycle when people were done with their meals and introduced the band, who at her direction broke into the first song of the evening, an upbeat instrumental piece that left the crowd chatting happily, half milling about the shoreline to watch the last few contests and half making their way to the food tents to get their meal.

Stella saw Eric's shoulders fall. He shook his head and stalked away toward the lodge. She hoped a good meal would ease his temper. She was glad the award ceremony was slated for after the meal. By then everyone should be in a mellow mood.

HE SHOULDN'T BE so damn happy about making another man miserable, Steel suspected, but showing up Eric Holden had been the most fun he'd had in a pig's age. Daniel Ortiz was steamed at him, but the deputy had acquitted himself well. He'd take a silver medal in the men's all-around. Eric wouldn't even get bronze.

He kept a low profile during the dinner hour, changing back into jeans and a T-shirt, wolfing down a burger and nursing a bottle of beer as the sun sank low over the western horizon. Some people danced to the music. Kids ran around and screeched in that after-dinner-games way that kids had done since time began, he suspected. By the time the awards were announced, a general feeling of goodwill pervaded the crowd. Steel took his place on the podium several times, including for all-around athlete, and bowed in recognition of the cheers he received, boosted by his family.

"I think Eric snuck off and left," Daniel said as they accepted the gold and silver medals placed around their necks by more of the teen volunteers.

"Good riddance," Steel said.

"He always was a prick," Daniel agreed. "Next year I'm taking you down, though."

"I don't doubt it." Would there be a next year? Maybe so, he thought, looking out at the happy crowd. If Runaway Lodge reopened, it would be good for the local economy. Maybe things would finally look up for Silver Falls.

"Ah, heck." Daniel turned his face up to the sky. A moment later Steel felt a drop of rain and understood what he meant. "We're going to get washed out!"

As the heavens opened up and a torrent of rain began to fall, shrieks of dismay punctuated the frenzy of motion as people leaped to their feet, began to gather their belongings and picked things up to carry inside.

The band was under cover, thank goodness, and Steel saw people letting down the sides of the awning under which they were playing to protect the instruments and equipment.

Steel headed for the nearest food vendor but quickly realized they had things under control. Anyone serving at festivals in this area had to have precautions for this kind of thing.

He began to gather the little clear globes that held the tea lights on each table. When he had an armful, he made his way to the lodge, where he bumped into Mary Turner.

"Have you seen Liz?" she asked him, stumbling among the crowd all trying to get inside at once.

"No."

"I can't find her anywhere!"

Normally, Steel wouldn't think much about a missing teenager at an event like this. She was probably with friends, or maybe she'd made a conquest of some boy. Teens didn't want to hang out with their parents at this type of thing.

But teenage girls had been ending up dead recently, and Liz seemed drawn to trouble.

"I'll look for her," he told Mary and pushed his way inside. There was a shortcut to finding Liz. He found Stella and her microphone.

"Can I borrow this? Liz is missing," he explained succinctly.

"Of course." She handed it to him, immediately beginning to scan the crowd as if she hoped Liz would turn up nearby.

He took the mic, turned it on and said, "Hey, folks, we're looking for a teenager, name of Liz…" He looked to Stella and covered the mic. "What's her last name?"

"Stanton."

"Liz Stanton. Fifteen, blonde, new to town. Liz, you

out there? If you are, please come to the stage." She'd probably be embarrassed, but he hoped she'd turn up just to get him to stop talking about her on the microphone.

A minute passed, then several more. Steel moved to the door and tried again, noticing the crowd was taking the search seriously. A few people slipped by him into the rain, and he heard voices calling Liz's name.

Mary was back at his side. "We've checked the treehouses and the greenhouses, too. She's nowhere."

"Sheriff Johnson, Sheriff Bolton, you want to join me up here?" Steel said into the microphone.

All around them people hushed and then burst into a new round of conversation. Steel heard the words "Silver Falls killer" more than once. People were quick enough to laugh at campfire stories until the lights went out—then they were all too willing to believe. Maybe Steel should have felt some vindication, but the last thing they needed right now was panic.

When he took in Stella's white face, he went to herd her and her family into a corner. He turned off the mic and pocketed it in case he needed it again. When Cab and Bolton met him, Bolton raised his eyebrows questioningly. Steel knew his current behavior was sorely out of sync with his carefully crafted undercover persona, but he also knew he wasn't going to let another girl die.

"Liz has been hanging around with Lara Whidby recently," he explained to Bolton. His boss immediately understood. "Lara was a friend of Sue Hill's," he added to make the connection clear to everyone else.

"I'll round up my deputies. You round up yours," Bolton said to Cab. "My people will spread out and look for her up the road. Cab, you want to stay here and organize a search on foot?"

"Glad to help," Cab said. He got right to work, walking through the crowd, gathering men and women and organizing them into small groups.

As the sheriffs and deputies headed outside, Steel went with them, Stella following close behind.

"I'm coming with you," she said. Steel didn't bother to argue with her.

"I'm coming, too!" Jed appeared at Stella's elbow, Aunt Virginia beside him, holding open the large black umbrella she always carried with her above their heads. Steel realized he hadn't seen them in quite some time. Had they been hashing out their differences?

"I don't think that's a good idea," Steel told him.

"You'll get yourself killed, you old lunatic," Virginia added, sticking close to his side.

"I'm going and that's that," Jed demanded.

"Then I'm going, too."

There was no time for a fuss. "We'd better check out the pit. She might have hitched a ride there." Steel grabbed Stella's hand, pulling her along with him, leaving Jed and Virginia to follow as best they could. They did a better job than he expected keeping up, bickering all the way, although that died down as they struggled to match Steel's pace. They had crossed the little bridge and were making their way uphill toward

Steel's truck when Steel caught sight of Lily Barnes hurrying away ahead of them.

"Hey," he called out.

She stumbled, turned back, spotted them and took off running. Steel caught a flash of long hair and anguished eyes before she veered off the crowded road into the woods. Steel followed.

Footsteps behind him warned him someone else had joined the chase.

Stella.

He had no time to think about that, though. Lily had a head start, and she was darting among the trees like a frightened deer.

This time when he caught up, he was going to get some answers.

AFTER STANDING AROUND all day, running felt great. Stella had been jogging every morning for weeks and practicing for the agility test daily on the obstacle course Steel had built for her, too. For once she felt like she could hold her own.

Lily was racing ahead like the hounds of hell were after her. Steel was gaining on her, though, and Stella was gaining on him.

As she dodged and darted through the trees, her lungs beginning to burn, her legs pumping beneath her, Stella figured out a more direct shortcut to cut Lily off, veered off the path the other two had taken and set out cross-country over rougher terrain.

She jumped a fallen log, raced around a mass of

blackberry bushes, scrambled up and over a rocky spit of land and jumped out in front of Lily.

Lily shrieked, then shrieked again as Steel caught up with her and grabbed her arm.

"Get off me! It's not my fault! Don't touch me!"

And Lily dissolved into tears.

Chapter Nine

"WHERE IS LIZ?" Steel demanded, keeping a firm grip on Lily's arm. He didn't want to scare the girl, and it pained him to keep questioning her when she was crying, but they needed answers.

"I don't know," Lily said through her sobs.

"Where is she?"

Stella intervened, stepping between the two of them. "My stepsister is missing," she told Lily, who was still squirming in Steel's grip. "We know she was seen with Lara several times. And we know Lara is your friend. What's going on?"

"I can't tell you," Lily said.

Stella stiffened. Raised her eyebrows at Steel. Lily did know.

Steel took over. "You can't tell us, but you know who she's with?"

Lily didn't want to meet his gaze.

They were wasting time, and Steel was ready to haul Lily to his truck and make her direct them to the killer, but as frustrated as he was, he could see that Lily was wavering, and he held himself in check.

"He's going to hurt Liz," Stella said calmly. "She's

only fifteen. Is that what you want?"

"No," Lily wailed. "But if I tell—"

"If you tell, what?" she asked when Lily broke off. "He'll come after you?"

"What do you care? You won't believe me anyway, even if I do tell the truth!"

Stella pulled back in surprise.

Steel's phone buzzed, and he automatically reached for it with his free hand.

"Lily, I swear I'll believe you. Just tell me," Stella urged.

"You won't," Lily said. "I know you won't."

"Steel here," he said into the phone.

"Steel? It's Marion."

"Of course I will—Lily, just give us a chance," Stella pleaded.

Lily turned her gaze to Steel.

Stella followed it in disbelief. "Steel?" she said. Her voice sliced through his distraction, and Steel felt a sick twist in his gut as he took in what was happening. Was Lily accusing him of the killings?

Would Stella believe her?

"You'd better get home right now!" Marion snapped in his ear. "Some guy in a red pickup drove up, broke into your trailer and lugged something in. Something heavy. What the hell are you involved in now?"

"Red pickup?" But he was still watching Lily's accusing gaze. He couldn't believe this. "How can I be the one who took Liz when I'm right here?" he snapped at the girl.

"Not you," Lily said in desperation.

And Steel realized he'd interpreted Lily's look all wrong. She wasn't accusing him; she was beseeching him.

"*She* won't believe me," Lily repeated, pointing at Stella.

"A Ford F-250," Marion said in his ear.

A red Ford? Did she mean...?

"She's *dating* him," Lily hissed.

"Dating?" Stella's head snapped toward Lily. "You mean...?"

Steel cut the call, pocketed the phone, lifted up Lily and tossed her over his shoulder.

"Steel!" Stella pounded after him as he ran off toward his truck. "What are you—"

"I know where Liz is!"

At the truck Steel set Lily down, yanked open the back door of the extended cab and pushed her in. He nearly groaned when he saw Jed and Virginia already buckled in their seats.

Stella climbed in the front passenger seat as fast as she could. He got behind the wheel.

"Where is she?" Stella said when she'd caught her breath. "We need to call the sheriff. Tell him what's happening."

"Liz is at my trailer," Steel said grimly. "And Eric Holden is setting me up—which means we're on our own."

STELLA'S MIND WAS still whirling from Lily's confession.

Eric had taken Liz? Had killed Sue—

She simply couldn't wrap her thoughts around it. Eric had a temper, but she couldn't imagine him luring girls like Sue to their deaths. He'd been a deputy for over twenty years—

Her thoughts tripped over each other. Over twenty years. Long enough to be around when the first women had gone missing.

Steel met her glance, turned to the road. "Don't overthink it."

"How could it be him?" She kept her voice low, but she knew Lily was listening to every word from the back seat. So were Jed and Virginia.

"Focus on right now. We've got to get to Liz before it's too late."

Luckily they didn't have far to go. Stella filled in Jed and Virginia. Mountain Rise trailer park was only a few miles away from Runaway Lodge, and they were getting close to it when sirens blared behind them. Stella turned in her seat.

"Silver Falls sheriff's department." She couldn't make out who was in the cruiser, though. "Are they following us?"

His radio kicked on. "Steel? You listening to me?" It was Sheriff Bolton.

"Is that...? Why do you have a sheriff's department radio?" Stella asked, noting it for the first time.

"I'm here," Steel said to Bolton. "Because I work for the Silver Falls sheriff's department," he told Stella.

Stella's eyes went wide. "You work for—"

"Got a report here. Hate to think it's true. You been playing us this whole time?"

"Is that report from Eric Holden?" Steel demanded. He didn't have time to fuck around. "Is he saying I've got Liz Stanton at my trailer?"

There was a silence. "Something like that."

"It's Holden who's been playing you. He's the one who took her there."

Another pause. "Holden's worked for the Chance Creek department for over twenty years, Steel."

"Yeah, think about that. Twenty years. Long enough to kill the last round of girls, too, back when my father and William Turner were trying to track down the killer."

"You were around, too. Helping your dad."

"What're you saying? You think Dad and William Turner were in on it? You think the three of us went on a killing spree? Or are you just blaming me? There were killings before the Chance Creek ones. Check out Livingston's records. Eric was practicing out there before he brought his game to Chance Creek. I was a teenager then. I was in school—playing football. Working my dad's ranch. Don't tell me I had the time or resources to pull that off."

Bolton was quiet. "I need you to pull over."

"Can't do that, Sheriff. I've got to get to Liz before it's too late."

"I've got backup coming. You pull over and let us sort this out. You let us take you in, I'll send that backup straight on to your place. Either way, I need you out of this. Pull over—that's an order."

"We can't let them take you in," Stella protested. "We've got to get to Liz."

Steel thought it through. "You've got to get to Liz. I'm going to pull over and get out of the truck. When the coast is clear, you keep going."

"Why won't Bolton believe you?"

"Focus," Steel told her. "Jed, you armed?"

"Sure am."

"What if they hurt you?" Stella asked.

"I'll be fine," Steel said. "Can you do your part? Stella, no heroics, you hear me? You drive. Jed, Virginia—one of you call Cab Johnson and tell him to get the hell out to Mountain Rise trailer park, just in case Bolton doesn't follow through. Cab was at Runaway Lodge—he can catch up fast. Fill him in on everything. Once you're there, be careful. If Eric sees you, he'll know he's lost control of things. He'll be even more dangerous."

"Got it."

"Okay, here we go." Steel swerved over to the shoulder of the road, slammed on the brakes, unclasped his seat belt and was out the door faster than Stella could cry out. She watched him race off through the rain. Watched the sheriff's cruiser skid to a stop behind them, the front doors swing open and two deputies race after him.

"Go," Jed said. "Hurry up, drive!"

"I'm going!" Stella slithered into the driver's seat, pulled the door closed, adjusted the seat and shifted into

Drive again. She put the pedal to the floor, peeled out and kept going, turning up the windshield wipers another notch. "I hope he's okay."

"I've got Cab Johnson on the line," Virginia said. She launched into an explanation, ending with, "Get your ass out here and save that little girl before I take you out myself!"

"Is he coming?" Stella fought to keep control over the truck as she swung around a tight curve in the road.

"He'd better be."

A few moments later, Stella spotted the sign for the trailer park and slowed down, putting on her turn signal. "I don't know which one is his."

"Take it slowly. Keep your eyes open. The killer might spot us before we find him," Jed said, but it was an elderly lady in a raincoat who leaped out from behind the wooden fence surrounding the park and flagged them down before Stella had even made the turn into the driveway.

"Steel! Hey—you're not Steel," the woman said, backing away when she caught sight of Stella and Jed.

"No, but we're his friends," Stella said, "and he thinks there's trouble at his trailer. Do you know which one it is?"

"Where is he?" the woman demanded.

"The Silver Falls sheriff's department has him," Stella said. "Someone called in a complaint about him."

"Silver Falls, but—" The woman straightened. "Never mind. That one is his." She pointed at a nonde-script single wide with white vinyl siding about three-quarters of the way down the row. "See that truck? Pulled up about twenty minutes ago. Guy driving it lugged something into Steel's place. Never saw him or that car before, and I knew something was up."

That was Eric's truck, a dull red in the low light, and any small hope Stella had been holding onto that maybe Lily was wrong disappeared. Eric—the man she'd been dating—was killing teenage girls.

"You're the one who called Steel?" she asked faintly.

"That's right. I'm his neighbor. He asked for my help a few weeks ago."

Stella thought fast. "Eric might recognize Steel's truck if we pull in there."

"Eric? Eric Holden? He owns that flashy thing?" The woman gestured to Eric's vehicle.

"You know Eric Holden?"

"I know everyone. He used to drive a GMC." The woman muttered about keeping up with everyone's purchases. "Park out here on the street," she went on. "I'm Marion. I'll help you sneak up on Steel's trailer." She must have noticed Stella's hesitation. "Done it a hundred times myself. I keep tabs on what happens around my home." She lifted her chin proudly, and Stella figured she knew exactly the kind of woman Marion was. The kind who drove you to distraction until you needed their brand of sneakiness.

It took a lot of arguing to convince Virginia and Lily to stay in the truck, but she finally did, telling Virginia to keep an eye out for Cab Johnson. She, Jed and Marion snuck up on Steel's trailer through a circuitous route through the dripping wet woods that surrounded the park as dusk thickened around them. Stella was finding it hard not to race up to the trailer, burst through the door and see what was happening inside, but she knew she had to be patient or probably wind up dead herself. Instead they came up behind the trailer in the gathering gloom. Soon night would really set in, and everything would get more difficult.

"You can get a good look through the back window into Steel's bedroom. He doesn't have shades," Marion whispered. She indicated a tree stump several feet away from the trailer. Jed loaned Stella a steadying hand as she climbed up and peered inside, raindrops slipping under her collar. There was a bed, the sheets in a tangle on top. A bedside table with a lightbulb but no shade. Behind them, in the corner, was a bureau of some sort.

Then Stella caught sight of something bright against the bureau's dark wood. A shock of blonde hair.

Liz.

Movement in the doorway of the room sent Stella jumping down from the stump. She grabbed Jed's and Marion's wrists and pulled them up tight against the trailer under the window, praying that if Eric happened to look outside, he wouldn't think to look straight down.

They could hear his muffled footsteps through the metal frame of the trailer. He seemed to mill around in the bedroom for a moment before his steps moved toward the front of the house again. Stella let out the breath she was holding. That was close.

"Now what?" Marion whispered.

Stella had no idea.

WHEN STEEL HEARD more sirens approaching, hope spiked through his chest. Chance Creek and Silver Falls had purchased their cruisers at two separate times, with the result that the sirens on their vehicles produced two separate and easily distinguishable series of noises.

This was a Chance Creek cruiser heading toward him.

When he'd taken off through the woods earlier, he'd heard Daniel Ortiz and Ned Haverstock shouting behind him. He'd given them the slip and hadn't seen any sign of them since, so he burst out of the woods at a long, straight stretch of the road that would give the driver a chance to see him—and stop the car before whizzing right by. He stood in the center of the road and waved his hands.

He couldn't blame his fellow deputies for being taken in by Eric Holden's charges. Everyone in these parts knew Eric was a trustworthy man. Who would imagine someone with over twenty years with Chance Creek county could pull something like this? Far easier to assume Steel Cooper was the criminal.

The sheriff's cruiser screeched to a halt, water sheeting through the air as it skidded through a puddle. Cab Johnson stuck his head out the window.

"What the hell are you playing at, Cooper?"

Steel didn't answer. Instead, he raced to the car, jumped into the back seat and said, "Drive!"

Cab drove, but he sent an unamused glance Steel's way in the rearview mirror. "If I hadn't just taken a call from your aunt, I would have run right over you."

"You're going to my trailer, right? Might as well give me a lift."

"I'm going to your trailer because Virginia thinks a kidnapped girl has been taken there."

"By Eric Holden," Steel added. "I'm not lying," he said when Cab's brows shot up. "Marion Wheeler saw him carrying something heavy into my trailer not half an hour after Liz went missing from Runaway Lodge, where as you know Eric has been all day—getting his ass whupped in the water Olympics by yours truly."

Cab kept driving, but he heaved a long-suffering sigh and shook his head. "If this is some kind of inter-county grudge match—"

"It's not. Think about it. A number of women died thirteen years ago. William Turner and my dad tried to catch the killer, but they failed—"

"William and your dad?"

"Then the deaths started up again. That's why I came back."

"You came back to fight crime."

Steel understood Cab's scorn, but it still stung. "I'm a deputy, Cab. Working undercover. Been trying to solve these crimes for three years. Sheriff Bolton will confirm that. But right now Liz is in my trailer with a man determined to kill her and pin it on me."

Cab pressed the accelerator, and Steel breathed a little easier, knowing at last they were getting somewhere.

"There's something else you should know," he admitted to Cab as the cruiser whipped down the road.

"What's that?"

"Stella, Jed and Virginia are heading to the trailer park, too. They've got Lily Barnes with them." He checked the time. "Probably already there."

"Bloody hell, Cooper. Got any other surprises up your sleeve?"

He had a few, but he figured the rest of them could wait.

"HOW CAN I get in there?" Stella asked Marion in a whisper as the rain tapered off around them. She pushed her soaking hair from her face.

"Bathroom window? It's always open. Doesn't have a screen, so Steel always keeps the door shut. Probably helps keep the mosquitos from getting into the rest of the place."

Stella wondered if Steel had any idea how closely his movements were monitored by his neighbor, but her information was sure handy.

"You can't go in there. You'll get yourself shot," Jed hissed.

"Got any better ideas?" Stella said. "We don't know what he plans to do with her."

As if on cue, the footsteps got closer again. A girl's voice—Liz's voice—carried through a partially open bedroom window. "I'm not taking that. I've heard what happens to girls like me. They end up dead."

"Little girls should talk less and listen more. Get those in you so I can get gone. Steel will be here any minute. So will the sheriff's department." It hurt Stella to hear Eric's voice. She'd let that man take her to dinner. Touch her—even kiss her.

"Get off me!" Liz shouted.

A slap rang out, and Liz began to cry. Stella moved, but once again Jed held her back.

"He'll get you, sure as shootin', if you aren't smart about it," he said.

"Take them," Eric snarled above them.

"No!"

Some kind of skirmish ensued, with Liz giving little cries. Thumps against the walls and floor were testament to how hard she was fighting.

"What if he's giving her pills? What if he's killing her right now?" she whispered. "I've got to get in there."

"Goddamn it!" Eric yelled. "You bit me!"

More sounds of struggle. Jed's expression grew grim. "It should be me going in there," he said.

"You won't get through that window," Marion hissed. "She might; it's pretty small."

"I'll get in," Stella said.

"You better take this." Jed drew his pistol from a shoulder holster Stella had no idea he'd been wearing under his cotton button-down shirt today. She probably should have guessed even before Steel had asked him about it. Jed being a retired deputy and all, he liked to be prepared.

"You remember how to fire one of these things?"

"Remember?" Stella practiced her shooting at the range at least once a week. She took the weapon and tucked it into the waistband of her jeans at the small of her back.

Marion led them carefully around the side of the trailer and pointed to a small open window.

"How am I supposed to get up there?"

They looked around. Jed pointed to a glint of light on metal, which turned out to be a short stepladder leaning up against the neighboring trailer's joey shed. It took far too long for Stella to tiptoe over there, grab the ladder and come back, all the while afraid Eric would spy her through a window.

True dark had fallen, however, and from the sounds of things Eric was still trying to force something down Liz's throat. There was a muffled grunt, and then Eric began to swear while footsteps ran toward the front of the trailer.

"Get back here," Eric called out, his heavier steps echoing Liz's path through the trailer. There was a shriek, a series of thuds and the unmistakeable thwack of a fist connecting with flesh.

Stella set up the ladder, climbed swiftly up it, careful not to slip on the wet surfaces, lifted a leg up and over the sill and slowly—slowly—edged inside. When her feet hit the ground, she cracked open the bathroom door just a bit, peered outside and bit back a curse.

In a flash she was out in the hall, the bathroom door closed again. She tiptoed down it and peeked into the kitchen, where Eric, swearing up a storm, was on his

THE COWBOY'S FORBIDDEN BRIDE

hands and knees picking up pills that had spilled all over the floor. Beyond him, in the living room, Liz lolled on the couch, hands duct taped together, the skin around her left eye bruised.

Had he succeeded in drugging her, or had he knocked her out? Stella wasn't sure, and in the second she spent trying to discern from this distance whether Liz was still breathing, Eric turned. Spotted her. Lurched to his feet.

His fist connected with her cheekbone before she could react, and hot pain exploded in her temple as her head cracked against the hall wall. A moment later, coming to, she saw Eric, Liz in his arms, leaving by the front door.

"Stop! Eric!" Stella scrambled to her feet, swayed as the room spun about her and reached for the pistol. When she caught her balance, she raced to the door, saw Eric's taillights and ran after his truck. "Call the sheriff. Call Steel! Tell them I need help!" she hollered over her shoulder at Marion. "Come on, Jed!"

They had to put a stop to this—now.

Chapter Ten

S TEEL WISHED LIKE hell he had his own truck. Riding shotgun with Cab Johnson made him feel helpless. The thought of Eric holding Stella's stepsister hostage had him sick with rage. The girl was barely fifteen. Eric was over forty.

Which made him twenty-seven when the first round of murders happened in Chance Creek, Steel thought. What had he been like back then? A young, cocky deputy drunk on his own power, dispensing his sick justice on women he'd deemed to have crossed the line? Had he gone after women in Livingston when he was even younger—fresh on the force?

What had made him change from targeting women on the outskirts of society to choosing victims from the heart of Chance Creek itself? Had he wanted a bigger challenge? And why hadn't his victims aged along with him? Did the man think he could somehow stay young if he slept with—and killed—teenage girls?

Steel thought about the way he'd goaded Eric today, how he'd used his own youth, strength and energy to upstage the older man. If Liz was hurt, it would be partly his fault; he'd seen Eric's temper before. Had known the man was close to his breaking point, at least when it came to Stella. Why had he pushed him so hard?

It had galled him to think there was even a chance Stella might end up with another man, he admitted to himself now. Despite his assurances to himself that he was completely committed to solving these crimes no matter what sacrifice it required, the truth was his own happiness had outweighed his promise to finish what Dale had started.

"You okay, Cooper?" Cab asked, shooting a quick glance his way.

"I'm fine."

"Working undercover, huh? For how long?"

Steel wasn't quite sure how to answer that, so he told the truth. "Since I was eighteen."

"Hell." Cab's quiet exclamation held more understanding than a whole speech could have.

"Yeah. Hell." Steel leaned back, wondering at the sudden pain that filled his chest. He'd been here before—in danger, chasing someone determined to hurt him or someone else. Why did this feel so damn raw?

"Wish I'd known."

"Too many people knew already."

Cab just nodded. "Don't even want to touch the fact we're chasing down Eric."

"Did you have any idea?"

Cab simply shot him another look, and Steel knew what he wanted to say: Did Steel think for a minute Cab would work with a man he suspected of killing teenage girls?

"He hid it well," Steel said. "Had a lot of resources at his fingertips to help."

"I'm running through everything I ever said to the man," Cab admitted. "Everything he ever said to me. I'm going to hate myself when this is done."

Steel pulled out his phone when it buzzed in his pocket. It was Jed. "Jed? What's going on?"

"Route 90. Heading east. Red Ford F-250. Eric's still got Liz."

"Wait—you're chasing them? What happened?" He turned to Cab. "Route 90. Now!"

"Stella tried to get her. Eric saw her coming. Now we're in pursuit."

"Who's driving? Stella?"

"Virginia. Stella's got the pistol."

Shit. "They're going after Eric," Steel told Cab. He related what Jed had said.

Cab pressed his foot on the gas lever. "Call it in." He jutted his chin toward the radio.

Steel did so, balancing the radio and phone. "Stay back, you hear me?" he told Jed. "Wait for us."

"You ever try telling Virginia what to do?" Jed asked waspishly.

Steel knew what he meant. Still.

"Go faster," he told Cab.

"BE CAREFUL, VIRGINIA!" Stella cried as the old woman took a curve in the roadway too fast and all of them slammed to the right.

"He's getting away—shoot him!" Virginia yelled back. "I should be the one with the gun."

"*I* should be the one with the gun," Jed contradicted from the back seat. "I'm the damn deputy here."

"You haven't been a deputy in thirty years." Virginia took another sharp turn, getting a little closer to the vehicle ahead of them.

"We have to get closer," Stella told them. "Where's Cab?" She clung to the door handle, trying not to let Virginia's driving kill her before she could save her stepsister. Her heart was beating hard, but her hands were steady, and she felt as clear in her thinking as if she'd drunk a shot of espresso. She was going to save Liz. There was no other possible outcome to this scenario.

"It's my fault," Lily muttered from beside Jed, hugging her knees to her chest. "It's my fault Sue died. It's my fault Liz is going to die."

Part of Stella wanted to comfort Lily, tell her no one was responsible for Eric's deranged actions but Eric. But there'd be time for that later. Right now they needed information. "Why?"

"I'm the one who introduced Sue and Lara to him," Lily explained. "I was friends with Rena. She invited me to party with her and Eric once. Told me to bring some friends along. I did."

Stella remembered Eric telling her he had "options" and shuddered.

"When Rena died, he started texting me. Telling me he was so sad—I tried to comfort him. I—I wanted him to like me. But he chose Sue instead. When she died, too…" Her voice broke into a sob.

"I'm going to flank them," Virginia announced, pulling Stella's attention away from Lily. The truck lurched forward.

Stella took in the curving road ahead. "You can't. If someone comes around one of those curves, we're dead."

"I've been driving twice as long as you've been alive," Virginia said. "I know exactly what I'm doing."

She swerved into the other lane. Jed swore when his head hit the window beside him. Stella, clinging to the trouble bar, realized things were about to come to a head. If she didn't do something, someone would definitely die.

"Just get close. Don't go beside them—leave room to drop back if you need to," she ordered Virginia. To her surprise, the woman did as she was told, holding the car in the far lane just behind Eric's truck, drafting him as if they were birds in a flock of geese.

"Go for his tire," Jed instructed Stella. She nodded. Exactly what she meant to do.

She rolled down the window all the way, braced her wrist on the sill, then decided that wasn't her best call. The truck was lurching and bumping on the country road. She lifted her wrist, braced it with her left hand, remembered to breathe.

Took aim.

Her first shot missed. Eric swerved but got his Ford back under control and lurched ahead with a burst of speed.

"Catch up to him!" Jed ordered Virginia.

"I'm catching up," she snapped back.

Stella ignored both of them and steadied her wrist again. She needed to make this shot. She couldn't see Liz in the vehicle. Knew she must be wild with fear.

She took aim again. Heard the echo of her father, who'd taught her to shoot so many years ago. *Remember to breathe. Take your time. When you're ready, make the shot.*

She pulled the trigger.

Eric's vehicle swerved again, and its back tires skidded off the road, one of them flapping badly. The difference in terrain between road and shoulder caught the truck and whipped it around. The vehicle spun straight into the ditch, where it came to rest at an angle, back wheels in the ground, nose to the sky.

Virginia slammed her feet on the brakes, swerved around them until the truck screeched to a halt, executed a quick three-point turn and parked on the opposite side of the road, facing Eric's Ford.

"Everyone get down and stay down," Stella said as she quickly climbed out, holding the pistol ahead of her, ready to shoot again. She heard another door open and looked back to see Jed climbing out, too.

"Give me that pistol."

"Get back in the truck!"

When shots rang out, Jed gave a cry of pain. Stella ducked and scooted behind the shelter of the passenger side door.

Virginia swung open the driver's side door and

launched herself out.

"Virginia—wait!" Stella cried, but the woman had already ducked around the open back door to get to Jed. Stella swore, dove into the truck and crawled across the front seats, popping out the other side just like Virginia had done moments before. "Stay down—under the seat!" she shouted to Lily, who was still inside the truck.

More shots rang out, ricocheting off the macadam ahead of her. Stella ducked around the open back door, racing to join the older woman in manhandling Jed, a splash of red spreading near his shoulder, in the back seat of the truck. Lily grabbed his arms and pulled him in, staying down behind the seatbacks as best she could. Virginia climbed in after him.

"Lay him on the seat. Put pressure on the wound," she ordered Virginia, who was already doing both those things. "Lily, get down." The girl ducked low in the foot well.

Virginia tossed Stella Jed's phone. "Call for help."

Stella punched in the first number that came to mind.

"Jed?" Steel's voice filled her ear. "What's happening?"

"It's Stella. I need you. Steel, I need you—"

"Already here."

A sheriff's cruiser screeched around the bend and squealed to a stop before it reached Eric's truck.

"Eric's got a weapon."

Steel's answer was lost in a volley of shots from Eric's truck. He was shooting at the sheriff's cruiser now.

"Call an ambulance!" Virginia yelled.

Of course. What was she doing? Stella broke the call with Steel and dialled 9-1-1. She explained the situation as quickly and succinctly as she could to the Silver Falls dispatcher.

"Backup is on its way," the woman assured her calmly. "So is an ambulance. Sit tight."

That was easy for her to say, Stella thought bitterly as she hunkered down in her truck. Liz was still with Eric. Maybe she was dead—killed by the man Stella had been dating. He wouldn't even have known Liz except for her, Stella realized, her throat filling with bile.

How could she have missed all the signs? Why wasn't she out there fighting for Liz?

How would she look her mother in the eye if she had to report that her stepdaughter—the daughter she'd chosen—was dead?

Stella pocketed the phone. Slid out of the truck again and crouched behind the open door. She could see Eric was focused on Cab and Steel.

"What are you doing?" Virginia half yelped, half hissed at her. "Stella, no!"

But Stella knew it was the only way. She began to walk toward Eric, pistol aimed at his head.

"WHAT THE FUCK?" Cab exclaimed.

Steel went cold when Stella stepped out of her truck and began to calmly pace toward Eric. She was a dim shape in the low light, staying clear of the headlights from her vehicle and theirs, but he could make out the way she held the pistol steady, her gaze fixed firmly on her target. She might just be able to take him out.

Who knew where Liz was in Eric's truck, though? A stray round could have unintended consequences, the reason why neither he nor Cab could take the shot.

"Go back," Cab intoned, although there was no way Stella could hear him. "Come on, go back."

Steel could not sit still and watch the woman he loved die. He swung open his own door.

"Get the hell back in here," Cab barked at him, but Steel shook his head. There was no other way. He had to keep Eric's attention on him.

"I beat you at every single event today, Holden," he shouted, "and I'm going to beat you again now."

He ducked behind the door as a volley of shots rang his way. When Steel looked again, Stella was even closer, becoming easier to see in the headlights from the sheriff's cruiser.

"Missed me," Steel yelled. "Always were a lousy shot!"

"Jesus," Cab spat. "Don't get me killed." He opened his door, slid out and used it to shield himself like Steel was on the other side of the cruiser.

"It's working, isn't it?" Steel hissed back. He popped up and ducked again almost immediately. Eric had honed in on him and was watching for his next opportunity. It was going to be tough to surprise him again.

So when Cab stood and fired a purposefully wild shot into the woods, wide of Eric's truck—and Stella— Steel was grateful to him. Now Eric swung his way.

And Stella got closer still.

Steel had to admire her determination and the calm, silent way she was advancing toward Eric. She was getting within an acceptable range to shoot him through the passenger window, but Steel had the feeling Stella would err on the side of caution out of a fear of hurting her sister—and that could cost her.

Instead of standing again, Steel knelt and took careful aim. He needed Eric out of the truck, but how could he manage it?

If he could block the man's windshield, it would help. If Eric couldn't see, he'd be afraid they were creeping up on him. But how could he manage it?

Steel looked up. The road here wound through a forest, and conifer branches arched over it. Could he...?

Steel dove into the cruiser, grabbed a shotgun from the rack above the seat.

"Cartridges?" he snapped.

Cab tossed him a couple, and Steel racked them up. He lifted the shotgun's barrel and fired. The tree branch he'd aimed for whipped back and forth as if a gale force wind had blown through, but it didn't fall—

Not immediately, anyway. After a momentary pause, a drawn out cra-a-a-ck sounded, and the large branch swung down almost gracefully before crashing directly on Eric's windshield. It hit with enough force Steel heard the safety glass crumpling. Just as he'd planned, almost simultaneously Eric pushed open his door and leaped out, shouting and swearing.

What Steel hadn't anticipated was that Stella would

use the distraction to get even closer to the truck. She must have made some sound.

Eric, who'd been facing Steel and Cab, whipped around, came face to face with her over the hood of his truck, lifted his pistol—

And Steel shot him in the back.

NOW STELLA KNEW what people meant by time standing still. As Eric burst from his truck, she sucked in a breath and Eric whipped around at the sound. She saw him blink in surprise as he took in her presence. Saw understanding cross his face as he took in the pistol in her hand. Heard Steel yelling. Saw Eric raise his weapon and point it at her heart.

And in that split second before she could pull the trigger, while she already knew she'd be too late to fire before Eric did, Eric's body jolted forward suddenly, his eyes wide. His mouth dropped open in an O of surprise. Then he fell—

Time sped up again. Blood spattered the hood of the truck. Stella fell back, a cry of surprise dying in her throat as Eric's lifeless body crashed to the ground out of sight.

Steel reached her, darting around the vehicle, just as the world went funny and the sky tilted.

"You all right?"

Yes. She was. She had to be. Stella blinked back the faintness, caught her breath, straightened. "Liz!" she cried. Steel half supported, half dragged her where she wanted to go. They opened the extended cab's back door together, and Stella cried out again in joy to see Liz's eyes open, body wriggling against the duct tape that pinioned her.

Steel made quick work of freeing the girl, and Liz scrambled to launch herself into Stella's embrace. Her words and tears made understanding her difficult, but Stella didn't care. She had forever to listen. Liz was safe. Eric was dead.

It was all over.

Rain began to fall as sirens blared and cruisers and ambulances pulled up, disgorging deputies and EMTs. Stella rocked Liz in her arms, crooning a litany of assurances to her. Steel stood watch, helped them into an ambulance when it was time and rode with her and Liz, while Virginia went with Jed and Lily in a second one.

Stella, Liz still in her arms, watched raindrops slide down the windows, shivering in spite of the warm weather and the blanket an EMT had put around her shoulders.

"Shock," Steel said, but he sounded far away. He gripped her hand, his solid body next to hers assuring her this wasn't a dream, no matter how strange she felt.

"Water's rising," she heard one of the EMTs saying. "We need to get across that bridge now before we're stuck on this side."

The other one whistled as the ambulance bumped over what she could only suspect was the bridge over Chance Creek. Out the small back windows she got a glimpse of the fast-moving water. That brought her out of her reverie. "I've never seen it that high," she said to

Steel.

He shook his head. "There's going to be flooding," he agreed.

The next few hours passed in a blur. Jed was whisked into surgery to remove the bullet that had entered his chest just below his left shoulder. Liz was taken to a private room, and the rest of them accompanied her. She was tucked into bed and checked over. Virginia brushed off all suggestions that she should be looked at, too.

"There's nothing wrong with me except too many years of this kind of crap," she snapped at an orderly. "I've been run off my feet today, and now I'm tired. I'm going to sit down right here. You're going to bring me a nice cup of tea and then get lost."

Mary and Maya arrived soon afterward, making it across the bridge to Chance Creek before the water got too high. They fussed around Virginia until she shooed them away, too, but she allowed herself to be ensconced in the best chair in the room with a blanket wrapped around her. Some minutes later, the orderly arrived with her tea and just as swiftly withdrew again.

Lily hunched in a straight-backed chair in the corner. Stella settled into one closer to Liz. She'd rest awhile and be right as rain. When Maya went out and returned with a strong chocolate mocha, Stella blessed her. Every sip of the sugary drink brought her back to herself.

"I've called Lily's parents," she said. "They're moving her grandparents out of their house—it's taking on water—so they'll get here as soon as they can. I told them she's doing fine."

"I should have done that."

"Drink up—I think you're still in shock," Maya said. "That was a brave thing you did saving Liz." Maya gave her a hug, careful not to spill her drink.

Once Virginia was set, Mary sat on the edge of the hospital bed with Liz, the girl tucked under her arm, stroking her hair and murmuring to her. Liz's tears slowed, although she gave a shuddering sob now and then.

Cab came in and questioned each of them in turn, taking copious notes about the sequence of events, especially when he talked to Lily, who cried through her explanation of how she, Lara and Sue had all been competing for Eric's attention—until Sue died and Lily realized Eric had to be at fault. "He would have killed me, too, if I'd said anything," she kept repeating. "He was a deputy. He said no one would believe me over him."

"Can't believe he was operating in plain sight," Cab said at one point. "I helped take down another serial killer a few years back. Totally different MO. I remember talking to Eric about it. The fucker was probably taking notes."

"You can't blame yourself," Stella said.

"Like hell I can't," Cab said, rubbed his chin and went on. "Sorry. I do blame myself, though. Feel like I'm getting something pretty wrong when one of my own men is the bad guy."

From the look of things, Steel was just as disgusted with himself. Stella wished she could make it easier on both of them, but she supposed they would all have demons to wrestle with after this.

"Listen to that rain," Mary said. "I guess the water Olympics would have broken up early one way or the other."

For the first time Stella remembered she'd run out of the event. It was a good thing Olivia had been in charge, after all. She asked for her phone and texted Monica, hoping all was well at the lodge.

It's fine. Everyone helped clean up, and we moved every-thing we could to the second floor. Then I sent everyone home and left with them. The lodge could flood, and I didn't want someone to have to come after me. I'm staying with Joan.

You think things will get that bad? Stella texted.

They're already that bad, Monica texted back. *I just heard Chance Creek is running over its banks. Runaway River probably will, too. Take care of yourself. Glad to hear all of you are safe, and I'll be keeping Jed in my thoughts.*

Thank you—stay safe yourself.

Joan's house is up high in Silver Falls. I don't think we'll take too hard of a hit here. It's you lowlanders I'm worried about.

When she was off the phone, Stella relayed the in-formation Monica had told her. Just as she finished, the door to their room opened, and a male nurse stuck his head in.

"We're requesting any able-bodied people to help fill sandbags. All the creeks and rivers are rising, and we're in a flood plain." He was gone as soon as he'd delivered his message, and they could hear him pacing down the hall, asking everyone he met to help.

Steel got to his feet immediately. So did Mary and Maya. Stella tried to follow them, but Mary pushed her gently down into her chair. "I need you to watch Liz—and Virginia. Can you do that? Keep them out of trouble."

Stella wanted to protest, but she still felt shaky, and her mother was right; someone needed to be here when Liz woke up. She thought Virginia might put up a stink, but she didn't, and when the rest of them left, she said, "I can do most things, but stacking sandbags isn't one of them anymore. Age isn't kind."

"I think you've kept it pretty well at bay," Stella said. "But it's good to know your limits."

"Your limits seem pretty broad," Virginia said. "You were brave back there. Stupid but brave."

"I did what seemed necessary."

"You did good," Virginia told her. She looked at Liz asleep on the bed. "Men and their need for mayhem. It never seems to stop."

"But there are good men, too," Stella said.

"Which is why we keep them around. Eternal optimists, that's what we are." She settled back in her blankets. "What the heck is keeping those doctors so long, anyway? They've been with Jed long enough they could have embalmed him by now."

Stella repressed a smile. "You like Jed, don't you? Under all that bluster."

"The hell you say." But that was the extent of Virginia's denials, and Stella figured she had the right of it.

Which gave her hope, in spite of it all.

Chapter Eleven

A S STEEL JOINED a group of volunteers to listen to one of the hospital administrators, he recognized Will Hostel at the front of the room as someone who'd graduated from Chance Creek high a few years ahead of him. He had a vague notion the man had left town for a number of years and come back only recently.

"I'll be coordinating the sand bagging," Will called out. "We've got permission to bring truckloads from the municipal supply that's used on our streets in the winter. I could use some volunteers to transport it. Anyone got a truck?"

Chuckles sounded as nearly every hand in the crowd shot up.

"Great," Will said. "Come on, let's get to work."

Given that the hospital stood in a location particularly vulnerable to flooding, Steel was happy to learn they had sandbags on hand. He and half a dozen others formed a caravan to pick up the sand from a few blocks away. Mary, Maya and the rest of the volunteers stayed to gather the bags from storage and ready themselves to fill them.

It was backbreaking work to fill the bags and haul

them into place to form a ring around the large building, especially with a hard rain still falling. They started at the side most likely to flood and moved outward, building up their wall of overlapping bags as they went. Hours passed, and the chatter that had punctuated their early efforts died down as muscles cramped and everyone grew tired. Thank goodness it was still warm, or soaked as they all were, they'd be freezing. Steel hoped things were okay at Thorn Hill—and the Flying W for that matter. There was nothing he could do about it from here except trust that Lance, Liam, Olivia, Tory and Noah would sort things out. At some point Steel noticed Stella, Liz and Lily were filling bags, as well.

"I thought you were watching Virginia," Steel said when he caught up with Stella.

Stella rolled her eyes. "You and I both know she doesn't need any watching, and Liz and Lily were getting restless. Lily's parents still haven't made it, but they said they'll be here soon. Anyway, when the doctors finally settled Jed in the room next door and said he could have visitors, Virginia was off like a flash to get to him. Claimed we would crowd him if we came, too, but I think she just wanted him to herself."

Steel raised his eyebrows. Whatever was happening between Virginia and Jed was stranger to him than the year's freak weather.

Stella smiled at his expression, and her quick grin gave him a second wind. Soon it would be sunrise—if they saw the sun today, which was doubtful in this weather.

"You think this will hold out the water?"

"I hope so." The storm showed no signs of slowing, which meant the water in nearby Chance Creek would keep rising. The lowest part of the parking lot surrounding the hospital was already flooding. Some of the volunteers had broken off to contact the owners of vehicles parked near there to move them. "Have you heard anything from home?"

"Liam says Pittance Creek is overflowing, too. Our house and yours will be okay; they're both built on high ground, but he, Noah, Lance, Olivia and Tory have been moving the cattle."

Steel made a face. "I should be there with them."

"He says it's under control. Says it sounds like the roads aren't passable between here and there, anyway. We're all stuck." She tucked an errant lock of hair out of her eyes. "Wonder what we'll find when the rain finally ends?"

"Whatever it is, we'll pull through," Steel said. "Our families always do, right?"

Stella nodded resolutely. "That's right."

When he opened his arms to her, she went to him willingly, pressing her sopping wet body to his. Steel let himself breathe her in. This was all he needed. Stella close by. His family safe. He could handle everything else.

"You must be exhausted," she said, squeezing Steel's shoulder. "Trade you?"

Steel started to protest, but he recalled Stella had been training for the body-drag portion of her deputy test. She was more than up to the task of carrying a few sandbags.

"Okay," he said, taking her place filling sandbags, promising himself he'd switch roles with her again soon.

As Stella took a filled bag from Liz and dragged it into place, Steel realized the girl had been packing scoops of sand into a bag without complaint. "You haven't gotten the best impression of Chance Creek, have you?" he asked.

He braced himself for the same couldn't-care-less act as before, but her eyes welled up, her tears joining the raindrops sliding down her skin. "Chance Creek isn't the problem. I am. I'm an idiot."

"No, you're not." Maybe she had made some poor choices, but she couldn't have known what she was getting herself into, and she didn't have enough life experience to recognize trouble.

At least, she hadn't when she first came to Chance Creek. She did now, Steel reflected, looking at the bruises on her head from when Eric had knocked her out. He suspected Liz was going to be a lot more careful in the future.

"I don't belong anywhere," Liz said bitterly. "I'm not like Justin. Working hard, making friends, doing the right thing—I don't know how it's always so *easy* for him. I guess he's like Mom was. And I'm like Dad."

Steel had heard about the twins' father, and he didn't think hanging out at the pit was quite as bad as embezzling money. On the other hand, he knew how one wrong step could lead to another. His own father's indiscretions had started out small enough. To brush aside Liz's concerns would be to do her a disservice.

"You've made mistakes," Steel told her gently. "Everyone does. Sometimes, when a person messes up too badly, their mistakes go on to define their life. But they don't have to. It's up to you whether you repeat them or learn from them."

She gave him a wry smile. "What am I supposed to learn from this? Don't live in a town with serial killers?"

"That's not the lesson, and you know it. You said it yourself: Chance Creek isn't the problem." He considered his next words carefully. "Whatever you're looking for, you'll find. That's the lesson here. You were looking for trouble, and you found it. But Chance Creek is a great place to live—if you want it to be. Give it a chance. Give yourself a chance."

"Are you sure the lesson isn't 'Stay away from the likes of me'?" Lily broke in. She was packing bags on the other side of Liz, but Steel hadn't known she was listening.

"You give yourself a chance, too," he said firmly. "It's never too late to decide to be someone different if who you are isn't working for you." Even Dale had redeemed himself in the end.

It occurred to Steel that he could tell everyone his father's real story now. He knew word of his own secret identity was already spreading.

"I spent years trying to find Eric, and so did my father before me," he told the girls. "No one can blame you for not figuring it out."

"But it was right in front of me!" Lily's voice broke. "Rena died… and I took his word for it that she was the one who messed up."

"Did Rena know Cecilia?"

Lily ducked her head. "Cecilia used to be her best friend. Then she kind of disappeared. She stopped coming to school much. Rena started hanging out with us." She made a face. "I'll bet you anything it was Cecilia who introduced Rena to Eric. He did the same thing over and over again, didn't he?"

Steel nodded, but inside he was seething. He remembered what Eric had said at the Burger Shack: girls like Rena couldn't be saved.

Steel decided then and there he was going to spend the rest of his life proving Eric wrong.

Lily gave Liz a curious look. "Except he took you next. That was different. He hadn't partied with you before. Why didn't he grab Lara? She still wanted him even after Sue died."

Liz nodded. "Lara's been texting me nonstop. She told me her parents wouldn't let her see you anymore, so I thought she was looking for a new friend. She kept hinting around that I should invite her for a sleepover. We'd barely met, so I thought that was weird."

"She was going to sneak out," Lily told her. "She was probably still texting Eric. He's always giving away phones," she told Steel, still filling her bag. "He gave one to Rena. I'm pretty sure he gave one to Sue, too, even though she said her mom bought it for her. He probably gave Lara one, and she was going to use Liz as an excuse so she could be out all night. She probably would have brought you along if you'd wanted to go," she said to Liz. "That's why she wouldn't answer my calls—she wanted to be Eric's girlfriend next."

Liz nodded. "I have a feeling she already told Eric about me, because I saw him at the water Olympics. He started talking to me when I was in line to buy pop. Said he knew my friend. I had no idea who he was talking about. I said I'd just gotten to town and was staying with the Turners. Seems like everyone knows them around here." She shrugged. "I could tell that freaked him out, but I didn't get why. He walked right off the line. An hour later I went to use the bathroom at the lodge, and he grabbed me when I came out—hauled me off and threw me in his truck."

"He was afraid you'd tell Stella about him. He had to *take care* of you," Lily said.

"Thank God for Stella."

"Yeah, your sister is badass."

Steel had to smile. Sounded like Liz was well on her way to settling in here.

He must have made a noise because Lily looked his way. "Don't worry, creeper, we know you helped get Eric, too."

Steel sighed. He hoped one day he'd live down that nickname.

"Hold the bag, Liz," Lily said. "I'll shovel the sand."

They got back to work.

ONLY WHEN THE sandbags were piled higher than the

water could possibly rise did Stella and the others allow themselves to rest. With so many helpers, a wall stretched right around the hospital, reinforced in places where it seemed like water might get deepest. The volunteers retreated inside when it was clear there wasn't any more to do. Now all they could do was be with their loved ones and wait to see what happened. It was daylight, but the rain still came down in torrents, meaning the roads wouldn't be passable out of town for some time.

The hospital staff had readied a few spare rooms where the volunteers could sleep. Lily's folks had come to take her home, since they lived nearby, and Liz had gone with Mary to watch over Jed and Virginia. Stella and Steel found a narrow steel cot in one corner of the space set up for sleeping and lay down together.

For a while they just rested. Listening to the rain pounding on the roof and Steel's steady breathing, his arms around her, Stella finally allowed herself to admit how exhausted she was.

She thought Steel had gone to sleep until he said, "I didn't get a chance to say how amazing you were." He propped himself up on one elbow and looked at her face. "If you hadn't done what you did, Liz could be dead and Eric might still be free." He kissed her. "I'd be proud to work with you as a deputy, you know."

"I'd be proud to work with you, too." Stella had barely begun to process what had happened in the last twenty-four hours, and it was only just now sinking in that Steel was, in fact, a sheriff's deputy. Had been for a very long time. "I'm sorry I doubted you. Sorry I believed what everyone said. It's not fair you had to live like an outcast in the town you were protecting."

"If everyone hadn't thought of me as a bad guy, I wouldn't have been doing my job right. But I am glad I don't have to hide anymore. I want to be with you—openly. Do you think that's possible?"

"Of course." She considered him. "Will you keep being a deputy?"

He thought it over. "For a long time, I thought when I caught the killer—caught Eric—I'd be done. It's been hell living like this for so long."

"You did it for Dale, didn't you?"

Something shifted in his expression, and she knew she was right.

"I wanted his death to be worth something. My dad wasn't innocent. He put himself in that prison; it's no one's fault but his own. But when your father came knocking with a problem, he jumped right in to help solve it. That's the way he was."

"People are complicated," Stella said. "I keep trying to sort out why my parents behaved like they did. Why was my mother so set on leaving? Why didn't my father fight for her more? I'm not sure I'll ever know. I guess it doesn't matter anymore, anyway. You and me; that's what matters. The decisions we make from now on. If you're ready to quit, I'll stand by you while you figure out what to do next. But if you're ready to stay on, I'll be proud to work in the next county over."

He shifted to his back, thinking it over. "Chance

Creek needs a rehab center for teens like you're trying to build, but it also needs law enforcement officers who understand that young people who use drugs are more victims than criminals. Maybe I will stay on, if I can carve out a niche that lets me help them. Looking forward to helping out more on the ranch, too."

"That sounds like a really good idea." She thought a minute. "You could even transfer to Chance Creek."

"I could, but are you sure you want to get involved with a man like me?"

"With a hero? Bring it on." Stella poked him with a finger.

"Hero?"

Was he kidding? "Yes, hero, Steel. You saved my sister—and me."

"You were doing pretty good there yourself," he put in.

"I nearly got myself shot," she corrected. "But yes, I did all right, considering. We did good together, don't you think?"

He nodded. "I do think that."

"And I think we can do a lot more good in the future, which is why I definitely want to get involved with a man like you." She lowered her voice. "In fact, I'd get a whole hell of a lot more involved if we weren't in a room full of people."

"I know exactly what you mean."

THERE WAS NO privacy to be had, so they opted for sleep instead. Steel wasn't sure how many hours passed before they woke and returned to Jed's room to check on their family members. When they arrived, they found Jed had other visitors.

"Eighty-four years old and he still took a bullet for you," Cab said from where he stood beside Jed's bed. "Can you believe it?"

"He's an example for us all," Steel said.

"Doesn't take a lot of skill to get shot," Jed grumbled, but he was obviously enjoying the attention.

Cab laid a hand on Jed's shoulder. "Truly. I wanted to congratulate you on being such an exemplary deputy, even so long after retirement." He turned to Steel. "I want to congratulate you, too. Get over here, Cooper."

Stella squeezed his hand before ushering him forward to shake hands with Cab.

"You did good work out there. Wish I'd known earlier you were on our team. I think some of your fellow deputies owe you an apology—Sheriff Holden, too."

"Time for all of us to move forward," was all Steel said. In a way he'd bought into his own undercover act. Had conducted himself like a man with things to hide. He looked forward to forging a new identity out in the open.

"Time for me to get going," Cab said. "Just stopped by for a minute, but I'm needed out there. We'll have a real celebration soon. Cake and everything. I'm sure Sheriff Bolton will want to take part."

"That won't be necessary." But hell if it didn't sound nice. "The roads in town are still passable?"

"Most of them. All the low-lying land is swamped.

Everything within a few blocks of Chance Creek, which means there's no way to get out to the ranches or Silver Falls," he added. "Anything close to a creek or river is flooded."

When they were gone, Steel was surprised to find himself still at the center of attention.

"You did good, Steel," Virginia told him. "Dale would be proud of you. I think he'll rest a little easier from now on knowing you finished what he started."

"I think it's about time we all held our heads up and learned to be proud of ourselves—both our families," Steel said. "No one needs to feel ashamed about the past anymore. And look at what we've done for this town. All of us." He looked around, trying to get used to the feeling of standing at the center of the crowd rather than the edge of it.

"Hear, hear," Stella said—and kissed him.

"Well," Virginia said. "What about that?"

"What about it?" Stella challenged her. "Don't you think I'm good enough for your nephew?"

Virginia hmphed and looked her up and down. "I guess you'll do." She snapped her umbrella open and shut, getting everyone's attention. "For goodness' sake, will you all give Jed a little room to breathe?"

THERE WAS NOWHERE to be alone in the hospital, but once again, Steel found them a quiet corner where they could sit on a cot, lean up against the wall and talk.

"I'd meant to save this for someplace more special," he began when they'd gotten comfortable, "But I have a feeling we'll be busy for a long time when the water goes down." He pulled a little velvet box out of his pocket, and Stella's heart stuttered before it began to beat again.

It couldn't be.

"I know I had no right to even dream of such a possibility, but after the night we made love in your pasture, I knew you were the only woman I wanted to spend my life with. Hell, like I told you that night, I've known it for years, even if I didn't let myself think it."

"Steel—"

"Let me finish." He opened the box and showed her the ring, a delicate swoop of platinum embellished with a diamond that glittered in the dull hospital light. "I love you. I have since the day I saw you flatten Leon with a math textbook."

Stella smiled.

"I've loved you for the way you've always stood up to injustice. The way you've been true to yourself. The way you've carried yourself with pride and the fierceness with which you've defended those weaker than you."

She was growing warm under his praise, and her hands were shaking. Was he truly proposing to her?

"I have waited so long to be able to throw off the past and step into the life I want to live. I want it to be right here on our families' ranches. I want to help keep our town safe. I want to have a family with you some-day—if that's what you want. Participate in all our town has to offer. Most of all, I want to be a man you can be proud of—and a man I'm proud of, too. Stella Turner, will you marry me?"

"Yes!" Stella leaned close, breathed in the scent of him, which was becoming so familiar. "I've always wanted this—for years. Long before it made sense. I think I've always known who you were."

"Who's that?"

"The one man in the world for me."

"You're all right with staying here in Chance Creek, no matter what we find out there when the water recedes?"

"Of course. This is my home. It'll always be my home." Never once during all the hard times had she wanted to leave the Flying W.

"Then let's do this together—you and me for the rest of our lives." He slid the beautiful ring on her finger, and Stella swallowed in a dry throat, thinking her heart might burst. It was beautiful, and Steel was everything she'd ever wanted. A true partner—on their ranches, at work—and in her heart.

"Now all I need to do is pass that test," she exclaimed, then whooped as Steel bowled her over and kissed her until she could barely breathe.

"I propose to you, and all you can think about is a test?" he demanded when they finally came up for air.

"I can't be a deputy with you until I pass it," she explained. And she pulled him close to kiss him again.

Chapter Twelve

IT WAS SEVERAL days before the water went down far enough that they could get home. Finally, they were given the all-clear, and Steel loaded Virginia, Jed and Stella into his truck. Mary, Maya and Liz were to follow behind, so he set a cautious pace.

Even when they were on the long stretch of highway between the ranches and town, he stayed well below the speed limit. The last thing they needed was to hydroplane into a pasture.

Slow and steady. That was how they would come back from this. After years feeling like he was racing the clock, Steel found he wouldn't mind the change in pace.

He tried to prepare himself for the worst, but when he pulled into Thorn Hill's driveway, they all were silent. There was standing water everywhere. The house looked like a hill fort surrounded by an enormous moat. Any crops that hadn't withered during the drought would now be drowned. Steel hoped the cattle were high and dry.

"Aren't you taking me home?" Jed demanded.

"Why don't you stay a day or two with us, keep Virginia company while we get things sorted?" Steel suggested, expecting a fight. "We'll make this our base and work together to take care of both ranches."

"I can do that," Jed said, surprising him.

Mary, Maya and Liz pulled up behind them and got out. "I was afraid to try the lane to the Flying W alone," Mary said worriedly. "It's lower than Thorn Hill's lane. But I'd like to get home to Justin."

"Why don't we stay here, as well?" Stella filled them in on the plans they'd made. "We'll fetch things from the Flying W when we can, bring Justin here, too, and just camp out for now." Everyone made their way inside, and Mary, Maya and Liz helped Jed and Virginia settle in the living room.

"I'll see what you have for food," Mary said. "Stella, go with Steel and figure out where everyone else is."

Stella joined Steel on the back porch, where they could survey the ranch. It was like being on an island in the middle of an ocean. "I've never seen anything like this in my life," she told him.

"Not sure when it's ever flooded so badly," Steel agreed. "Let's find Lance—see what he's been doing while we've been gone."

"Wait—who's that?" She pointed to a speck in the distance that was moving over the water—and getting closer.

"It's Olivia. She's in a canoe!" He had to chuckle at the surprising sight of her paddling over their pastures.

They waited for her to approach, helping her to secure the little boat and climb up to join them.

"Good thing we kept this old thing," she said, hugging Steel. "The Turners have one, too. I never thought I'd be herding cattle in a boat, but you've got to make do."

"How's the herd?"

"Doing just fine. We got most of them to high land before it got bad. Rounded up the stragglers by boat. The water isn't more than a few feet deep anywhere. The cattle waded through it while we paddled. Now we're keeping an eye on them and hauling feed out to them. That's the worst of the work."

"Liam and Tory are okay?" Stella asked.

"They're fine," Olivia assured her. "Noah's good, too. So is Justin. We've all been working together to keep things running." She seemed almost cheerful.

"It'll be a mess when the water goes down," Stella said.

"There'll be plenty of work for everyone, that's for sure. What about you two? Everything good?" Olivia asked.

"More than good." Stella showed off her ring. When Olivia pulled her into a fierce hug, she laughed. "Like you said, I bowed to the inevitable."

"Well, that suits me just fine," Olivia said.

"Me, too."

It gratified Steel that his sister had already accepted Stella, but he couldn't take his gaze from the submerged fields around them. "Something like this can change a town forever." He was thinking of all the other ranches. Some would be luckier, less damaged by the flooding. Others would be even worse off. "People will give up.

Move away."

"Not everyone will," Stella said. She met his gaze, and he was happy to see the determination in her eyes. "The fighters will stay."

"JED AND VIRGINIA are expecting us at one sharp," Steel told Stella several days later. The creeks and rivers were back in their banks, leaving the mess everyone had foretold behind. Both families were working together to clean up the damage to the outbuildings. Neither family's homes had taken on water. They were lucky; many homes in Chance Creek and Silver Falls had been damaged.

Stella hadn't had a chance to speak with Monica for days, and she meant to make up for that this morning. "I'll be back in plenty of time," she told Steel. "I'm taking Olivia with me to see Monica and Joan. We're supposed to talk about the rehab center, but really I want to make sure Monica is okay. Sounds like there was damage to the lodge."

They met the other women at Joan's house in town, where Monica was still staying, since the lodge had taken on water. They sat on the porch sipping the coffee Joan made them.

"Have you been home yet to see the damage yourself?" Stella asked Monica.

She nodded. "I'm glad we got all the furniture upstairs. There's some water damage on the first floor, another excuse to get my sons home. Your fundraiser was a roaring success, by the way. We've had time to count donations, and you've raised more than we expected. Good thing, too. Chance Creek has hard times ahead, and that means more need for rehab."

"I'm glad it worked out, and I'm sorry I ran out of there and left you two to finish it all up."

"I'm just glad Liz is safe," Monica said, patting her hand.

"Both your families have done a lot for the area," Joan said. "I look forward to working with you two to secure more funding to run the rehab and stabilization programs. We'll have to wait for things to get back to normal, so we'll tuck the money away in the bank in the meantime."

Stella enjoyed their chat and looked forward to working more with Joan. On the drive back to the ranches, Olivia considered the ring on Stella's finger. "You really love Steel, don't you?"

"More than anything."

"Good." Olivia gazed out the window at the dark clouds once again building on the horizon. "I have a feeling we're all going to need each other to get through the next few months."

"I think you're right. What do you think Jed and Virginia want to talk to us about?" she asked, taking the turn toward Thorn Hill, where they had all agreed to gather, Mary determined to return the hospitality the Coopers had extended to them after the flood.

"Beats me."

Though Jed and Virginia had called the meeting, Steel tugged Stella to her feet when everyone was settled in the living room and formally announced their engagement. Everyone already knew, but there were still cheers and congratulations all around when they announced their wedding date.

Noah had an announcement, too. "Mary, Justin, and Liz were looking for a place in town, but they've decided to stay on the Flying W instead. We need all hands working together right now, and they've agreed to help get the ranch back in order."

"One other thing," Stella said. "I met with Joan this morning. Despite everything, we did manage to raise enough money to get started on the expansion of the rehab center to include services for teens. There's lots more to do, but we're on our way."

"Wait—does that mean we Turners win?" Noah grinned.

"Hold up—it was all my idea, remember?" Olivia said. "Besides, Steel shot a serial killer. That ought to count for double."

"That's right. Anyway, with Stella marrying into our family soon, I think the rehab center expansion should belong to us Coopers no matter how you look at it," Tory jested.

"We're basically all one family anyway now, if Steel and Stella are getting married," Lance said. "The Coopners."

"You mean the Turnpers," Maya corrected him with a grin.

Jed stepped forward—holding Virginia's hand in his own. "Settle down. Settle down. We have an announcement."

"What's up, Uncle Jed?" Stella asked as everyone else's laughter died down.

"Well, it's a strange state of affairs... I think the only way to get you all up to speed is to tell a story."

"What kind of story?" Maya asked.

"Hush your mouth and you'll find out," Virginia said, thumping her umbrella on the floor.

Jed cleared his throat. "A long, long time ago, there was a foolish man," he began.

"That's him." Virginia poked Jed with her umbrella.

"Who's telling this story?"

"Just make sure you get it right."

"Hush, woman. And this foolish man," Jed went on, "invited the prettiest girl he knew to the Founder's Dance, because he meant to marry her soon and he was damn proud of it."

Stella felt Steel reach for her hand. She squeezed his fingers in acknowledgement. They'd heard some of this, but now she wanted to know how it ended.

"But there were darker forces at work," Jed said. "In the form of Foster Crake, who wanted the pretty girl for himself."

"I'm the pretty girl," Virginia said.

"He came up with a trick—and it worked all too well. He said the pretty girl meant to stand me up and go to the dance with someone else."

"With a boy I was tutoring," Virginia said with a humph.

"It made me jealous as all get out," Jed said. "Foster

told me she would pretend to be my date until the very last minute and then humiliate me in front of all our classmates. So I fooled her; I took someone else."

"And the pretty girl—that's me—got steaming mad," Virginia said with a nod.

"There wasn't any chance she'd accept my proposal after that," Jed said. Virginia poked him again, and he sighed. "Not for a very long time anyway, you have to admit that, my love."

Stella blinked. *My love?*

"But there wasn't a single god-darn day I didn't want to propose. I never married anyone else because there wasn't anyone else I wanted to marry, but I always carried the wedding ring I bought for you, because I hoped that someday—" He broke off and cleared his throat. "That someday I'd be able to put it on your finger."

He lifted Virginia's hand, where a beautiful ring sparkled.

"Oh, Uncle Jed, I'm so happy for you," Stella burst out. "When's the wedding?"

"As soon as we can make it. We're no spring chickens," he said.

"Speak for yourself," Virginia said, but she seemed mighty pleased, Stella thought.

"People will be coming for Steel and Stella's wedding soon, anyway," Maya said. "We can make it a double header."

"Sounds good to me," Stella said.

"Me, too," Steel said.

"It's a deal," Jed said. "One other thing." He cleared his throat. Shuffled his feet a little. "We have a request."

Stella traded a look with Steel. She couldn't remember the last time Virginia or Jed had ever asked for anything, even if they demanded things all the time.

"I'd like to bring my bride to my home, the way I would have when I first meant to marry her. We don't want to put anyone out, but when we win the Ridley property, and I'm pretty sure at this point we have it sewn up between our families, there'll be plenty of room to build something new for anyone who wants a place of their own."

"Of course, Uncle Jed," Stella said.

"Sounds like a perfect solution," Steel said. "We'll find a way to make everyone fit."

Chapter Thirteen

B Y THE TIME Halloween rolled around, the families had settled into a new normal. There had been a few more storms, and more water damage around town, but they had been prepared, and their ranches had come through all right.

At first there'd been talk of canceling the Harvest Festival, at which the Founder's Prize was to be awarded, but the prevailing sentiment was that the town needed a celebration, and as usual, plenty of volunteers pitched in to make it happen. As Steel got ready for the occasion, he knew today was only the beginning of the festivities. Tomorrow, he and Stella would get married—as would Jed and Virginia.

He and Stella had agreed to wait to start a family of their own. They wanted to get themselves and their jobs in order first and to just spend time together. Stella had passed her deputy exam with flying colors, and Steel's transfer to the Chance Creek department had been approved, so now they saw each other at work as well as at home.

On the drive into town, he was saddened but not surprised to see how many places were for sale. On the other hand, plenty of places were in the process of being fixed up.

"You were right," he told Stella, who rode in the passenger's seat. "Not everyone is giving up so easily."

"I don't remember Chance Creek ever being so quiet, though."

Steel was thinking the same thing. After a hard summer, everyone was gearing up for a hard winter, he mused.

The mood was different at the Harvest Festival. It was a simpler affair this year than the Spring Fling had been, during which the Founder's Prize had first been announced, but there were still food booths, live music and games. Everyone seemed to be having a good time.

During the evening Steel met up with many old friends. The Cruzes were there, as were the Mathesons, the Halls, and the crowd from Westfield. But what made him happiest of all was when he spotted Liz with a bevy of other girls working at Fila's food booth. Fila, Camila and Juana had taken them under their wings, and all of them were laughing and chatting as they worked.

"I'm so glad Liz is getting involved with the community," Stella said as they wandered away with their food. "I was worried she'd never be happy here."

"That's the silver lining to all of this, I think," Steel said. "We're all in this together now, and everyone knows it."

Everyone turned at the sound of microphone feedback. Steel looked to see the announcers were getting up on stage. Steel took Stella's hand in his and waited.

As SHE LOOKED around at the gathered crowd, Stella was so glad to see how many people had stayed. Regardless of who the prize went to, plenty of families had spent the past year chipping in for the good of the town. Now, with everyone pulling together like never before, she was sure Chance Creek would come back from all this better than ever.

"The Founder's Prize was conceived of as a way to encourage good citizenship and giving back to the community," the announcer said. "And I think we've seen that in spades this year. While countless people have given their time and energy to Chance Creek, I think you all will join me in saying that the Turners and Coopers have gone above and beyond. Therefore, the Ridley property will be awarded jointly to both families." The man grinned. "They're pretty much one family at this point, anyway."

There was laughter and cheering, and Stella embraced Steel and kissed him, as all around her Noah and Olivia, Liam and Tory, Lance and Maya embraced, too. Even Jed and Virginia got in the act, Virginia allowing Jed to give her a peck on the cheek. Stella was proud of her family and happy that Jed and Virginia were finally going to get to live the life they had denied themselves for so long.

"I never would have guessed last spring this is how it would all turn out," Stella told Steel.

"Life certainly has its twists and turns." He kissed her again. "But I can't argue with where it got us."

THE NEXT DAY Steel found Virginia in her room at Thorn Hill in her wedding dress. Olivia and Tory were with her, helping her get ready.

"I'm proud of you and all you've done," Virginia told him. "For this town. For this family. For Dale."

"Thank you." Steel embraced her.

"Now, when are you going to get to work on babies? I'm not going to live forever, you know."

Steel rolled his eyes. "I already told you—"

"A fat lot of excuses is what you told me." She jabbed at him with her umbrella. "Get to it, young man."

Jed and Virginia's ceremony was simple but charming, the arbor under which they stood decorated with greenery. Virginia wore a mauve wedding gown with a lace bodice and a draping skirt. The flowers in her bouquet were white, so elegant Stella thought they suited her perfectly. Jed stood straight and proud in his best suit.

Reverend Halpern took special care officiating, and Steel thought the whole town had turned out to wish them well. Through it all Jed and Virginia beamed like the high school sweethearts they were.

Steel and Stella stood up as their bridesmaid and groomsman. There shouldn't have been any dust left in the air after all the rain, but there must have been because by the time the ceremony was in full swing, Steel's eyes were watering from the grit.

"That's us in five or six decades," he whispered to Stella when he conducted her up the aisle after Jed and

Virginia had kissed with unexpected verve.

"Let's hope," she answered.

After a light lunch and plenty of dancing, everyone needed a bit of a break before the second wedding of the day. Chairs were set up all over the lawn, with more inside, for their guests to rest and chat.

Steel kissed Stella before they split up to get ready for their own wedding. "Ready for this?"

"I'm ready. Don't you dare stand me up. I'm not waiting for you for sixty years."

"Nothing could keep me away."

MARY AND ENID both helped Stella change from her bridesmaid dress to her bridal gown. Maya, Olivia and Tory were on hand, too. Stella had chosen an off-the-shoulder princess-waisted gown with lace details. It made her feel like royalty. She hoped Steel liked it.

"Oh, you look so beautiful," Mary said when she was dressed, stepping back to admire her.

"Resplendent," Enid agreed.

"Steel won't know what hit him," Olivia said. "But he's already a goner for you."

Mary fluffed Stella's gown, while Enid fetched her veil.

"Want to know a secret?" Mary asked. "Enid, Leslie and I have decided what kind of project we want to take on."

Stella patted at her hair before accepting the veil, a little apprehensive. The last thing Chance Creek needed right now was a spa.

"We're going to take over the Top Spot Café. We got advance notice it was coming up for sale, and we've already put in an offer. That place is begging to be turned around. We'll keep it simple—home cooking at its best."

Stella blinked. "I didn't know you wanted to get into the restaurant business."

"It won't just be a restaurant," Enid said. "It will be a way for us to help teenagers in the community. We plan to start a mentorship program for them. We can employ some of them ourselves, but we also want to match teens with opportunities for jobs and mentorships with other businesses, as well as run evening programs for them. We could arrange visits to colleges in Billings and Bozeman, have local businesspeople come talk to them about their work—and coordinate volunteer projects, too. Whatever it takes to keep them involved and active."

"That would be wonderful!" Stella embraced her.

When her mother hugged her back, Stella realized this was the first time they'd done so for real in—years. They'd been paying lip service to being mother and daughter. Now she felt a real connection to Mary.

"I'm sorry I ever doubted your ambitions," Mary said. "I suppose you choosing to be a deputy felt like you were choosing your father's side. And there never was a side—there were only misunderstandings."

"You're okay with me being a deputy?"

"More than okay. I'm proud." Mary hugged her again. "Now go marry that man of yours and be happy for the rest of your life."

"Will do." She couldn't think of a better way to spend her days than right here with her family—and his—in the place that had always been her home.

Chapter Fourteen

T HERE WAS A flurry among the guests when a light shower fell during the rest period between the two ceremonies, but it cleared up quickly. When Steel stepped out into the sun, Lance by his side, he was gratified to see a rainbow arcing across the sky.

"Seems like a good omen," Lance commented.

Steel shrugged. "I'm not worried about omens. I know Stella and I are going to have a happy marriage and a good life, because I'm going to work every damn day to make sure we do."

Lance grinned at him. "You're pretty calm for a man on his wedding day."

Steel was. They weren't out of the woods yet—far from it—but the constant uncertainty that had plagued him for over a decade was now gone from his life.

Every day would bring a new challenge, but he was ready to face them all.

That sounded like his kind of happily ever after.

THE RAINBOW THAT arced overhead as Stella ventured down the aisle on her uncle's arm was just the icing on the cake of a perfect day. The sunlight glittering off the wet grass and trees gave everything a shimmery, other-worldly quality.

Members of her newly expanded family sat on either side of the aisle and stood on either side of the altar, the line between Turner and Cooper meaningless now. When she took her place across from her husband-to-be—who cleaned up very nicely in her opinion—Camila, Olivia, Maya, Tory and Liz stood beside her. Carl, Noah, Lance, Liam and Justin stood beside Steel.

Stella touched the diamond engagement ring on her finger, a reminder of all she and Steel had been through. Diamonds were forged under conditions of extreme pressure, after all.

She and Steel had come together under such conditions. As had Chance Creek. Looking out at the assembled guests, Stella's happiness knew no bounds, not just for herself and Steel but for her town, which stood strong and united no matter what happened.

And when they'd spoken their vows and bound their hearts together, she went up on tiptoe to meet Steel's kiss with her own, knowing that everything that mattered was right here—and she'd never let him go again.

"Ready for the rest of our life?" he whispered.

"Ready."

Chapter Fifteen

New Year's Eve, four years later

"WHERE'S MOMMY?" IVY asked sleepily.

Carl Whitfield dropped a kiss on top of his daughter's head. Three and a half years old, she was a spitfire. Dark-haired and dark-eyed like her mother, sturdy like her father. Living proof that dreams really could come true.

"Mommy's bringing out the desserts," he said, pointing across the interior of Elms, the beautiful, modern café and music venue that used to be the Top Spot Café. Its tired old booths and pitted walls had been replaced by sleek furnishings, countertops and light fixtures that wouldn't have been out of place in a city. Tonight, the venue was closed for their private event. Camila had pitched in to help Mary Turner, Enid Cooper and Leslie Falk put on a New Year's party for all their friends, and she and her business partner, Fila Matheson, had been cooking all day, along with Camila's cousin Juana and a bunch of teenagers they were mentoring.

Carl expected Ivy to perk up at the idea of dessert since she loved sweets, but instead she snuggled deeper into his embrace. He had found a quiet corner to sit in, if you could call any place in the restaurant quiet, and was cradling Ivy on his lap. He doubted she'd make it to midnight, even though it wasn't that far off.

"I think there might be a stampede for that dessert table," Noah remarked from where he was sitting nearby.

"You going to be the first? Or wait until it's over?"

"I think I'll wait." Noah smiled at the sight of Ivy on Carl's lap. "Fatherhood sure suits you."

"It does. Everything about my life here suits me." He could barely remember the frantic decades out in California when he was starting his business. Moving to Chance Creek was one of the smartest things he'd ever done. Marrying Camila tied for first place, though. He hadn't known what community meant until he'd come to this tight-knit town. He'd been afraid that waiting to find the perfect ranch might mean he'd lose her, but he'd been right to hold out for what he wanted. Laurel Heights was everything he'd ever dreamed of in a ranch.

Camila was the public face of the family these days with her ever-popular restaurant. He was content to stand back, wait for her orders for the fruit and vegetables she needed him to grow for the dishes she wanted to serve and then fulfill them the best he could. With the help of his old business partner, Sven, and a rotating cast of visitors from Mexico, as Camila's family took turns helping out and going home, he had been able to transform part of his Montana ranch into a paradise of geothermally heated greenhouses in which to grow the ingredients of all Camila's favorite Mexican dishes.

He loved the adventure of it all. Loved ranching cattle, too. Loved always having people around and getting the fun of pampering Camila whenever she took a break—which wasn't often.

And then there was Ivy.

"I like being a stay-at-home dad," he said to Noah. "Along with being a rancher, of course."

"And a purveyor of fine vegetables," Noah said with a grin. "And hot peppers and avocados and whatever else it is you grow over there."

"That's right." But it was getting to spend much of his days with his tiny daughter that brought him the most joy. He'd come to marriage and fatherhood later than lots of men, and he was soaking up every last minute of it.

Camila caught his eye from across the room and raised a questioning brow. Carl nodded. All was well with him. A few minutes later, she appeared with two plates in hand, passed one of them to Noah and handed the other to Carl.

She took a seat next to him and leaned against his shoulder. "I'm getting sleepy, too."

"Midnight on New Year's Eve should come at ten o'clock for ranchers," Noah said, digging in to a piece of chocolate cake. "We've all got to be up early tomorrow."

"It's worth it to be with everyone tonight, though. I wasn't sure if this would work out. Wondered if everyone would prefer to be at the Dancing Boot or something like that," Camila said.

"Too many kids among us for the Boot," Carl said. "I think this is perfect. There's still dancing, still drinks to be had, but you don't have to pay a bundle for the babysitter."

"Or stay home alone," Noah agreed. "I think it's perfect, too."

"I think everything's perfect," Camila said, reaching up to give Carl a kiss on the cheek, the swell of her belly pressing against his hip. They were expecting a boy in a couple more months. Were still fighting over names.

"You got that right," Carl said and kissed her back.

CAMILA COULDN'T BELIEVE how lucky she was. She had a career she adored, could be as creative as she wanted with the meals she offered at Fila's, and had a wonderful business partner and coworkers. Now that they were coordinating with the ladies of Elms to mentor two to three teenagers each semester, teaching them the workings of their restaurant and how to cook, Fila's was always lively. She loved the teenagers' energy and loved the sense of community it brought. Add in her cousins coming and going and the constant round of community events they attended, and her life was full.

Four years ago she'd thought she might spend her life alone. Now she woke up every morning next to a man who seemed determined to make all her dreams come true. At first when they'd moved to Laurel Heights, Camila hadn't known what to make of it, feeling like it was Carl's concern. He'd made it clear very quickly that he wanted to raise the ingredients that she craved to make authentic food.

These days she knew that the more difficult the request, the more enjoyable the challenge for Carl, and she worked to come up with dishes that required unusual vegetables and fruit that no one in Montana had ever heard of. Carl happily went about the process of figuring out how to grow them in his greenhouses.

She'd been a little afraid that having a baby would make it hard to keep up with the restaurant, but she hadn't counted on how much Carl would take to parenthood. Of course, he had a lot of help. Sven and her cousins loved having Ivy around. Her daughter was already confident with growing things in the greenhouses and being around the horses and other critters on the ranch. She was around grown-ups so much that she was equally confident around them, too, and often could be heard demanding attention from one of them.

Soon a little boy would join them.

"What are you thinking?" Carl asked, murmuring in her ear since Ivy seemed to have fallen asleep despite the clamor of the crowd.

"I'm thinking I'm happy. Just one-hundred-percent, completely happy."

"That makes me happy."

"I love our home, our ranch, our little family…"

"Our growing little family." He caressed her belly.

"Our neighbors, our town…"

Carl slid his hand down to wrap his fingers in hers for a moment. "Let's remember this night, whatever happens. This perfect night in our perfect lives."

"Absolutely." And she kissed him again.

NOAH TURNED AWAY from Carl and Camila and got up to look for Olivia. He found her with Mary, Enid and Leslie in the kitchen, where happy chatter competed with the thump of stove doors and the clatter of dishes coming out of the dishwasher.

"Can I help?" Noah asked, trying to stay out of the way of a trio of teenagers who were putting away dishes as fast as they could.

"Can you carry these trays out to the main room?" Olivia asked, handing one to him that was laden with more desserts.

"Sure thing. Then I'm going to come steal you for a dance."

"I can't dance now," Olivia protested. "There's too much to do."

"And a million hands to do it. I need my wife." His wife. The words still made him happy after all this time. Life with Olivia was everything he'd dreamed it could be. At work he'd been promoted to head up the parole department, and at home he had two ranches that needed all the help they could get. He'd discovered he liked the freedom of pitching in to projects but allowing Liam to head up their endeavors. With the arrival of baby William last year, there was plenty for everyone to do.

He'd even grown used to having his mother and stepsiblings around, and he liked the way their family had grown. All the generations together on the Flying W—and Thorn Hill—meant there never was a dull moment and always someone to help.

"One dance," Olivia said when he returned to the kitchen and took her hand.

He didn't answer but tugged her gently out to the dance floor and took her in his arms, swaying slowly despite the upbeat tempo of the song.

"This is nice," Olivia admitted a few minutes later. "We need to do this more often."

"I'm down for that," Noah said. "Anytime."

OLIVIA BREATHED IN the familiar scent of her husband and was reminded how once upon a time she wouldn't have dreamed of looking to a man for comfort or support. Now she took Noah's presence in her life for granted. He'd pledged himself to her, and Noah was a man of his word.

He was so strong and determined. A rock she could anchor herself to when life seemed out of control. He was a good father. A wonderful husband. Knowing he'd always be there meant she could let go of her worries and concentrate on all the good in her life.

Last year when she'd finished her library degree, Noah couldn't stop talking about it to everyone they knew. This year, when Marta Langly stepped into a supporting role and Olivia had been given the head librarian position at the Chance Creek public library, she thought he'd burst with pride.

Olivia could hardly believe she'd made it this far,

but as soon as she really buckled down, she found her studies suited her far better than she'd expected, and now she looked forward to entering her library early every morning, turning on the lights, getting ready for each new day, surrounded by the books she so loved.

And then there was William, the light of her life. Her precious little tow-haired boy. She laughed to think she and Noah had worried at all about how they could balance work and parenting. With so many couples on the ranch—and so many friends in town—childcare was the least of their worries. They hadn't decided whether to expand their family yet, but Olivia thought they might.

She tilted her head back and kissed Noah on the underside of his chin. He chuckled, bent down and gave her a proper kiss.

"I should go find William. Last I saw him, Virginia was holding him," Noah said.

"We'd better grab some dessert first," Olivia said, nodding to indicate the crowd that had gathered around the trays of food.

"I've got all the sweet stuff I need right here." Noah growled playfully against her neck. "Actually, Camila already brought me a plate."

"I'd better catch up then." But she stayed where she was a moment longer. "Mmm, that feels good, but I've got work to do, and you've got a baby to find."

"Later?" he asked and finally stepped back.

"Definitely."

"IT'S BEEN A good year, hasn't it?" Maya said, picking a beautiful berry tart off Lance's plate of desserts.

"It has," he agreed. They were crowded around a tiny café table with Liam and Tory, but he didn't mind the squeeze. It had been a fun night, and he and Maya had danced already to a number of songs, shaking off all the long days and nights that had gotten them so much closer to their goals.

"What do you think about grad school?" Tory asked.

"It's hard, but we're taking it nice and slow," Lance said, "so it's not as intense as finishing our undergrad degrees, right, Maya?"

"That's how I feel, too. The work goes deeper, but we're taking it more slowly. I think we've got our rhythm down."

Lance knew what she meant; between chores at the ranches, school, studying and working at the Chance Creek history museum, they kept awfully busy.

"Any thoughts about starting a family?" Tory patted her belly, which had just begun to swell.

"Not until we finish grad school," Lance said, although he had to admit it was getting harder—for him at least—to put it off. His siblings were starting families. They would be among the last to get to that part of life at this rate.

"It would be a lot to take on." Tory nodded. "Glad I finished law school before we got pregnant." She smiled at Liam.

"It was worth the wait, but I'm getting impatient to

see the baby," Liam said, resting a hand on Tory's thigh.

"We're looking forward to having children, too," Maya said, "but I'm enjoying this part. Getting to be with Lance, going to school and working together. We make a good team."

"That we do." Lance was still awed by the fact he had this woman by his side, and he knew when they did start their family, it would only increase his satisfaction with his life. Once, he'd struggled to know where his place was in this town, but now he felt he inhabited it completely. His work on the ranch, his schooling, his care for the historical museum—it was intoxicating to feel like he had so much to give to his community.

He'd never expected to feel so solid about his ranch and his family, either. The Coopers had taken a new place in Chance Creek—had settled squarely into the number of families who gave the town its structure and its strength, and that made him prouder than he had words to express.

He took Maya's hand. "You're still the best thing that ever happened to me. Always will be."

Maya smiled back at him. "Can't wait to see what happens next."

Liam surged to his feet. "You two are sappy enough to make a man sick. Come on, Tory, let's dance."

"Sounds good to me."

"Thought they'd never leave," Lance said as they watched the other couple thread their way through the crowd and find a space on the dance floor. He leaned closer to Maya and kissed her. "I mean it; I couldn't ask for anything more in life."

"I love you," Maya said when they pulled back. "I always will."

"I am looking forward to our family," he told her. "But I'm just fine with now, too."

"We can still practice, even if we can't get pregnant." Maya arched one eyebrow. "It's getting late."

"It's not midnight yet." But his pulse gave a throb. Practicing with Maya was always a good time.

"We could celebrate at home. Just you and me."

"Hell, yeah." Lance stood up. Offered her his hand. He didn't need a crowd to celebrate the new year. Not with Maya by his side.

MAYA CLUNG TO her husband's hand as they said their goodbyes and slipped out the front door. It was a clear, frigidly cold night and stars twinkled overhead, the air cutting through her lungs as she took deep breaths.

Life was so wonderful that sometimes she thought she might be dreaming it all and dreaded waking up. She couldn't remember how she'd managed to navigate her days before she had Lance by her side.

He was tender, caring and damn funny. Together, they managed to joke their way through the hardest times. That was a good thing, because in the year or two after their marriage, life had been hard. Adjusting to going to school while still accomplishing their chores at home had taken a lot of compromise. When they'd taken on building a small house on the Ridley property—or the North property, as they'd all come to call it in the Cooper/Turner clan, since the property edged both Thorn Hill and the Flying W on the north end of their ranches—it had almost been the straw that broke the camel's back.

It had forced them to make decisions that they hadn't been entirely ready to make: How many children might they someday have—and how many bedrooms and bathrooms should they build? What style of home did they prefer? Did they want bedrooms upstairs or down? A million little details that could be hard to decide at the end of a day that was already too long.

They had sorted them out in the end, though. Jed and Virginia had taken the homestead on the Flying W, as Jed had requested after finally becoming engaged to Virginia. Mary and the twins had stayed in the house with them, Mary helping with chores that the older couple found difficult, and the twins providing lively company for them before heading off to college at Montana State. These days Liz was pursuing a fine arts degree and Justin was going for a degree in livestock management and resources. They came home often on weekends to help out with chores and connect to family. When Maya thought back to the way Liz had been so lost when she arrived in Montana, she always breathed a prayer of thanks that her stepsister had found her way.

Noah and Olivia had taken on the old home at Thorn Hill and were slowly accomplishing a series of projects to fix it up while maintaining the historical elements of the house. Maya wasn't sure how they managed it with everything else they did, but each time she visited, it seemed like something had been accomplished—and something else was midstream, meaning there was always a pile of boards or boxes of flooring in a corner, but Maya was sure the end result would be a beautifully restored home.

Liam and Tory had decided to expand upon their cabin, almost doubling it in size in anticipation of the children they were planning. Steel and Stella had built their home on the opposite side of Pittance Creek from her and Lance on the North property. Maya had appreciated how easy it was to accommodate all the members of their large family, and there was already talk of what would happen when the twins were out of school. For two families who had spent a hundred years feuding over one thing or another, they were all mighty cozy now, she thought.

"You're quiet," Lance said when he pulled up in front of their beautiful two-story home.

"Thinking about how good we've got it."

He parked the truck and cut the engine, then leaned over to steal another kiss. "We've got it damn good."

"Yes, we have," she agreed, leaning in to kiss him again.

"We gonna sit out here and freeze to death, or are we going inside?" Lance asked some time later with a chuckle.

"It's pretty out here with the stars, but that big warm bed of ours is calling my name."

"Mine, too. After all, we need to get a lot of practice

in before it's time to get real about our family."

"Exactly." She kissed him one last time. "Lots and lots and lots of practice."

"HOW ARE YOU feeling?" Liam asked Tory. "Is it okay to keep you on your feet like this?" They were slow dancing, and he liked the way her belly pressed against him, a little bulge that reminded him of their child they had created together. Ever since Tory had become pregnant, he'd felt so protective of her—and proud of her, too, which she found funny.

"You're proud of me for getting pregnant? I worked a hell of a lot harder to get my law degree," she always said.

He was proud of her for that, too, of course, and he was happy that Chance Creek now had a lawyer far younger than any of the others in town, who were all nearer to retirement than they were to their college years. He knew other people in town felt the same way. It took lawyers and doctors and teachers and all kinds of service providers to keep a place thriving.

"I'm fine," she told him now, nestling in his arms. He had realized that his tough, determined wife liked his protectiveness now that she was carrying his child. He knew she would always be a fierce defender of those who needed her help, but he also realized that when she came home from work, it helped to have him there solidly by her side. Some nights when she arrived she sought him out, came into his arms and just rested there. He'd come to understand she was soaking up his strength, replenishing her reserves with some of his. It made him proud to think that she could depend on him that way, and he made sure to always have time to stand there for as long as it took before she took a deep breath, let it out, her shoulders finally releasing some of their tension, and straightened, ready to meet his kiss.

"It's almost midnight," he told her, checking his phone.

"Another year, all fresh and new to fill, coming right up," she said.

"It's going to be a good year," he assured her. He'd made great strides in bringing the Flying W—and with the Coopers' help, Thorn Hill, too—into becoming a provider of organic beef, and they were all reaping the benefits of carving out the niche for themselves. These days people were lining up to buy certified organic beef. They had increased the herds on both ranches, and the surplus they'd earned was allowing for all the building and renovating of homes on both sides.

"I think it's going to be a spectacular year," Tory said. "Because I'm going to spend it with you."

Liam knew he was smiling. He was always smiling now that Tory was his wife. "Can't wait to see our baby. Can't wait to spend the year with you."

"Me, neither."

TORY WAS GETTING tired. The baby seemed to take it out of her in a way that law school and everything else didn't, but she didn't regret her decision to start her family in the slightest. When she'd set her sights on being a lawyer years ago, there had been several reasons for her choice. One, she wanted to set herself firmly apart from her father's criminal ways and what she saw as her family's troublemaking reputation. Two, she wanted respect. And three, after a childhood dominated by money problems, she wanted the steady paycheck she knew that kind of career would give her.

She'd been determined to have the kind of inner strength and moral compass that would allow her to champion clients and do her best for them amid the high-stress corporate world. When she changed her mind, and decided to join a family practice here in Chance Creek, at first she'd thought the work wouldn't be nearly as complicated or challenging.

She'd been wrong.

Now she was glad she didn't have to go it alone. If she had, she was sure she would have survived— thrived, even—because she loved a challenge. But she wouldn't have been as good a lawyer as she was today without Liam by her side.

Liam had become her rock. Always there for her. Always a port in the storm when disputes between her clients and their adversaries got too heated or too heartbreaking. Every day he held her until she felt she had the strength to go on. At night he rubbed her feet as they unwound on the couch and watched a movie. He picked up the slack when she couldn't get to the store or the post office. He found something fun to do on the weekends when she could easily have brought her work home and kept at it straight through them.

She knew that when their baby was born, a little boy they'd decided to name Wade, Liam would make it possible for her to have the best of both worlds, so she could keep up nearly two-thirds of the hours she normally worked at her practice and be home for the rest of the time with her son and any siblings they decided to have.

Tory leaned in against her husband and pressed a kiss to the side of his neck where it met his shoulder, the crisp fabric of his shirt cool against her cheek.

"I love you so much, Liam Turner," she whispered.

"I love you, too. Forever and always," he murmured back.

"TWO MINUTES TO midnight," Jed said as he took his wife's hand and led her carefully to the dance floor, carving out a space for them so they wouldn't be jostled by the others swaying around them.

He would never admit it to another living soul, but the phrase *his wife* still brought him almost to tears every time he thought of it. He had wanted Virginia for his bride since the day he first noticed girls were… girls.

It pained him to think of all the harsh words that had passed between them in the years after they fought, before they found the way clear to marrying, but he'd accepted decades ago that their fighting had merely been an unusual—and lengthy—very lengthy—courtship. Virginia needed to be fought over, even if that meant he'd had to fight *her* for her own hand in marriage—for years and years.

And oh, their strange relationship had made for some very good times over those same years, despite all that fighting. Good times indeed, he thought with a private smile. Wouldn't his great-nephews and nieces be surprised if they knew just how good?

Because even if he and Virginia had spent decades laboring under the false idea that the other had betrayed them, that hadn't kept them from having a relationship of sorts anyway. A rather exciting relationship. If he was honest, during their early years, their feud was what made it possible to be together at all.

It wasn't until that feud heated up and they'd begun to argue in earnest, flinging accusations and imprecations at each other every chance they got, that Jed realized there had been a fundamental flaw in their plan to marry back before Foster Crake had driven them apart.

Virginia was terrified of marriage.

She was raised by her old-fashioned parents to think that the day a woman wed was the day she ceased to exist as an independent person. She thought she was meant to defer to Jed in all things, and Virginia wasn't the type who enjoyed deferring.

So while it had been his own stupid jealousy that caused their rift, Jed realized it rather suited Virginia to sustain it. It pained him more than he cared to admit now that what he'd wanted so badly hadn't been the right choice for her. For a time he'd preferred to fight with her than to own up to it. That interlude gave Virginia time to make different plans.

It was a funny thing. At his age no one much mentioned his career except for a passing reference now and then. It wasn't surprising; his great-nephews and nieces barely remembered a time when he worked. They remembered Virginia's accomplishments even less. Virginia had also had a career. She'd been a math teacher at Chance Creek High, and she'd taught mental discipline to generations of Chance Creek students. Always demanding the best of them. Always holding them to a high standard. She'd given as much to the community as anyone else.

Virginia had been proud of that career, even if no one else noticed it.

Eventually, angry as he'd been that he'd lost her, Jed noticed that pride, noticed the cause of it and took a moment to really listen when Virginia was yelling at him.

Then he'd understood. Virginia couldn't marry—not yet. She needed time.

He'd decided to give it to her.

And in return, he'd gotten as much of Virginia as she'd been able to give to him—which turned out to be a fair amount more than he might have expected. They'd muddled through the intervening decades. He and Virginia had had more of a relationship over the years than anyone else knew, even if it hadn't been nearly as much of one as he'd always craved.

"Two minutes to another year," Virginia said, allowing him to lead her in the dance, a concession that made him swell with pride of his own. She wouldn't let just any man do that. Only him.

"Two minutes I'll cherish as much as all the other minutes I get to spend with you."

Virginia's eyes closed. Was she savoring this moment as much as he was? Being married to her was like getting a huge ice cream sundae at the end of a steak dinner on some special occasion—except the celebration happened day after day after day.

"We've done good with this family," Virginia said. "We've done good for everyone."

"Sure have. We helped make this town a special place."

She opened her eyes and looked up at him, nodding. "That's true."

"We've come a long way, haven't we?"

She nodded again. "That we have, and I like it."

That was as much a declaration of love as he was likely to get, Jed knew.

But it was enough.

VIRGINIA ALLOWED JED to lead her around the dance floor. If she was honest, it was nice not to have to make every decision about every last thing these days. Moving into the Flying W with Jed had been a treat. As had taking up their relationship where they'd left off—although it pleased her no end that not a single person in this room—aside from Jed—knew that their relationship had been far more robust—and interesting—over the years than one might think.

She wondered what Jed really thought about their

journey to the altar. Was he as torn as she was, sometimes wishing she'd allowed him to marry her far sooner so they could have known domestic bliss all these years together, and other times knowing that the sweetness, and thrill, of their encounters over the years was all the sweeter—and more exciting—because of their feud?

They'd had some good times in between all the fighting.

She'd never forget the first time she'd cornered Jed at the Harvest Festival when she was twenty-one. They'd argued all day each time they bumped into each other.

Then they'd met at the refreshment booth. Jed had tried to buy her a cup of punch. She'd thrown it in his face and stormed away. He'd followed her outside, just like she'd hoped—

And she'd kissed him. A long, hot kiss that burned with all the pent-up anger and desire she'd held inside her since the night he'd stood her up at the Homecoming Dance.

When they'd pulled apart, Jed had peered into her eyes for a long moment, then grabbed her hand, tugged her around the far side of the community center and kissed her again in a totally different way.

She'd lost her virginity that night in a field out back under a sky of stars that glittered like the ones out tonight. Jed had proposed to her afterward.

She'd said no—in no uncertain tones, which had led to another row—

And another bout of lovemaking.

"Can I at least take you home?" Jed had asked when they were sated, breathing hard, staring together up at a moon so huge it seemed to fill the sky.

"No," she'd said. "I'm my own woman, Jed Turner. Don't you forget it."

"I won't wait forever," he'd said.

We'll see about that, she'd told herself.

She supposed none of the other couples dancing with them would understand their strange lives. The way she and Jed had turned a feud into something that could sustain them through the years. He had his life. She had hers. Sometimes the want they buried through their busy days sparked up into a surprisingly strong storm—and swept them into a night—or several nights—or a week of passion, but then they sailed their ships back to their respective ports and went on, as if they'd never connected at all.

So they'd still be faring, she thought, if she hadn't woken up one morning earlier this year at the old age home where she and Jed had both lived for some time with her right hand so stiff and sore that when she reached for her trusty umbrella, she wasn't able to grasp the handle. Sitting straight up in bed, it was as if her eyes opened for the first time in years. When she'd said no to Jed's proposal all those years ago, she'd wanted time to establish herself—to live a little. She'd still been furious with him about his slight, but in truth she'd gotten in the habit of ruling her own life. More time had passed, and she'd gotten used to enjoying her trysts with Jed—and their blow-ups, which were almost as fun.

When the time had come, she hadn't thought twice about moving into the Prairie Garden old age home. Jed had followed her there rapidly, and they'd had fun sneaking around the joint, in between sending its denizens into an uproar now and then during their fights.

But life was passing—fast.

That day she'd asked for a sign. A staunch believer in the faith the younger generation seemed to take or leave, she sent up a prayer for clarity. An hour later, on her usual morning fact-finding round, she heard about the Founder's Prize and understood it was time to act. Settler's Ridge—or the Ridley property, as everyone in town called it—abutted her land and Jed's. It was an acquisition worthy of their legacies, and it was a reason for the two of them to re-involve themselves with their families, move back home, get everyone safely married off—

And finally bring their relationship out into the open.

Now here she was, a married woman. A dutiful wife.

Virginia snorted.

"What's that?" Jed asked, but she didn't have to answer, for right then the crowd around them, led by Noah, began to count down to midnight.

"Ten… nine…eight," they called out.

"Did I ever tell you I'm the happiest man in the county?" Jed asked her.

"A half dozen times today, at least," she said.

"And I'll say it a half dozen times more before I go

to bed tonight."

"Seven…six… five…"

"No doubt," she said waspishly.

"I think you're pretty happy, too."

"Four…three…two…"

Virginia nodded, surprising herself, and allowed Jed to pull her closer. "I am pretty happy," she said.

Jed dropped a kiss on the top of her head.

"Good."

"One…zero… Happy New Year!"

All around them couples kissed and whooped and celebrated, but Virginia stayed in the arms of the man she loved. The man who'd shared her life in the most unconventional way. The man worth fighting… and fighting for.

"Love you, Virginia," Jed murmured, kissing her again.

"I love you, too."

"I'M SO HAPPY they found each other after all these years," Stella said as she and Steel watched Virginia and Jed kiss at midnight. "Can you imagine waiting so long to marry the one you love? I can't let myself think about the years they wasted. It's too sad."

Steel nodded, but the way he was looking at them made Stella wonder what he really thought. He caught her expression, and a smile tugged at one corner of his mouth. "I have a suspicion," he admitted. "It's one I can't prove, though."

"What suspicion?"

"That we might have been played. All of us."

"What do you mean?" She took in their relatives again. Virginia was as elegant as usual. Jed was dressed in his Sunday best.

"I don't know what I mean, really," he admitted. "Just that the two of them don't seem to be walking around with any regrets. I mean, if it had taken me sixty years to marry you, I think I'd be cursing the loss of all that time."

"Maybe they don't want to waste any more time on recriminations."

"Are you serious? Jed and Virginia live for recriminations."

It was true, Stella thought. Those two never met an argument they didn't relish. "You said they were playing us."

"Not just us—everyone. Look at the two of them together. They went from not being able to be in the same room together to being as lovey-dovey as anything. They had no trouble moving in together. No trouble making a life together..."

"You think they had some kind of relationship before?" Stella shook her head. She didn't buy it.

"I don't know. Maybe I'm wrong."

"I think you must be. No one gets away with anything in this town without everyone else knowing."

"That's true. You'd have to be awfully sneaky to keep it up so long."

Stella knew what he was really saying. If anyone could, it was her uncle and his aunt. She watched them dancing. Caught the satisfied expression on Jed's face. That wasn't a man who felt cheated in any way in life. Had he been able to get over the hand that fate had dealt him for so many years so quickly? Or was Steel right—had he and Virginia had some kind of clandestine thing going on?

"They couldn't have been sneaking around all this time," she told Steel firmly.

"You're probably right." But the admiration she saw on his face as he studied the other couple told her he didn't really believe that.

Now Stella wasn't sure what to believe either. Steel's hunches about people tended to be right. It was a skill she was learning to develop for herself as a deputy.

"Enough about them," Steel said. "Let's talk about us."

"What about us?" But she knew exactly what he meant. The night of their wedding, they'd made each other a promise: four years of life in the open. Four years of Stella getting to pursue the career she really wanted. Four years for Steel to try out wearing a uniform. Then they'd make some decisions about what to do next.

"How would you like to spend the next four years, wife of mine?"

"I get to pick anything I want?" she teased him. She knew exactly what the rules were.

"That's right. Anything your heart desires. I mean that, Stella. Even if you want to chuck it all and go live on a desert island, you tell me, you hear?"

She still tingled all over at the way Steel talked. The way his hands rested on her hips. At work she was every bit the deputy. Strong, decisive, capable. The best she could be. At home she could be sweet sometimes. She could let Steel be the tough guy. Allow him a hand in helping her achieve her dreams.

"I've loved being a deputy."

"I know. You're damn good at it."

"I'll probably want to get back to it again someday."

Steel stilled. "Someday?"

"I want a family now. I want to have my children while I'm still young and energetic, and I want to be with them for the first few years. I don't want to divide my time. Is that all right?"

"That's just fine," he assured her. "In fact, it's better than fine. I'm ready for kids, too. I didn't know if I'd ever be."

"What do you want to do for the next four years?" Stella loved that they were taking it in chunks rather than trying to decide forever all at once. It allowed for so many more possibilities.

"I want to take time off from being a deputy, too," he said simply. "I want to work the ranch awhile, plain and simple. I can help Liam and the others grow the business, get my hands dirty and work the land—our land. I want to solidify my connection to this place so I can pass it on to our kids, and I want to be here for you and them through their first few years. Does that make sense?"

"It makes all the sense in the world, and it makes me

so happy," Stella said, drawing him near. "I don't want to worry about you while I carry our babies."

"I know exactly what you mean." He held her protectively. "We can't say how many years any of us will be given on this earth, but we can make choices that give us a better chance. Like you said, someday it will be time to get back to protecting our town, but we deserve a chance to be a family for now."

"Damn straight we do." She reached up on tiptoe to press a kiss to his cheek. "Happy New Year. Now take me home and let's get to work."

"Happy New Year." He kissed her back. "You want to make a baby—tonight?"

She nodded. "Didn't go off birth control these past couple of months for nothing, you know."

Steel's grin grew. "Grab your coat, honey. Time to really get this party started."

STEEL TOOK ONE last look around at the people gathered in the café before slipping out the door with Stella. All the people he loved were together in one place, although he noted Lance and Olivia had disappeared some time ago. More and more lately he found himself overcome with gratitude for the path his life had taken these past few years.

Serving openly as a deputy next to Stella in the Chance Creek department had cleared the cobwebs from his reputation and opened up a number of horizons for him. For the first time since he'd returned home, he'd been able to make friends with the kind of people he wanted to spend time with. He'd been present for family dinners, community festivals, birthdays, Christmases and other special occasions as a participant, not as a shadow on the outskirts of the fun.

Being a deputy in the public eye redeemed the way he felt about himself, too. He could hold his head up high as he moved about town. He was accepted—welcomed, even.

That felt good.

Now he wanted to bring his work home. He wanted to spend his days with his brother, sisters and in-laws. Wanted to continue the work the others had started to maximize their ranches' earning power—for everyone. Wanted to support Stella through her pregnancy—and the first years when their children were young.

As imperfect as his family was, he'd had that—a mother and father who were around more often than they were away. He wished those times had been happier for all concerned, but there was much about them he recognized as good. All those fishing and hunting trips with his dad. Learning about horses and cattle. Coming back to the house to find a home-cooked meal on the table. His mother's love always evident in the way she was there.

He and Stella would have it much easier than Dale and Enid ever had. The prosperity of the ranches and their own savings from their work meant they wouldn't struggle. And they had two families' worth of love and support to depend on if times got tough.

As Steel helped Stella into his truck and drove the

winding roads out to their home on the North property, he couldn't help feel that life was going to be pretty sweet from here on in.

When he'd parked in front of their home, Stella waited for him to come around and open the door. He appreciated that she let him be a little old-fashioned now and then, and he couldn't help pause for a kiss on their way inside.

"Remember our first time?" she said when he drew back.

Steel looked up at the stars twinkling overhead, then turned to the field where he'd built the obstacle course for her. "I will never forget our first time." He chuckled. "Or the amount of dirt that went down the drain of my shower that night."

Stella laughed, too, a light sound he loved to hear. "I know exactly what you mean. I had to scrub the bathroom afterward to hide how much I'd tracked in; I didn't want anyone asking any questions."

"Too cold for mud tonight."

"Too cold for getting naked outside and taking it nice and slow, the way I want to," she agreed. "Good thing we have that skylight in our bedroom. We'll still be able to see the stars."

"Good thing."

Steel led her inside, figuring he'd have his chance to take her outside under the sky again someday. Tonight they needed the warmth of the big bed they'd positioned under the skylight in their bedroom. A nest of soft covers. A bottle of champagne he'd hidden away.

When they finally lay down together, Steel undressed Stella slowly, delighting in every inch of skin he exposed, skimming his hands over her, kissing her until she wriggled underneath him.

When he bared her breasts, he took a good long look at her, thinking he'd never be tired of what he saw. This was the woman he'd wanted for so long, and who'd freely chosen to spend her life with him. He still found it hard to believe he could be so lucky, and that need to assure himself that it was true made him linger for a long time, kissing her creamy skin, teasing her and tasting her and enjoying himself until Stella shifted again, her desire clear.

"I thought you said we were going to take this nice and slow," he said.

"I changed my mind. We can take it nice and slow next time. Get your clothes off."

"Yes, ma'am." He shrugged out of his shirt, easy to do since she'd already unbuttoned it. She worked at his belt until she freed it, then moved her fingers to the button of his jeans. When that was undone and his zipper down, she helped him shuck them down. He kicked them off the end of the bed.

"Better?"

"Not quite." She tugged at the waistband of his boxer briefs, then gave a hard yank, setting him free. "Now we're getting somewhere."

"You're insatiable."

"You have no idea." Stella tugged him back down on top of her and sighed when he settled his weight against her. When her hands slid to his waist, and then lower still, he knew what she was asking.

"You really stopped using birth control?"

"You said you didn't mind a couple of months ago. I was tracking things to make sure we didn't accidentally get pregnant until enough time had gone by and I could check with you."

"I don't mind. I'm happy," he assured her. "I know for sure I want this. You sure?" He had to check.

"Positive. It's funny—since I was on the pill this isn't going to be different from what we always do, but it feels like it will be different."

"It will be; I've got to work extra hard to get this job done." When she grinned up at him, he grinned back.

"I sure hope so," she told him.

If he hadn't been hard before, he certainly would be now, but the truth was he'd been aching since they'd been back in town. "You want things fast, right?"

"You got it. Start slow, then go fast," she corrected.

"Will do." Steel nudged himself against her, and they both sighed. Their lovemaking was always satisfying to him, but he knew this night would be special— and so would the rest of their nights together. As he pushed inside her, his desire grew. They were making a family—a baby. Right now, maybe. Soon at any rate, if the stars aligned. He and Stella would bring a new life into the world through this testament to their love.

"What's wrong?" Stella whispered.

"Nothing. It's… everything's right." His voice was husky, but his emotion hadn't unmanned him in any way. If anything, his resolve grew and his pace increased.

Stella moved with him, biting her lip, matching his pace, her hips meeting his. When she closed her eyes and arched back, he knew she was giving herself to him utterly, giving him leave to make love to her, to lead this excursion into the next phase of their lives.

Steel paced himself, wanting to make this last, but the sight of her body bared to him, the feel of her surrounding him, the heat and sweet friction and the desire inside him to give her everything overcame his control. Steel plunged into her, gathering her close in his arms, and she tangled her fingers in his hair, urging him on with her whispered pleadings and the lift of her hips to meet his.

When Steel felt her crashing over the edge into her release, he followed with her, bucking against her, crushing her to him, riding the wave of their orgasms together toward the shore.

They collapsed in a tangled heap afterward, both of them breathing hard, and when Stella laughed, Steel joined in.

"I don't know why I'm surprised how damn good that feels every single time."

"I don't know why I'm surprised every time I wake up in the morning and you're still here and I'm still here and this house is still here," he answered.

"We're so lucky," Stella said. "And soon we're going to share that luck with our baby."

"You think you're pregnant yet?"

"Not yet. Rest up a minute, then we'll try again."

He'd try as many times as it took, Steel resolved. And then he'd try some more for good measure.

Steel rolled over and fished out the champagne he'd squirreled away in a cooler. When he pulled out two glasses and filled them, Stella looked impressed.

"Look at you thinking ahead."

"I know how to treat a woman."

"You do." She took a glass from his hand.

"To all of us," Steel said. "You. Me. Our baby. Our family. To Chance Creek, too."

"To all of us." Stella took a sip. "And to another wonderful year together."

"I'll drink to that."

And he did.

Be the first to know about Cora Seton's new releases! Sign up for her newsletter here! www.coraseton.com/sign-up-for-my-newsletter

Other books in the Turners v. Coopers Series:

The Cowboy's Secret Bride (Volume 1)
The Cowboy's Outlaw Bride (Volume 2)
The Cowboy's Hidden Bride (Volume 3)
The Cowboy's Stolen Bride (Volume 4)

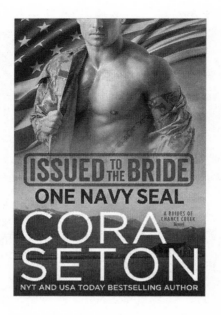

Read on for an excerpt of **Issued to the Bride One Navy SEAL**.

Four months ago

O N THE FIRST of February, General Augustus Reed entered his office at USSOCOM at MacDill Air Force Base in Tampa, Florida, placed his battered leather briefcase on the floor, sat down at his wide, wooden desk and pulled a sealed envelope from a drawer. It bore the date written in his wife's beautiful script, and the General ran his thumb over the words before turning it over and opening the flap.

He pulled out a single page and began to read.

Dear Augustus,

It's time to think of our daughters' future, beginning with Cass.

The General nodded. Spot on, as usual; he'd been thinking about Cass a lot these days. Thinking about all the girls. They'd run yet another of his overseers off Two Willows, his wife's Montana ranch, several months ago, and he'd been forced to replace him with a man he didn't know. There was a long-standing feud between him and the girls over who should run the place, and the truth was, they were wearing him down. Ten overseers in eleven years; that had to be some kind of a record, and no ranch could function well under those circumstances. Still, he'd be damned if he was going to put a passel of rebellious daughters in charge, even if they were adults now. It took a man's steady hand to run such a large spread.

Unfortunately, it was beginning to come clear that Bob Finchley didn't possess that steady hand. Winter in Chance Creek was always a tricky time, but in the months since Finchley had taken the helm, they'd lost far too many cattle. The General's spies in the area reported the ranch was looking run-down, and his daughters hadn't been seen much in town. The worst were the rumors about Cass and Finchley—that they were dating. The General didn't like that at all—not if the man couldn't run the ranch competently—and he'd asked for confirmation, but so far it hadn't come. Finchley always had a rational explanation for the loss of cattle, and he never said a word about Cass, but the General knew something wasn't right and he was already looking for the man's replacement.

Our daughter runs a tight ship, and I'm sure she's been invaluable on the ranch.

He had to admit what Amelia wrote was true. Cass was an organizational wizard. She kept her sisters, the house and the family accounts in line, and not for the first time he wondered if he should have encouraged Cass to join the Army back when she had expressed interest. She'd mentioned the possibility once or twice as a teenager, but he'd discouraged her. Not that he didn't think she'd make a good soldier; she'd have made a fine one. It was the thought of his five daughters scattered to the wind that had guided his hand. He couldn't stomach that. He needed his family in one place, and he'd done what it took to keep her home. That wasn't much: a suggestion her sisters needed her to watch over them until they were of age, a mention of tasks undone on the ranch, a hint she and the others would inherit one day and shouldn't she watch over her inheritance? It had done the trick.

Maybe he'd been wrong.

But if Cass had gone, wouldn't the rest of them have followed her?

He'd been able to stop sending guardians for the girls when Cass turned twenty-one five years ago, much to everyone's relief. His daughters had liked those about as little as they liked the overseers. He'd hoped when he dispensed of the guardians, the girls would feel they had enough independence, but that wasn't the case; they still wanted control of the ranch.

Cass is a loving soul with a heart as big as Montana, but she's cautious, too. I'll wager she's beginning to think there isn't a man alive she can trust with it.

The General sighed. His girls hadn't confided in him in years—especially about matters of the heart—something he was glad Amelia couldn't know. The truth was his daughters had spent far too much time as teenagers hatching plots to cast off guardians and overseers to have much of a social life. They'd been obsessed with being independent, and there were stretches of time when they'd managed it—and managed to run the show with no one the wiser for months. In order to pull that off, they'd kept to themselves as much as possible. He'd only recently begun to hear rumblings about men and boyfriends. Unfortunately, none of the girls were picking hardworking men who might make a future at Two Willows; they were picking flashy, fly-by-night troublemakers.

Like Bob Finchley.

He couldn't understand it. He wanted that man out of there. Now. Trouble was, when your daughters ran off so many overseers it made it hard to get a new one to sign on. He had yet to find a suitable replacement.

Without a career off the ranch, Cass won't get out much. She might not ever meet the man who's right for her. I want you to step in. Send her a man, Augustus. A good man.

A good man. Those weren't easy to come by in this world. The right man for Cass would need to be strong to hold his own in a relationship with her. He'd need to be fair and true, or he wouldn't be worthy of her. He'd need some experience ranching.

A lot of experience ranching.

The General stopped to ponder that. He'd read something recently about a man with a lot of experience ranching. A good man who'd gotten into a spot of trouble. He remembered thinking he ought to get a second chance—with a stern warning not to screw up again. A Navy SEAL, wasn't it? He'd look up the document when he was done.

He returned to the letter.

> *Now here's the hard part, darling. You can't order him to marry Cass any more than you can order Cass to marry him. You're a cunning old codger when you want to be, and it'll take all your deviousness to pull this off. Set the stage. Introduce the players.*
>
> *Let fate do the rest.*
>
> *I love you and I always will,*
> *Amelia*

Set the stage. Introduce the players.

The General read through the letter a second time, folded it carefully, slid it back into the envelope and added it to the stack in his deep, right-hand bottom drawer. He steepled his hands and considered his options. Amelia was right; he needed to do something to make sure his daughters married well. But they'd rebelled against him for years, so he couldn't simply assign them husbands, as much as he'd like to. They'd never allow the interference.

But if he made them think they'd chosen the right men themselves...

He nodded. That was the way to go about it.

In fact...

The General chuckled. Sometime in the next six months, his daughters would stage another rebellion and evict Bob Finchley from the ranch. He could just about guarantee it, even if Cass was currently dating the man. Sooner or later he'd go too far trying to boss them around, and Cass and the others would flip their lids.

When they did, he'd be ready for them with a replacement they'd never be able to shake. One trained to combat enemy forces by good ol' Uncle Sam himself. A soldier in the Special Forces might do it. Or maybe even a Navy SEAL...

This wasn't the work of a moment, though. He'd need time to put the players in place. Cass wasn't the only one who'd need a man—a good man—to share her life.

Five daughters.

Five husbands.

Amelia would approve.

The General opened the bottom left-hand drawer of his desk, and mentally counted the remaining envelopes that sat unopened in another stack, all dated in his wife's beautiful script. Ten years ago, after Amelia passed away, Cass had forwarded him a plain brown box filled with envelopes she'd received from the family lawyer. The stack in this drawer had dwindled compared to the opened ones in the other drawer.

What on earth would he do when there were none left?

End of Excerpt

The Cowboys of Chance Creek Series:

The Cowboy Inherits a Bride (Volume 0)
The Cowboy's E-Mail Order Bride (Volume 1)
The Cowboy Wins a Bride (Volume 2)
The Cowboy Imports a Bride (Volume 3)
The Cowgirl Ropes a Billionaire (Volume 4)
The Sheriff Catches a Bride (Volume 5)
The Cowboy Lassos a Bride (Volume 6)
The Cowboy Rescues a Bride (Volume 7)
The Cowboy Earns a Bride (Volume 8)
The Cowboy's Christmas Bride (Volume 9)

The Heroes of Chance Creek Series:

The Navy SEAL's E-Mail Order Bride (Volume 1)
The Soldier's E-Mail Order Bride (Volume 2)
The Marine's E-Mail Order Bride (Volume 3)
The Navy SEAL's Christmas Bride (Volume 4)
The Airman's E-Mail Order Bride (Volume 5)

The SEALs of Chance Creek Series:

A SEAL's Oath
A SEAL's Vow
A SEAL's Pledge
A SEAL's Consent
A SEAL's Purpose
A SEAL's Resolve
A SEAL's Devotion
A SEAL's Desire
A SEAL's Struggle
A SEAL's Triumph

The Brides of Chance Creek Series:

Issued to the Bride One Navy SEAL
Issued to the Bride One Airman
Issued to the Bride One Sniper
Issued to the Bride One Marine
Issued to the Bride One Soldier

The Turners v. Coopers Series:

The Cowboy's Secret Bride (Volume 1)
The Cowboy's Outlaw Bride (Volume 2)
The Cowboy's Hidden Bride (Volume 3)
The Cowboy's Stolen Bride (Volume 4)
The Cowboy's Forbidden Bride (Volume 5)

About the Author

With over one million books sold, NYT and USA Today bestselling author Cora Seton has created a world readers love in Chance Creek, Montana. She has twenty-eight novels and novellas currently set in her fictional town, with many more in the works. Like her characters, Cora loves cowboys, military heroes, country life, gardening, bike-riding, binge-watching Jane Austen movies, keeping up with the latest technology and indulging in old-fashioned pursuits. Visit **www.coraseton.com** to read about new releases, contests and other cool events!

Blog:
www.coraseton.com

Facebook:
facebook.com/coraseton

Twitter:
twitter.com/coraseton

Newsletter:
www.coraseton.com/sign-up-for-my-newsletter

721263376R00186